BOOK BLURB:

From birth, the Savage brothers were taught by their father, Deuce, that life is like a sandwich; any way you flip it, the bread comes first. They were taught to get money, not fall in love, so they left a wreckage of broken hearts on their road to getting money. Yet, now, as mature men, they realize that you're not rich until you have something that money can't buy. And money certainly cannot buy the women that have stolen these brothers' hard and stubborn hearts.

Taye "City" Savage and Akira White's love story started in the projects. Ten years ago, they met when Akira was only a young girl and City was a grown man getting his hustle started. City and Akira's bond was strong, and their fate was inevitable, so they thought. However, before their bound could be sealed, life happened. They were torn apart by unimaginable circumstances, and they never saw one another again until a decade later. Yet, by that time, both City and Akira were involved, but they weren't so loyal to Nova and Davion that they could ignore the passion in their hearts that they still harbored for one another.

The only thing that ever mattered to Keandre "Money" Savage was the hustle. He had never fallen in love, not even with his girlfriend of five years, Zoe Moore. Money and Zoe had the typical hood love that involved lots of fussing, fighting, and other women. Yet, Zoe was the only one in the relationship that was in love. Money only kept her by his side because she was the last woman standing. Along the way, he had ruined Zoe with every woman that he cheated on her with, and every lie he told. Now, Money is finally ready to shed his immature ways and settle down. Yet, Zoe finds herself in a desperate state of mind when she realizes that she is not the woman that Money has chosen to settle down with.

Shamar Savages' only love has been his love for art. When his brothers financed his baby, Savage Ink, his only focus was his tattoo shop. Yet, he soon realizes that despite not even wanting it, he was falling for his friend and frequent dip, Taraji Green. However, Taraji had the same mindset as Shamar. Her only focus was becoming the baddest hair stylist in Chicago; not love. The last thing she wanted was a committed relationship with anyone, not even one of the infamous Savage brothers.

Sometimes, the last thing a person wants to do is fall in love, but love sucks them in any way. That is exactly what happens with these Savage brothers and the women that adore them. As life always has it, love ain't that easy to obtain, especially when loving a man that was raised by the streets and whose first love is the hustle. In yet another urban tale by Jessica N. Watkins, death, sex, and chaos leads to unforeseen tragedy and unexpected love.

ABOUT THE AUTHOR:

Jessica N. Watkins was born April 1st in Chicago, Illinois. She obtained a Bachelors of Arts with Focus in Psychology from DePaul University and Masters of Applied Professional Studies with focus in Business Administration from the like institution. Working in Hospital Administration for the majority of her career, Watkins has also been an author of fiction literature since the young age of nine. Eventually she used writing as an outlet during her freshmen year of high school as a single parent: "In the third-grade I entered a short story contest with a fiction tale of an apple tree that refused to grow despite the efforts of the darling main character. My writing evolved from apple trees to my seventh and eighth grade classmates paying me to read novels I wrote about kids our age living the lives our parents wouldn't dare let us". At the age of twenty-eight, Watkins' chronicles have matured into steamy, humorous, and realistic tales of African American Romance and Urban Fiction.

In September 2013, Jessica's most recent novel, Secrets of a Side Bitch, published by SBR Publications, reached #1 on multiple charts.

Jessica N. Watkins is available for talks, workshops or book signings. Email her at authorjwatkins@gmail.com.

DAVID WEAVER PRESENTS

EVERY LOVE STORY IS BEAUTIFUL, BUT OURS IS HOOD

by JESSICA N. WATKINS

EVERY LOVE STORY IS BEAUTIFUL, BUT OURS IS HOOD
by *Jessica N. Watkins*

PROLOGUE

-TEN YEARS AGO-

AKIRA WHITE

"Akira!"

At the sound of my mother's voice, instantly, my eyes rolled toward the ceiling.

"What does she want?" I muttered to myself.

"Akira!" my mother's voice irritatingly shot through the air again.

I sucked my teeth and cringed.

"*Akira*! Bring yo' ass here!"

"Hold on, boo," I spoke into the phone, telling my boyfriend, City. "My mama keeps calling me."

He chuckled, knowing my annoyance with her, and told me, "A'ight."

I sat the cordless phone on my bed and regretfully left my bedroom. I knew that she couldn't want much of anything because she barely talked to me. Her ass was rarely at home. I took care of myself. Whatever I couldn't do for myself, City took care of it.

Every Love Story Is Beautiful, But Ours Is Hood
by *Jessica N. Watkins*

At the age of twenty-nine, my mama was heavily in the streets. She had been selling pussy since she was fifteen years old. Back then, she used to trick for a famous Chicago pimp, Jeffery Savage, better known as Deuce in the streets. He saw her one day when she was outside playing Double Dutch with her friends. Besides her tattered, dirty clothes and run-over shoes, he noticed her exotic features and mature curvy figure that made her look almost twenty, instead of the young girl that she was. Since my mother was being raised by her grandparents back then and they were too old to look after her properly, it took very little for Deuce to convince her to start hooking for him. That's how she got pregnant with me a year later. My father was one of her Johns that she never saw again.

Now, fourteen years later, the streets and the addictions that she'd developed along the way had turned my mother's once beautiful, modelesque looks into battered and worn features that made her look twenty years older. Hooking was all that she had ever known. She sold her body to men that were also run-down so bad that they *had* to pay for pussy. She used that money to feed her addictions. Nine times out of ten, my mother was high off of one thing or another or drunk. Her money went toward her lifestyle, not

Every Love Story Is Beautiful, But Ours Is Hood
by *Jessica N. Watkins*

taking care of me. We lived in the Dearborn Homes, one of the few housing projects still standing in Chicago at the time. My mother had government assistance, so her bills were few. So, the only reason why I went without clothes that fit, food, and lunch money at school was because her addictions were more important than her only child.

Luckily, City and I had finally hooked up about a year ago. Since then, he had been doing whatever he could to feed and clothe me because my mother wouldn't. He lived in the Dearborn Homes as well. He'd known me since birth because Deuce is his father. I had developed a crush on City as soon as I was old enough to be attracted to boys. He was five years older than me, however. He was fine as hell and had been hustling since he was seventeen. I knew that he couldn't even see me beyond the older girls that were all over him. However, a year ago, I was finally bold enough to shoot my shot, and City was surprisingly just as attracted to me as I was to him.

Unlike my mother, I valued my body. So, City and I had never had sex. In fact, I was a virgin.

Once I reached the hallway, I met my mother's wide eyes. Instantly, I got irritated because I knew by her fidgeting that she needed a high, and she needed it *quick*.

EVERY LOVE STORY IS BEAUTIFUL, BUT OURS IS HOOD
by Jessica N. Watkins

"Yes, Mama?" I asked her regrettably.

Still fidgeting, she whispered, "I need you to do something for me."

Frowning, I asked, "What?"

I heard movement behind her, so I looked up and saw one of her Johns. He was some old, crusty dude that looked gross. He had to be in his sixties. His skin was dark, and so were his eyes. His skin looked rough like leather. He was fat and sloppy. There were bumps on his face oozing puss. I had seen him multiple times coming in and out of my mother's bedroom. Soon afterward, she would run outta here and come back the next day or two days later. He usually came around on the first. That day was December 2nd.

Rolling my eyes from him to her, I asked, "What do you need me to do, Mama?"

Her John moaned, "*Me*."

I couldn't believe my ears. My eyes instantly bore lethally into my mother's.

Still fidgeting, she explained, "He don't want me. He wants *you*—"

"No!" I shrieked in disgust.

My mother had reached a new fucking low! No matter her addictions, she had *never* asked me no shit like this!

EVERY LOVE STORY IS BEAUTIFUL, BUT OURS IS HOOD
by *Jessica N. Watkins*

"Akira, please—"

"Mama, are you serious?!" I instantly cut her off. Tears pooled in my eyes. I couldn't believe it. I always knew that my mama was a hoe and a drug addict. I knew that she barely gave a fuck about me. But gawd damn! *This?* I couldn't take this.

When I turned to storm into my room, I felt my mother grab me doggedly by the elbow. The first thing I thought was that she was so hungry for that high that she was going to let this nasty-ass man take my body and my virginity, so I turned around swinging.

"You bitch!" my mother cursed as she started swinging back.

I heard the nasty man fuss, "I ain't got time for this shit!"

When my mother heard that, she stopped swinging and instantly went to run after him like a thirsty puppy.

I heard her begging him, "Wait! Please! I'll make her do it! Don't leave. I'll make her have sex with you."

That disgusted the hell outta me. Instantly, tears filled my eyes. For years, I had dealt with the effects of my mother's habits: the lying, manipulation, the bouts of sickness, and her stealing everything that I managed to get myself. But *this*? This was a new low.

As I heard the front door slam, I raced into my room, closing the door behind me. I instantly went to the phone on my bed. Putting it to my ear, I heard the dial tone and realized that City had hung up. I hurriedly dialed his number. Unfortunately, it just continuously rang with no answer.

"Shit!" I cursed as I hung up and threw the phone.

Tears were running down my face. All I could envision was my mother willing to give me to that nasty motherfucker. That mental picture made my stomach turn. I needed to talk to City so bad because I'd come to the conclusion that I couldn't stay in the house with my mother any longer. I quickly threw on my coat and gloves, figuring that I would go to City's apartment for the night. After grabbing my keys, I raced toward my bedroom door. Yet, by the time my hand wrapped around the doorknob, my mother came barging through.

"You fucked that money up for me!" Her eyes were beady and unbelievably evil as she screamed at me.

I couldn't believe that she was really that mad. I couldn't believe that she needed a high *that* bad.

EVERY LOVE STORY IS BEAUTIFUL, BUT OURS IS HOOD
by Jessica N. Watkins

I went to move around her. I wanted to get the fuck out of there. I wanted City. I *needed* City.

"You could have done that for me!" she screamed. "I know you fuckin'!"

I kept walking, realizing that my mother was willing to sell her daughter's body for some crack. I always had at least acknowledged her as my mother. However, at this point, I didn't give a fuck about her. She was nothing to me. I never wanted to see her again. My plan was to go to City's place and never go back home.

"Don't you walk away from me!" my mother snapped as she snatched me by the shoulders and violently spun me around. "I needed that!"

I stared at my mother in disbelief. This wasn't my mother. I had seen her feigning. I had seen her do anything for a few dollars. Yet, none of the things she'd done had anything to do with me. Now, she needed me, and she was willing to do whatever to get me to make this money for her.

I didn't like the way that she was looking at me. I suspected that she felt some kind of way because he didn't want her anymore. She was looking at me with envy, as if she wished that she was still young and pretty like me. There was panic in her eyes, as if she'd suddenly realized that she could no longer sell her wretched body, so she didn't have a way to support her habits.

"Mama, let me go," I cried, trying to get out of her grasp.

Suddenly, she charged at me. She was like an enraged animal, seething and salivating at the mouth with anger. She was fighting me like I was some bitch off the street. Despite her addictions and her inability to be a mother, I didn't fight her back that night to hurt her; I was defending myself. I could barely do that, however, due to the snug winter coat and gloves that I was wearing. But despite how much the drugs and alcohol had deteriorated her body, her need for a high gave her the strength of a man. Tables and lamps toppled over as she tossed me around. She threw me into the wall, tables, and the island that separated our small living room from the smaller kitchen.

I prayed that someone would hear my screams. I prayed that someone would come knocking. But at eleven at night, I could hear the music and sounds of people laughing and hollering inside of their apartments over my own screams.

When she started to choke me against the island, I began to panic. The look in her eyes was so frightening. It was

EVERY LOVE STORY IS BEAUTIFUL, BUT OURS IS HOOD
by *Jessica N. Watkins*

as if she was no longer fighting me because I wouldn't help her. She was now taking some rage out on me that had nothing to do with what had happened that night.

As I clawed at her hands around my neck, I tried to speak. I wanted to remind her that this was *me*, Akira, her daughter. But she wouldn't stop. My hands stopped trying to free hers from around my neck and started to reach for anything that I could use to stop her before I lost consciousness.

I gripped the first thing that I was able to as tightly as I could with the wool glove. I started swinging, without even knowing what was in my hand, until I saw the blood gushing from her neck. I gasped just as my mother stumbled backward. Finally able to breathe, I gasped with sheer terror in my eyes as my mother looked at me with bulging eyes of disbelief. She reached for the knife that was still stuck in her neck. She was still seething with unbelievable strength because she actually pulled the knife right out.

"Ahhhh!" I screamed as the blood squirted from her neck and splattered against the walls.

I watched with horror as she gripped her neck to stop the bleeding. My hands covered my mouth and gripped my face in horror. I held in a terrified scream just as she hit the floor and her eyes traveled to the back of her head.

Suddenly, the front door swung open. I stared towards the door with bulging eyes. I was so relieved when I saw City come rushing inside. Rage was in his eyes. I assumed that he had heard some of the commotion over the phone and had finally come to save me. I was so relieved, as he quickly rushed towards me. But his swift footsteps stopped as soon as he saw my mother's lifeless body lying in a pool of her own blood. He quickly rushed back toward the front door and closed it.

Appreciating his presence, I finally broke down crying, and my knees hit the floor.

"Baby, c'mon."

I had heard City, but I couldn't move.

Tears streamed down my face. "Mama," I whimpered in a raspy voice over and over again. "Mama, mama, mama..."

Then, I could hear City's voice closer, "We gotta get the fuck outta here."

Staring at my mother's body, I could only mumble, "I didn't mean to."

"I know you didn't, but the police don't give a fuck about that, baby."

EVERY LOVE STORY IS BEAUTIFUL, BUT OURS IS HOOD
by *Jessica N. Watkins*

Everything was making it hard for me to think clearly; stabbing my mother, visions of that old, nasty man lusting for me, and her blood. I couldn't wrap my young mind around all of this.

Suddenly, I felt arms on my shoulders, and I jumped in fear. Realizing that it was still only City, I threw my arms around him and began to wail pitifully. I felt him pick me up into his arms and begin walking toward the door as he assured me, "I know you didn't mean it, baby. I got you. I'll take care of everything."

****

After getting me into his apartment and seeing all the bruises on my face, City didn't blame me for what I'd done. Then, as he cleaned my wounds with peroxide and alcohol and bandaged them, I told him what had happened. Afterward, he was so pissed off that he wanted to kill my mother again himself and that old-ass man.

The next week went by, and I stayed in City's apartment, going to school during the day as if nothing was wrong. Besides feeling the guilt of killing my mother, I actually felt relief. I didn't have to live in a dirty, nasty home barely kept by a mother who cared about dick, drugs, and alcohol more than she gave a fuck about me. I was fed, clothed, and taken care of by City. I had already fallen in love with him long ago. But, that week, a bond grew between us that I knew would keep me in love with City forever.

A week went by before my mother's body was found. That day, as I walked home from school, the police presence was thick in my building. Then I saw the yellow crime scene tape and huge crowd surrounding my old apartment. I hurried in the opposite direction, toward City's building. My heart was beating over a hundred miles an hour with fear. I just knew that I would spend the rest of my life in prison, away from the world and City. But he had assured me that no one saw him carrying me out of my apartment that night. Then he had secretly gone back inside during the middle of the night and cleared up any evidence that would've made it appear that I was still living there. My mother's body was only discovered because of the horrible stench that was so overbearing that the neighbors called and reported it to building management. Then the maintenance man came by and found her rotting body.

Every Love Story Is Beautiful, But Ours Is Hood
by *Jessica N. Watkins*

For days afterward, I lived with City waiting for the police to come and get me. People in the projects told me whenever the police came by looking for me to question me, but they never snitched and told that I was living with City, though. Finally, they came to my school and pulled me out of algebra class one day. I was questioned about my whereabouts and my mother. Just like City had schooled me to say, I told them that, because of my mother's habits, I lived with a friend and there were so many Johns and feigns coming in and out of her apartment that there was no telling who had killed her.

And that was that. The police never pressed further because my mother was a junkie prostitute whose murder nobody really cared about. For another week, I forced out the thoughts of the night that I killed her. I went about my days as if nothing had ever happened, going to school and laying up under my boyfriend once he came back in from serving on the block.

Despite the thoughts of my mother, all was perfect in my world, until one Monday afternoon when I decided to ditch school. I had cramps so bad. I was laying on the couch alone in City's place with a heating pad on my stomach. Most of the times, City's brothers, Money and Shon, who sold dope with him, and their crew would be all over his place. His youngest brother, Shamar, would always be there after school before their mother made him go home for curfew.

City, Money, and Shamar had the same parents, Deuce and Valerie. Shon was their half-brother. Shon's mother was Deuce's bottom bitch, Tierra. She was one of his prostitutes who was so loyal that he'd grown feelings for her. The projects were well aware of the beef between Tierra and Deuce's wife, Valerie. The beef got real heavy when Shon was born three days after Money. Then Tierra had more kids by Deuce. She gave birth to twin boys, Jeremiah and Josiah, four years later. Then, Yummy, the first Savage baby girl, came along a year after that. They all lived in the projects in various buildings. It was known between Valerie and Tierra that they were sharing a man, and the beef was so heavy that Tierra tried her best to keep her kids away. However, Shon was now deep in the dope game with City, and her other kids snuck over to City's apartment whenever they could.

It was rumored that two years after Yummy was born, Deuce knocked up another one of his prostitutes. She had a baby girl named Tanisha, whom for years, Deuce hadn't claimed, although she looked just like a Savage kid, with their signature dark skin, big juicy lips, and slanted eyes.

Every Love Story Is Beautiful, But Ours Is Hood
by Jessica N. Watkins

Anyway, today of all days, I was in City's apartment alone. It was early in the morning when there was a knock on the door. As City had taught me, I grabbed the nine millimeter off of the table before going to the door.

"Who is it?" I asked, peering through the peephole.

On the other side of the door, I saw a chick with her face scrunched up as she spat, "Who the fuck is you?!"

At that point, everything that City had taught me had gone out of the window. I snatched the door open, sneering. "Akira! Who the fuck are you?"

Her guard seemed to ease when she looked me over and realized that I was much younger than her. "Where is City?" she asked, waving her hand dismissively. Then, she marched right by me and into the apartment.

I stood motionless in the doorway, staring at her and wondering who she was. I didn't even feel the cold December air whipping into the apartment. It made my skin crawl the way she comfortably sat on the couch and removed her coat.

"*Hellooo*?" she spat, snapping her fingers to get my attention. "Where the fuck is City? And who are you? Some lil' runner he hired?"

I ignored her questions and asked, "Who are *you*?"

by *Jessica N. Watkins*

She didn't like my obliviousness to who she was. Nope, not all. She cocked her head to the side and spat, "I'm City's woman. The bitch that took a case for him and been in fucking prison for two years. Now where the fuck is my man?"

My heart sank. My fourteen-year-old soul was crushed. I was heartbroken. How could I not know this? But, then I realized; shit, two years ago, I was only twelve, so of course I wouldn't have known anything about her. Even still, she might have thought she was City's girl, but clearly, she was one of many. As long as I had known him and his brothers, I hadn't heard anything about her.

I could look at her and tell that she wasn't a project bitch either. Even though she was fresh out of prison, she spoke differently. If she didn't know where to find City, then she definitely wasn't from around here.

Suddenly, I walked out. I was going to find City to clarify some shit. Yet, when I left, I didn't know that it would be my last time in that apartment.

As I marched towards the stairs, I could hear this bitch on my heels spazzing out. "Who are you?! Are you fuckin' City?! Is your little ass fucking my man?!"

I didn't owe this bitch an explanation, so I wasn't telling her anything. Because of the bond that City and I had,

EVERY LOVE STORY IS BEAUTIFUL, BUT OURS IS HOOD
by *Jessica N. Watkins*

I wanted to hear this from *him*. But, clearly, by my reaction, she knew that I had some connection to City.

All the way through the building and down the six flights to the courtyard, since the gawd damn elevators were always broken, I could hear her nagging-ass voice behind me. "Who the fuck are you?! You hear me, lil' bitch?! You bet' not be fuckin' my man! City is *mine*!"

She was getting the attention of others as I stormed through the building with her behind me. By the time I got to City in the courtyard, there was a whole crowd behind us.

City saw my puzzled face and was curious until he looked behind me. Then, it was as if all of the dark brown color in his face had flushed away. I could even see Shon and Money's eyes buck as they noticed this chick yapping behind me.

"City, who the fuck is this lil' bitch?!" she yelped.

I stared at him right in the eyes, waiting for him to shut her up and claim me.

Yet, all he said was, "Nova, when you get out?"

"I got out early for good behavior, motherfucka, but you 'bout to cause me to go back! I called myself surprising yo' ass, but I get here and find this lil' bitch in your crib. Who is she?!"

We all waited for his answer, the whole hood. Everybody had seen me with City here and there. I was the "lil' young chick" that City had no business with. Nobody believed that he was with me for me. Nobody believed that he was with me because of our connection and chemistry and nothing more because he wasn't even fucking me. However, as I looked between City and this Nova bitch, I realized that what I thought we were must have been a fairytale.

He didn't deny me, but he didn't claim me either.

"C'mon now. Stop acting a fool out here," was all he said to Nova.

That was all that I needed to hear. I turned on my heels and ran away. I didn't know where I was going because without City, I had nothing. I wished for him to stop me, but amongst the snickers from the crowd that I ran through, I didn't hear City's voice calling for me.

I kept running with tears in my eyes until I was a few blocks away at my high school. It was first-period lunch, so I started searching for my best friend, Lola.

"Lola!" I screamed when I saw her amongst a group of girls laughing.

When she turned and saw my tears, she ran toward me. "Best friend, what happened?!"

EVERY LOVE STORY IS BEAUTIFUL, BUT OURS IS HOOD
by Jessica N. Watkins

After telling her everything, she ditched the rest of the school day, and we went to her apartment, which was in the Ickies. I cried all night with visions of Nova and City in my head. Throughout the night, Lola assured me of the love that City and I had.

"Fuck that bitch!" Lola sneered. "That's *your* nigga. You been with him for a year. He been takin' care of you and you ain't even fuckin' him. Y'all got a connection."

Lola was right; City and I did have a connection deeper than anyone could imagine. Lola didn't know about what happened the night of my mother's murder. When it came to my mother, I barely spoke of her and was too embarrassed to bring my only friend to my home. I never told my mother about any school functions, in fear that she would actually show up. Everyone thought that I was pretty much on my own, which I was. But no one knew the hell that I went through at home, not even Lola. And I most definitely hadn't told her about the night that I killed my mother. But I knew; I knew the bond that had been created between City and me that night, so I knew that Lola was right. Despite whomever this Nova bitch was, me and City's connection ran deep. He was all that I had, and I needed him. So, I wiped my face, left

Lola's place, and made my way back to City's apartment, ready to get my man back.

But just as I had climbed the last set of stairs and entered the hallway that led to City's apartment, my eyes met City's. I was relieved when I saw so much love in his eyes for me. However, I was heartbroken when I noticed that, as he stared lovingly at me, he was cuffed and being escorted by three police officers in tactical gear with his brothers, Money, and Shon, being hauled off in the same way behind him.

From then on, I was all alone, and I never saw City again until...

CHAPTER ONE

- TEN YEARS LATER–

AKIRA WHITE

On a cold evening in January, I was sitting on the passenger's side of my man's Porsche truck. My fiancé, Davion McCoy, was a reserve linebacker for the Chicago Bears. The year prior, he'd gotten drafted days after he proposed to me on graduation day when we got our bachelor's degrees at Southern Illinois University.

The last ten years had been a drastic change from my days in the projects. After being left all alone, I stayed with my best friend, Lola, for two days until her mother wondered why I didn't have a place to live. After finding out that my mother was dead, she took me in. For two years, I enjoyed finally being a part of a happy home. Then there was a knock on her door. When the police officer appeared on the other side, we all got nervous, especially because he wasn't dressed like a regular police officer. He introduced himself as Detective Russell White, who was looking for his daughter, Akira. He was the John that had knocked up my mother.

EVERY LOVE STORY IS BEAUTIFUL, BUT OURS IS HOOD
by *Jessica N. Watkins*

Actually, when he had sex with my mother, he was just some knucklehead seventeen- year-old who was buying pussy from a pretty prostitute who was strolling near one of his crew's hang outs back then. He eventually got his life on track, went to the police academy, and quickly made his way up the ranks with training and a degree.

He'd learned about me when my mother's murder was broadcasted quickly during a brief segment on the news when they flashed a picture of her fourteen-year-old daughter. He remembered the night he'd spent with my mother and quickly realized that I was his because we were nearly twins. He had been searching for me ever since.

That was eight years ago. My father took me from Lola's home that day and spoiled me. He had taken every chance to make up for lost time and the horrible life that I had succumbed to since birth. I wanted for nothing, and he took great care of me.

Now, I was the fiancé of an NFL player. Life was surreal for me.

"Where are we going, baby?" I asked Davion.

We had been riding for a while since we left our new condo, purchased with his signing bonus money in the South Loop, so I was curious.

Every Love Story Is Beautiful, But Ours Is Hood
by *Jessica N. Watkins*

"Neko invited me to this party at his cousin's crib. They say it's supposed to be real dope."

I left it at that. If Davion and his closest teammate, Neko, were partying during the season, then I let it be. They weren't able to do it often, so I wanted Davion to enjoy himself.

I relaxed my head back on the headrest and nestled behind my scarf since Davion refused to turn up the heat. He'd fussed that I should have worn a longer dress when I asked him to. It was the dead of winter. We had just celebrated the New Year a week before. Snow and ice were on the ground, and it was cold as shit in Chicago. But as I said, this was one of the rare times that my man wanted to go out during the season, so I had dressed the part. Given his position, Davion wasn't filthy rich, but with his annual $500,000 NFL income, I was well taken care of. I wanted to work, but he didn't want me to. So, I spent my days shopping for clothes and my favorite pastime, makeup. I had studied so many YouTube makeup artists' how-to videos that I was able to beat my face that night. Then I perfected my huge natural kinky twist out, which I had dyed blonde to pop off of my dark brown skin. My light brown eyes burned through the blonde and highlighted the exotic, dark features that I had inherited from my father. I wrapped my 5'6", two-hundred-pound frame in an olive green, Gucci bandage dress and paired it with tan Louboutin heels decorated with gold studs.

As we drove through the city, I realized that we were heading further and further south. After about twenty-five minutes, we pulled onto a block in Matteson.

"Where are we?" I asked as Davion parked in front of a brick house.

Even though I was still inside of his truck, I could hear music spilling from the house, which was a few feet away from where he had parked. I looked curiously at the decorations inside of the snow on the lawn.

"This is Neko's cousin's house," Davion told me as he turned off the engine.

"So, it's a house party?"

"Yeah," he answered quickly and hopped out.

I looked down at my bare legs and Louboutin's in disappointment. Had I known that we were going to be at a house party, I would have thrown on some sneaker wedges and jeans. I should have known, however, when I strutted out of the walk-in closet that I'd had built in one of the extra bedrooms in our condo and saw that Davion was only in jeans, a tee, and Giuseppe boots.

EVERY LOVE STORY IS BEAUTIFUL, BUT OURS IS HOOD
by *Jessica N. Watkins*

Nevertheless, after Davion opened the passenger's door for me, I allowed my man to take my hand and lead me through the snow toward the front door. Along the walk up the side drive, I noticed the "Welcome Home" signs in the snow in the yard. I figured someone was returning home from the military, college, or something and kept chucking through the snow.

The door to the house was unlocked, so we walked right in. The house was filled to capacity; niggas upon niggas upon niggas. Even though we were in a nice neighborhood, these were some hood motherfuckers in this party; I knew it. My life had gone in a different direction than when I was young, but I had not lost all elements of the projects. And though most of the projects had been torn down in Chicago by then, I knew project niggas and bitches when I saw them.

Yeah, I definitely should have worn some gym shoes, I thought as Davion guided me through the thick crowd.

As I followed behind him, I took in the scenery. Beyond the house full of people, I saw the balloons and various signs. One that read, "Welcome Home, City," caught my attention. Without realizing it, I stopped dead in my tracks and stared at it in disbelief.

Ain't no fucking way.

Every Love Story Is Beautiful, But Ours Is Hood
by *Jessica N. Watkins*

I felt a tug on my hand. I looked up and saw Davion looking at me with concern as he said something that I couldn't hear over the loud, banging music. I waved my hand as if nothing was wrong. He turned and kept walking. I followed him with my heart beating out of my chest.

It couldn't be him, I thought.

It had been ten years, but I could never forget my first love. Taye 'City' Savage was the love of my life, and I had compared every man to him until I realized that I would never find a love or connection like that again. Memories of our past tried to force their way to the forefront of my mind as I followed Davion through the crowd, but I pushed them back. I assumed that the person that this party was in honor of could not be *my* City. The last time that I'd seen him, he was being arrested. I had heard through people in the Dearborns that City's apartment had been raided that night. Many had been arrested, but City had pled guilty to everything to spare his brothers. At fourteen, I didn't know how to contact him after he was locked up. I waited for him to send word to me. When he never did, I assumed that Nova was everything that she had claimed to be and that I was nothing but a fourteen-year-old girl who he had played.

Every Love Story Is Beautiful, But Ours Is Hood
by *Jessica N. Watkins*

It took me months to finally stop crying. However, I had never gotten over it because nobody had ever loved me the way that City had... not even Davion.

Every once in a while, the night that I stabbed my mother forced its way through all of the bad memories that I had buried on top of it. Though I was in a house full of banging music, screaming, and drunk people, memories of that murderous night overshadowed everything going on around me. The guilt started to choke me. Every detail of that night replayed in my mind, including how City took care of me. I remembered the bond between us that strengthened during the days that followed and that shattered into pieces when Nova showed up.

"Baby!"

Davion's voice brought me out of my hypnotic trance.

I looked up to Neko's smiling face as he greeted me, "What's up, Akira? You a'ight?"

I forced a smile and answered, "I'm fine. Whose party is this?"

"My cousin, City. He got out of prison this morning."

His answer caused my heart to drop to my feet. I couldn't believe that I was having this reaction to City after all of this time. I swallowed, but the lump in my throat caused me choke and cough.

Davion put a soothing hand on my shoulder. "You okay, babe?"

I nodded quickly to assure him that all was well. "Yeah," I answered before I cleared my throat. "I'm okay."

Over my rampant thoughts, I heard Neko explaining to Davion, "My cousin, City, was that nigga back in the day. Them Savage brothers wasn't nothing nice."

I felt faint. Suddenly, my mouth was dry. Not only had I never expected to see City again, but I never expected for my past to come back. City didn't only remind me of love that I had never obtained again and a broken heart; he also reminded me of what I had done to my mother.

Neko shouted, "Aye, what's up, cuz?!"

My eyes nervously darted up. I was relieved when I saw two women.

"Aye, Davion and Akira, this is my cousin, Tanisha, and this Zoe, my cousin's girlfriend."

They waved, and I nodded. Then I quickly turned away as if I was giving something else my attention before they could recognize me. I got even more nervous as I recalled Tanisha, the daughter that Deuce had once never claimed.

Every Love Story Is Beautiful, But Ours Is Hood
by Jessica N. Watkins

Instantly, I felt my stomach turn. I could no longer hide the feelings that all of these memories were bringing on. The anxiety was suffocating me.

As Tanisha and Zoe engaged in conversation with Neko, I stood on my tiptoes and said into Davion's ear, "Baby, I'm not feeling good."

He looked so disappointed.

I immediately assured him, adding, "You can stay, but I think I need to go home. I'm not going to enjoy myself. I'll take an Uber home."

"What's wrong?"

I frowned and rubbed my stomach to add emphasis. "I feel nauseous all of a sudden."

He smiled. "Pregnant?"

I giggled. "No, fool."

He pretended to pout. Then he replied, "Okay. I'll walk you out and wait for the Uber with you." He then whispered something to Neko. I was relieved when Davion then started walking me toward the front door.

As we made our way, suddenly the music stopped.

"Aye, I just wanna thank everybody for being here and welcoming a nigga back home."

Every Love Story Is Beautiful, But Ours Is Hood
by *Jessica N. Watkins*

I was so mad that the sound of his voice stopped me in my tracks. My eyes followed the smooth, deep rumble and peered beyond the crowd. There he was on the stairs; all dark skin, 6'5" of him. I wanted to look away, but I couldn't. Who knew that prison could be so good to a man? His dark, black skin was flawless. His build was big and brawny. His looks were epic. Every swagged-out, bad boy feature that I'd adored about him had only been enhanced over the last ten years. I stood there stuck, staring at those slanted, dark eyes surrounded by so many heavy lashes that they almost made his eyes look feminine. I adored the goatee and mustache that he'd grown out. It had matured his face and surrounded those big, juicy lips that I remembered kissing. Instead of the fade he'd had back then, he now had dreads that cascaded down his back, making him look like an African king.

"Baby," I suddenly heard in my ear.

I jumped, tore my eyes away from City, and remembered where I was and who I was with.

"I'm sorry," I simply whispered, swallowed hard, and kept walking. I hoped that I hadn't stared at City so obviously that Davion had noticed.

But who I did see notice me walking through the crowd was *City*, since Davion and I were the only people

EVERY LOVE STORY IS BEAUTIFUL, BUT OURS IS HOOD
by *Jessica N. Watkins*

leaving during his speech. We locked eyes, and I saw him squint as if he was trying to recognize me. I quickly turned my head and allowed Davion to usher me through the front door.

Once outside, I took out my phone and scrolled through the Uber app as City's voice soared from inside the house and pierced my soul.

"I'm sorry, baby," I told Davion. "I just really don't feel good."

I wondered if Davion could see my hands shaking. I wondered if he could hear the nervousness in my voice. But I think that he was so eager to get back in that party that he paid me no mind.

"It's cool, baby. I'll be home in a little while."

"Don't rush," I insisted. "Enjoy yourself."

Shit, I needed some time to digest all of this. *A lot* of time!

Luckily, there were many Uber drivers in the area, so one arrived within three minutes. I kissed Davion goodbye and rushed inside of the waiting Tahoe, running away from the cold that had settled in during the three-minute wait and away from the good and bad memories.

TAYE 'CITY' SAVAGE

I was in the middle of thanking everyone for coming when I noticed motherfuckers actually walking *out* of my welcome home party during my gawd damn speech. But then shorty's beauty caught me off guard. Her familiarity fucked me up. I recognized her from somewhere, but I couldn't put a finger on it. I shrugged it off in order for Nova, who was standing close by, not to notice and kept talking.

"A nigga been gone for what feels like forever, and it's so good to see everybody. Thank you for coming out. I fucks with y'all the long way. I want everybody to have a good time. Bottles is poppin' in this bitch, so turn up. Deejay, start that shit back up."

Just as the crowd started to clap and cheer and the music started bumping again, I was swarmed by family members and people I knew from the hood as I descended the stairs.

Ten years ago, I knew that the name Savage was epic in the projects. From the age of seventeen, I had worked hard on building my own name outside of my father's epic shadow. What my father had done with hoes, I had started doing with

Every Love Story Is Beautiful, But Ours Is Hood
by *Jessica N. Watkins*

drugs. I was on the way to building an empire with my brothers when my spot was raided. Since I was the oldest and it was my organization, I took the fall for it all so that my brothers could stay free. In exchange, I wanted my brothers to keep our name alive in these streets. What Money and Shon did was beyond that, however; they created a legacy. The Savage name was even more epic in the hood. The Savage empire was financed through drug money, had funded other businesses, and had been run by my brothers for the last ten years.

When I spotted 'ol boy coming back in the party, I excused myself from everyone and headed toward him. I saw my cousin, Neko, following me with his eyes and then beeline toward me. Neko must have thought that I was about to check this lame-ass lookin' boy for walking out of my party because he reached me just as I reached that goofy and said, "Aye, aye, cuz, this my boy and teammate that I was telling you about that I invited, Davion."

"What up, bro?" I greeted as I shook up with him. "Looked like you were on your way out at first."

"Nah, my fiancée wasn't feeling well. Sorry about that."

EVERY LOVE STORY IS BEAUTIFUL, BUT OURS IS HOOD
by *Jessica N. Watkins*

Fiancée? Surprisingly, hearing that made my jaw clench.

"Oh, that was your girl," I spoke closely so that he could hear me over the music. "She looks familiar, like I know her from the Dearborns. What's her name?"

"Akira."

I fucking knew it. I could never forget her. "Akira White?" I asked just for confirmation.

His eyebrow curled curiously as he answered, "Yeah."

To ease homeboy a little bit, I told him, "Yeah, I remember her little ass from back in the day." Then I left it at that. But as he and Neko chopped it up with me and offered me skybox seats to their games, I couldn't help but remember the pretty young thang that I fell for back in the day. Akira was the little girl that I had loved, despite her being five years younger than me and not giving me no pussy.

Akira was my heart back then. I was a street nigga that gave zero fucks, but back then, that little girl snatched a piece of my heart, and I couldn't get it back from her virgin ass no matter how hard I tried. We had known each other since we were shorties because her mother was one of my father's hoes. Since I was five years older than her, she was always just a shorty to me, at first. Even when my father let her

EVERY LOVE STORY IS BEAUTIFUL, BUT OURS IS HOOD
by *Jessica N. Watkins*

mother go because she was too hooked on the pipe, I still saw her mother selling pussy for a high. I used to wonder where her daughter was, if she was out in the streets. Then at the age of seventeen, when I first started selling dope successfully, Nova, a bad-ass chick two years my senior that I was able to bag because of my bread, took a case for me when we were stopped by the police and searched. She put my work in her purse and was given some time, because the hating-ass prosecutor knew that she was taking the wrap for a man and wouldn't snitch. That's when Akira caught my eyes. No matter how many times I threw her a couple of dollars, she never gave me that pussy, which made me like her even more. Eventually, I had spent so much time with her that having sex with her was the last thing on my mind. I just wanted to take care of Akira. I loved her that much. I hated the living conditions that her mother had her in and wished that she was older so that I could legally just take her out of that bullshit. Then, I walked in on her mother lying there dead and saw the look of pure fear in Akira's face. That day, a bond grew between us that I never forgot.

Back then, I wanted to make shorty mine. No matter her age, I was willing to be patient until she was ready to give me that pussy. In the meantime, I wanted to love on her.

by *Jessica N. Watkins*

When Nova popped up that day, I was so taken off guard that I didn't know what the fuck to say. I couldn't disrespect Akira, but Nova had done something for me that many women would've never done.

Before Nova took that case for me, she was one of my hoes that was fighting for the number one spot in my life. In her eyes, when she took that case for me, it was her slam dunk on every other bitch that I was fucking with. I had all plans to explain that to Akira, but I got raided that night. After that, my main focus was saving my brothers, who had gotten arrested with me. While I was pleading guilty, Akira was in the back of my mind the entire time.

I shrugged off the thoughts of Akira and excused myself from Neko and his lame-ass homeboy. After a few months of being in prison, I forced myself to let Akira go. She was so young that I didn't want to fuck up her potential by tying her to a dude that was doing a ten-year bid. Though Akira was always in the back of my mind, it wasn't hard to move on, I must admit. Nova was a ride or die bitch for me and never left my side over the past ten years. When other hoes forgot about me, Nova never did. She wrote me constantly, visited at every opportunity, and worked closely with my brothers to turn our spot on the block into an empire. Akira may have had my heart then, but Nova had earned my loyalty now.

Nova had taken care of me with no question in every sense of the word, so I owed her that much.

CHAPTER TWO

ZOE MOORE

I was stumbling through the hallway of Nova and City's house. It was nearly four in the morning, and this gawd damn party was still crackin'. I was drunk *and* high. The last thing that I wanted was another fucking drink. I wanted nothing but my bed. Since my man, Money, was still partying with his brothers, I was on my way to lie down in one of the guest bedrooms until he was ready to go.

Inches from the bedroom, I felt a hard tug snatch me back and pull me into the bathroom as I was passing by.

"What the fuck are you doing?!" I spat at Money's brother, Shon, as he slammed the bathroom door shut.

When he looked me up and down, licking those big and juicy, signature Savage lips, no matter how hard I wanted to fight it, my pussy leaked.

"*No*," I told him, but he knew that my body wanted differently. "Money is right downstairs."

"You think I don't know that shit?" he fussed as he tugged at my jeggings.

EVERY LOVE STORY IS BEAUTIFUL, BUT OURS IS HOOD
by Jessica N. Watkins

I swatted his hand away. "You're drunk."

"I know. So." He shrugged. "Gimme that pussy," Shon ordered as he grabbed the back of my neck.

Like always, it took very little for him to persuade me. I was Money's woman, but Shon had had a hold on this pussy for a year, and no matter how hard I tried, I could not get it out of his grasp.

"Fuck, Shon," I mumbled against his mouth as he reached into my jeggings and began playing with my already throbbing clit.

"You ain't got no panties on," he moaned at the realization. "That was for me?"

I winced, trying to be quiet as I ground against his fingers that were rotating roughly in a circle against my clitoris. "Yes, it was for you."

He growled, knowing that I liked that shit. When he yanked my jeggings down, in my heart, I knew that I should have stopped him. I could hear my nigga a few feet away downstairs. This was the kinda kinky, risqué shit that Shon did that always had me impatiently waiting on the next time I would get the dick again.

by *Jessica N. Watkins*

Suddenly, he swung me around. I gasped as he pushed my head into the sink, put my left foot on the toilet and dove into my syrupy center, dick first.

"Ahhh!" I gasped from the sensation.

He didn't even allow me to brace myself; like the savage he was, he held on to my waist and tore this pussy up. I bit my lip as my face contorted into ugly expressions and tears formed in my eyes from the sensation of the pressure and pleasure.

At the age of twenty, I was the luckiest bitch in the hood to have the most outlandish luck of having, not one, but two Savage brothers fucking me. Honestly, when I met Money at the age of fifteen, I never thought that we would end up together. He was a Savage brother getting money, and I was a naïve little girl, three years younger than him, that he randomly fucked here and there. As the years went by, our fuck sessions grew closer in between. After three years of being just a dip and fighting off all of his other hoes, I was still standing as his girl. When I was nineteen, I moved into his crib. I didn't need to work, so I never went to college. There was no need. My man took care of me. Now, things were still the same. Money was still getting money but on a higher level. He was taking good care of me financially. He was also very

EVERY LOVE STORY IS BEAUTIFUL, BUT OURS IS HOOD
by *Jessica N. Watkins*

much still a hoe, and I was still fighting off other bitches! The last straw was when he told me about a baby he had with this bitch named Bliss a year ago. That shit hurt my soul. Men cheat. Some women are able to deal with that, and I was one of those women. Money was a man of reputation, popularity, and wealth. You don't walk away from a Savage brother and give him to these other hoes. So, despite the heartbreaker, I stayed with my man.

Yet, I ran to Shon. Money and Shon were not only brothers, but they were also business partners. They did everything together. So, as a single man, Shon was in my home often. I fed him nightly, and he slept in our extra bedrooms often. I never looked at him that way, however, because he was Money's brother, of course. Yet, no woman, or hell, not even any straight men, could ignore how fine Shon was. He and Money had different mothers, so despite the signature Savage lips and height, he had a physical difference from Valerie's sons. He had inherited his mother's light skin and wavy dark hair, which he kept in a messy man bun. He had high cheekbones, almond-shaped eyes, heavy eyelids, and bronze skin.

Despite Shon's good looks and the fact that Money was a hoe, during my first year in a "committed relationship" with

by *Jessica N. Watkins*

Money, I was faithful through all the hurt, heartbreak, and hoes. But that day that I found out about Money's side baby, I just wanted to talk to Shon and vent. Yet, as Shon held me tightly, I wanted to hurt Money like he had hurt me. When I started kissing Shon, he was game. I wasn't surprised. Though they worked closely together and were brothers, there was a constant competition that stemmed from Shon because he had always felt like had to prove his importance from childhood, since he was the "side baby" who was born days apart from Money. Shon would never admit it, but he competed with his brothers and constantly fought for approval from their father and the hood because so many people thought he was the legendary mistake. Even though his mother gave birth to three more of Deuce's kids, Shon had kept that competitive mentality, which formed him into the man that he was today.

So after we had sex the first time, he took every opportunity to fuck me. Sometimes he planned it, other times he lustfully took it. He would just show up when he knew Money wasn't home or take it when Money was only a few feet away.

"Yessss, Shon," I moaned.

"Gawd damn, this pussy wet. Is it mine?"

Every Love Story Is Beautiful, But Ours Is Hood
by *Jessica N. Watkins*

"Yes," I lied, knowing better.

If bitches couldn't take me from Money, Shon definitely couldn't. He knew that, which was why he pulled stunts like this.

He grabbed my long, natural ponytail and started ramming into my pussy. I feared that the slapping sound of his pelvis colliding with my wet ass could be heard outside of the bathroom door, but the music and voices on the other side of it were still so loud.

I gripped the sides of the sink, attempting to take all of the dick. "Oh my *Gooood*."

"I'm cumming, baby. *Fuuuuck*."

I braced myself as he pounded and pounded, causing intolerable pressure in my core until he burst inside of me.

Shon had stopped caring about wearing condoms with me long ago. He *wanted* me to get caught up. I knew it, so I fought it. The more I fought, the more he tried. It was the competition of it all. But no matter what Money had done to me, I would never let him catch me being disloyal. No matter how disloyal he was to me, he expected loyalty from everyone around him. Those that were disloyal to him paid a deadly price. Money's lethal reputation was known in the

EVERY LOVE STORY IS BEAUTIFUL, BUT OURS IS HOOD
by *Jessica N. Watkins*

streets. No matter how Shon tried to compete with that, he lost to Money's wrath.

With a growl, he pulled out of me.

"Don't move," he told me as I felt his cum dripping out of me.

I wasn't scared of getting pregnant. Unbeknownst to him and Money, I was on birth control. I dealt with Money's shit, but I was to be damned if I brought kids into our bullshit.

After Shon wiped me clean with wipes that were under the sink, I pulled my jeggings back up, happy that the party sounded like it was still going on downstairs.

"I missed that pussy," Shon told me with rugged breaths.

"She missed you too." I had. Sex with Money was full of heartbreak on my end. I constantly worried about who he was fucking. Fucking Shon was careless, free and a vacation from the constant hurt that I felt when I was with Money.

After we dressed, I told him, "Give me something."

He reached into his pocket and handed me a few pills. They were a mix of Mollies, Oxy, Xans, and Percs.

My pill habit had formed from the hurt that Money inflicted, which he never tried to heal, and the confusion and guilt of being lost in Shon's lust. I didn't know how to deal with either issue. I didn't want to feel anything. I wanted to be numb, so I started relying on being high on prescription drugs to float through it all daily when weed was no longer strong enough.

I popped a Xan. Then I chewed it so that it would settle into my system faster.

Shon then kissed my forehead and opened the bathroom door, leaving out without even checking to see if someone was outside in the hallway. I shook my head and waited, giving him a few minutes to arrive back downstairs to the party before I did.

AKIRA WHITE

I lay in the darkness for hours unable to sleep. The memories were stalking me and giving me living nightmares. Although City had always been in my thoughts, I had forced myself to forget about the night that I killed my mother. Now, those thoughts were stalking my mind. By three in the morning, I was still wide awake, so I heard Davion entering our condo.

"Shit," I groaned as I rolled over, turning my back to his side of the bed.

I closed my eyes and attempted to lay as still as possible as I heard his Giuseppe boots walking heavily on the hardwood floor in our hallway. I watched him stumble into our bedroom. I could hear him grunting as he attempted to take off his clothes without falling. I peeked through the darkness at him and chuckled as he tripped while trying to step out of his jeans.

"Fuck," he mumbled.

As soon as he was naked, he stumbled toward the bed, and I played dead. But no matter how still I lay, I felt his lips on my cheeks within seconds of him crawling under our

Every Love Story Is Beautiful, But Ours Is Hood
by *Jessica N. Watkins*

down comforter. I cringed because his cold lips felt clammy. Still, I laid there playing dead, and yet, he didn't give a fuck. He rolled me over, parted my legs and started kissing around my lace bra.

"Baby," I tried to mumble sleepily.

He mumbled, "Yes, bae?"

I smelled the stench of Hennessy and frowned. "I'm sleepy."

He chuckled and said, "It won't take me that long."

Like always, I just shut up and took it.

You know when you are with a man that you are passionately in love with that fucks the living shit out of you? When you're just on cloud nine because you have everything in one man?

That was *not* my life!

I groaned inwardly as Davion's kisses traveled down my stomach and landed on my dry, uneager crevice. Though the wetness of his tongue added moisture to it, my pussy was not at all pleased with the way that he licked it like he was scared of it. He ate pussy like a scared little boy. He really thought he was good at it, though. I lifted my head and watched with amusement as he shook his head vigorously like he was eating this motherfucker to death. On cue, I moaned as if it felt like the shit, but on the inside, I was laughing my ass off.

There was no need in telling Davion how to eat my pussy. He thought he knew everything and could do no wrong. Not only was Davion popular and every woman's dream, he was good-looking. His thick and tall football build was coated in tanned skin. His dark hair was always in a curly fade that left enough coils on the top to run your fingers through. Though he had tan skin, it was decorated with tattoos that covered his arms, back, neck, and legs. Although he was a college boy who had never committed a crime in his life, he had the swag of the niggas I loved in the projects. That is what initially attracted me to him. His good looks and reputation left him with an abundance of women who fought to be on his arm. Those women would never have the audacity to tell him that he couldn't fuck or eat pussy. So, he fucked me his way because he had been getting away with fucking like this since he started getting pussy in his teens.

He never stayed down there long, so I was put out of that misery within minutes. Yet, misery quickly returned as he flipped me over and slid his five-inch dick inside me.

Not only could he not eat pussy, but his dick was average in size and performance. It was average length, but wide. It could have been halfway decent had he fucked me any other way besides from the back. Bible, he only fucked me doggy-style. He claimed it was because he liked to be in control. In my mind, I knew it was because that was probably the easiest position for him to get his average dick past all of this ass and thighs and get the deepest in my pussy.

He began to moan and grunt, and I instantly rolled my eyes into the back of my head. I was thankful that he was behind me so that he couldn't see the way that I frowned in annoyance as he pounded my pussy as if he was hitting one wall.

"Yeah, take this dick, baby."

Oh, shut the fuck up!

I know it's a wonder why I'm with him since he can't fuck. Well, my father had taught me to settle down out of comfort. He schooled me to never be with a man who fucked me good, but didn't and couldn't take care of me. So, when I met Davion, who was one of the stars of the football team and sure to be an NFL draft pick, I settled for comfort, love, and commitment from a good man. All of that was more important than passion, chemistry, and good sex.

I was not a sexually satisfied woman, but I was a lucky one.

EVERY LOVE STORY IS BEAUTIFUL, BUT OURS IS HOOD
by *Jessica N. Watkins*

TAYE 'CITY' SAVAGE

Finally, the last party guest had stumbled out of the house. I was drunk, and my dick was rock hard.

I hadn't fucked in ten years; ten...long...fucking...years. I was ready to bend Nova over the moment I held her in my arms when I walked out of those prison gates that morning. But the moment I felt the shade in her touch, the fantasy of fucking her went away.

Nova had always been loyal, but loving was never her forte. That was cool with a nigga like me when I met her because I wasn't trying to settle down with her. Twelve years ago, Nova was a hot-headed chick trying to prove her worth to a young hustler by fucking me and taking a case on my behalf. She was a bougie chick from the burbs that fantasized about being the ride or die bitch to a street nigga. Once she got what she wanted, her focus was to keep me by proving her potential to be an asset to my empire, but never proving her love.

I thought that would change once I got back home, but hadn't shit changed, except there was no correctional officer in the room when were together. She acted like we were still

Every Love Story Is Beautiful, But Ours Is Hood
by *Jessica N. Watkins*

in the visitation room and there were restrictions. I figured it was because we had had little time physically together before she took that case for me, and then, as soon as she was released, I was locked up. All of our time had been verbal with little physical interaction. I figured she had to get used to me again. Yet, I found it odd that Akira had looked at me with more admiration and love in a few seconds than my own fucking woman.

But at the moment, I gave zero fucks about any of that. I had ten years' worth of backed up frustration to take out on some pussy.

"I feel you looking at me, City." She ended her statement with a smirk as she undressed in front of the dresser.

"I wasn't trying to hide it. You know how long it's been since I've seen a naked woman. I'm just enjoying the view."

And the view was most definitely something to enjoy. Nova's body had been manufactured to perfection. Over the last ten years, her petite body had matured by the help of my money. She had gotten implants, fat transfers, and butt injections. The only thing real on her was her short haircut and light skin. I preferred natural curves, but after all of the

EVERY LOVE STORY IS BEAUTIFUL, BUT OURS IS HOOD
by Jessica N. Watkins

years I had spent locked away from a woman, fake or not, her body had my dick already leaking precum.

When I started walking toward her, she knew what time it was. Once I was in front of her, I leaned her against the dresser and took her mouth. It was the first time that we had kissed with our tongues meeting in years. Yet, I felt no passion from the woman who had spent ten years driving five hours to visit me every other weekend. There had been more passion in her hustle than there was in this kiss. This was the first time that I had been able to hold her, and when I wrapped my arms around her tiny waist, she responded like this was some everyday shit.

I ain't no weak nigga. I was as savage as them all. But every man wanted his woman to treat him like he was that nigga in the bedroom, especially after doing a bid, but Nova was emotionless.

She left my arms and went to her knees like it was a job and not something she had waited a decade for. There was no drive in the way that she pulled my dick out and started sucking it. There was no energy, no passion, and no lust. I was expecting her to slob all over this rock hard, nine-and-a-half-inch dick almost too wide to fit in her mouth. But,

EVERY LOVE STORY IS BEAUTIFUL, BUT OURS IS HOOD
by Jessica N. Watkins

nah, she sucked this motherfucker like she had been forced to do it every day at gun point.

But I had been so deprived that I shrugged that shit off, closed my eyes, and waited eagerly for this nut.

Yet, I felt it; there was no love in the room with us. There was just loyalty.

EVERY LOVE STORY IS BEAUTIFUL, BUT OURS IS HOOD
by *Jessica N. Watkins*

KEANDRE 'MONEY' SAVAGE

This bitch, I thought as I shook my head at Zoe. I put my eyes back on the road before I crashed. With my eyes on the road, I sneered. For the life of me, I couldn't understand why this girl got so high off pills that she could barely keep her eyes open. I knew an addict when I saw one. Back in the day when I was still on the corner serving, I came in contact with hypes every day. Zoe might not have been sticking a needle in her arm or snorting lines, but she was definitely dependent on prescription medication.

When I first peeped it, I wasn't tripping. Shit, every other person I knew popped a Xan, Narco, or Perc here and there. Nowadays, those drugs were just as profitable as mollies and cocaine. Plus, when she was high, she wasn't on my ass about what bitch she thought I was fucking every time I left the crib. It was when she was dysfunctional and started stealing from my stash when I started to have a fucking problem.

I blamed myself, though. She barely smoked weed and had a drink only here and there until I had that baby on her a year ago. Ever since, though she had stayed with me, emotionally and mentally, she was barely in the relationship because she stayed high all the time. But I knew she did it just to deal with my shit, so I let her do it out of guilt.

Once we got to the crib, I started to shake her awake. "Zoe... Zoe... Zo—"

"What?! Shit!" she snapped as she jumped out of her sleep.

I just chuckled and shook my head. "We at the crib. Get yo' ass out the car. C'mon. It's cold as fuck outside."

It was like five degrees, but the sun was rising at six in the morning and shining so bright that Zoe's dark eyes squinted as she looked confused out of the window. Realizing that we were indeed at the crib, she slowly got out of the car. I took a moment to shake my head at her dumb ass as she climbed out of my Range Rover, before I got out of the truck too and got the hell out of the cold.

I regretfully followed Zoe up our driveway and toward my building just a few minutes away from City and Nova's crib. My walk was slow because I was preparing myself for the drama awaiting me. After a long night of fun and celebration, the last thing I wanted to do was ruin it, but I had been putting this conversation off long enough.

EVERY LOVE STORY IS BEAUTIFUL, BUT OURS IS HOOD
by *Jessica N. Watkins*

Once in the crib, we removed our shoes at the door and walked on the cozy beige carpet, until we reached the master bedroom on the second floor. We were both beat. Lately, life had been hectic with preparations for City's release. Since he had been released that morning, the day had been nonstop partying. I just wanted to lay the down, but I had to holla at Zoe about this right fucking now.

I sat on the bed, watching her undress. She was moving so slow because she was high as fuck. She looked good with every piece of clothing she took off. But after five years of bullshit, my dick barely got hard when I saw her naked. We barely had sex. The only reason I'd fucked her on New Year's Eve was because I was drunk and she woke me up with some sloppy toppy. Our relationship was just an arrangement. She was more like a roommate now than my woman. I can't say that I ever loved her because I was so young when I cuffed her that I didn't even know what love was. I wifed her because she had stuck it out. She fought for her position when all my other hoes had quit. Every nigga I knew had a main bitch, so I picked her to be mine. And I had felt like I'd made the right choice back then. But with every bitch I got caught up with, the more depressed she got, our relationship just turned into two people living together and

EVERY LOVE STORY IS BEAUTIFUL, BUT OURS IS HOOD
by Jessica N. Watkins

trying not to get on one another's nerves. We both failed miserably at that, however.

We were only still together because she refused to leave and give me to another woman, and I was man enough to know that if I left her, she would have nowhere to go.

Nevertheless, I couldn't deny how good she looked. She was thick as fuck as a teenager and was even thicker now. She was a petite 5'5" and had so many curves that I got dizzy watching them. When niggas were paying to build their women's bodies, I liked chicks with them Southern, homegrown curves. I didn't like those fake injection booties, those big-ass bubbles that looked like they were being held up by two sticks. Urgh! Fuck that! I liked cornbread thick, and Zoe was definitely that with skin the color of Jiffy Mix.

No matter the hoes I had on the side when me and Zoe first met, she was my favorite back then. That was why she had become my number one. And even though the excitement had been sucked out of our relationship, I didn't want to hurt her further... but I had to.

"Why you got that look your face?"

I looked up suddenly, not realizing that my thoughts were written all over my face.

Every Love Story Is Beautiful, But Ours Is Hood
by *Jessica N. Watkins*

Regretfully, I sighed and told her, "I gotta holla at you."

She instantly got nervous. I could see the fear in her eyes. I had told her some fucked up shit in the past. She had found out some fucked up shit over the years too. But this here was going to take the cake.

She folded her arms. Her voice shook nervously as she asked, "What?"

Again, I sighed slowly and replied, "Umm... "

Fuck it, I thought. I figured I'd spit it out. Like I said, no matter the hoes she had found out about, or the times I had disappeared on her, no matter the phone calls I didn't answer, no matter the text messages she'd found in my phone, and the hoes that called, she had never left me. I had had a baby on her, but she was still with me. So, fuck it...

"Bliss is moving in for a lil' while."

As expected, her eyes bucked, and she started going clean the fuck off. "*What*?! Are you fucking crazy?!"

As she snapped, she took quick, heavy steps toward me. I met her in the middle of the floor. She tried to swing on me, but I was too quick for her. I grabbed her arms to stop her.

EVERY LOVE STORY IS BEAUTIFUL, BUT OURS IS HOOD
by Jessica N. Watkins

"Look, I know it's a fucked up situation," I started, still holding her arms to stop this from turning into a physical fight. "But you know her crib caught on fire, and I ain't tryin' to have my son with no place to go."

Like always, when I mentioned my son, Zoe looked sick to her fucking stomach. Suddenly, the anger was gone. Her fire was put out, and she fell weak. "You're crazy! After I forgave you for knocking that bitch up and having that little side baby, you—"

"Watch your fucking mouth," I threatened through gritted teeth as I gave her a slight shake and let her go with a small push.

"*No!* Fuck that!" she yelled. But no matter how mad she was, she knew better than to run up. She just stood in the middle of the floor screaming until she turned red and tears came to her eyes. "How much shit do you expect me to fucking take from you, Money?! Gawd damn! I already gotta deal with her being in your life for eighteen years. Now you want to move the bitch in?!"

"Just until I can find her another crib and—"

"That's bullshit! You're on bullshit! Nigga, you got money! Who the fuck do you think you talkin' to? You can get her a place!"

Every Love Story Is Beautiful, But Ours Is Hood
by Jessica N. Watkins

"I am, but in the meantime, she—"

"Fuck the meantime! Get that bitch a hotel! Why she gotta stay here?!"

"Because I don't want my son stuck in some fucking hotel for weeks anymore. I want him to be able to run around, play, and fuck shit up like kids supposed to. He been stuck in that hotel for two weeks already."

Tears were forming in Zoe's eyes as she glared at me, shaking her head. I knew she couldn't believe that I would pull a move like this, but she knew I cared for my son more than anything, even more than I cared for her. That's what fucked her up.

"Where the fuck is her family? Why can't she stay in one of the spots?"

I looked at her ass like she was crazy. "C'mon now. You sound stupid. You know I ain't havin' my son stay in no fucking trap house. You know she ain't got no family here. Plus, she ain't takin' my son out of the state." Again, she looked sick at the sound of me giving a fuck about my son, and I ignored that shit. "She's gonna be in the vacant condo downstairs. You act like she's gon' be in one of the spare bedrooms or some shit. It'll be three thousand square feet between you and her. She ain't gon' be in your way. You shouldn't even see her. I'll make it my business to find her a place as soon as I can."

At that, I walked out of the bedroom. I knew that Zoe was too afraid of me walking out of the house and to one of my hoes to keep talking shit. She wasn't going to like it. Hell, Bliss didn't like it. But this was the only option, and they were going to fucking deal with it because, without me, they didn't have shit.

I could still hear her crying as I made my way downstairs to the den where I was opting to sleep for a few hours. Yet, those tears didn't faze me. Zoe probably wouldn't get much sleep that night, but I would sleep just fine.

CHAPTER THREE

AKIRA WHITE

When I saw Lola's name and picture pop up on the screen of my Galaxy, I answered right away. I had been waiting all weekend to tell her what had happened, but I never had a moment since Davion was around or I was at his game. Now that it was Monday morning and he would be at workouts and practice all morning, I had all the time in the world.

"What's up, girl?" I answered as I turned down The Real on the seventy-eight-inch curved TV hanging on the wall in my master bedroom. I got cozy under the covers as I adjusted the wireless Bluetooth headphones in my ears. When I was alone in my bed was when I was the happiest because I didn't have to worry about Davion trying to fuck.

"Hey, best friend," Lola greeted.

"What's going on?"

"*Working*... unlike yo' ass, heffa."

"Whatever, bitch."

We both giggled.

Every Love Story Is Beautiful, But Ours Is Hood
by *Jessica N. Watkins*

Lola and I had remained very tight since our days running around in the projects. But after graduating from college, she moved to Miami with her fiancé. He had been on the football team with Davion, but he got drafted by the Dolphins. We had moved up considerably in our worlds from our days in the Dearborns, but we were still very much those little project girls at heart.

"Bitch, you *choose* to work," I teased.

"Because I ain't about to let this nigga think he can tell me what to do because he takes care of me," Lola sassed.

"Whatever. You're at work, but are you busy or nah?"

She sucked her teeth and replied, "Hell nah, girl. What's the tea?"

I giggled. I knew this chick wasn't busy. She was an executive assistant to the head of pediatrics at Miami Children's Hospital, who was always out of town at conferences. So, Lola barely had shit to administer but her fucking Facebook page.

"So...," I started. "Neko invited me and Davion to his cousin's house party this weekend. As soon as we walked in, I started recognizing people. You would not fucking believe whose party it was, girl."

"Whose?" she asked eagerly.

EVERY LOVE STORY IS BEAUTIFUL, BUT OURS IS HOOD
by *Jessica N. Watkins*

"City."

Lola gasped so loud that I was sure her whole damn department had heard her. "Shut the fuck up," she whispered into the phone. "He finally got out?!"

Of course, Lola knew everything about City. I had cried over him for months while lying in the bed that we shared after her mother took me in. She knew how much I loved him. She knew how close we were. But what she didn't know was why. I still had never told her how City and my bond was created that night that he walked in on me and my mother's lifeless body.

I shook off the horrific memories replaying like a bad movie in my mind. "Yes, girl."

"I know you were freaking out."

As I lay there replaying the night of the party in my head, a smile spread across my face, thinking about how good City looked. "Hell yeah. I never expected to see him again."

"What did you say to him?"

"Not a gawd damn thing. Girl, I got the hell up out of there."

"Why?"

Just thinking of speaking to him made me blush in embarrassment. "Because it would have been too weird."

Every Love Story Is Beautiful, But Ours Is Hood
by *Jessica N. Watkins*

"I know you don't have no feelings for him still. You were only fourteen, girl."

"Hell nah," I lied.

Did I still want to be with City as I was back in the day? No. I had long since gotten over that. However, the love that I had for City still burned hot in my heart as I lay under the covers hiding from the icy winds seeping in through the windows.

"But he had the nerve to hit me up on Facebook yesterday talkin' about can we talk. What do we have to talk about?"

When I saw his instant message the night before, I damn near dropped my phone in my drink. It was only a few short sentences: "What up? How you been? Can we talk?" But it blew me away, so I didn't respond. He hadn't said shit to me in ten years, and suddenly, he wanted to have some what-you-been-up-to conversation? Hell nah! I could admit that I never loved a man like I loved him, but I had grown up to realize that maybe I shouldn't! That kind of love hurts like hell.

"Maybe he wanna catch up," Lola offered.

"Catch up on what? The last ten years he been in prison?! Girl, bye!"

TAYE 'CITY' SAVAGE

"What's up, Deuce?"

My father insisted that me and all of his kids call him Deuce. He and my mother were both fourteen when they had me, so he felt way too young to be called "Dad" back then. He had been more of a big brother to me anyway. I was alongside him while he pimped. I had collected money from many of his hoes. He'd taught me the ways of the streets when I was barely through puberty.

My father and I dapped each other up. Then I sat at the bar next to him in V75 Chicago, a lounge on the Southside of the city where all the hustlers and dope boys kicked it at heavy.

"Finally got time for your old man?" Deuce taunted.

I chuckled. "It's been a lot goin' on since I got out. You know how it is."

He nodded in agreement. Although my father had never done a long bid in prison, he had been locked up here and there for various crimes back in the day. As a pimp with a line of hoes, my mother stayed bailing him out of jail. Now, my father's business was virtual. Most women no longer sold pussy on corners. They sold it on Craigslist, Backpage, and whore houses in Nevada when he felt like traveling. Yet he still had a few faithful hoes that stood on the corners of the Windy City to get his money.

After telling the bartender to bring us two double shots of 1738, my father turned toward me. "Lookin' good. You don' swole up."

A deep chuckle left my throat. I was never a little nigga, but I had gained about thirty pounds of muscle on top of my already thick frame while I was locked up. My only option behind those bars was to work out to keep my mind clear, so that's what I did.

"Now that you don' had some time to chill and get you some pussy, you ready to work?"

That was my father; always focused on getting to the money. Although he got money from selling pussy, he was well informed on how the Savage drug empire went since it started with his investment and he'd introduced me to the connect.

"Are you going to take your empire back over or let your brothers continue to run it?" Deuce pressed.

"I don't know, honestly. Money and Shon have run it smoothly."

That was understatement. At the time that my spot was raided, our little organization was putting a couple thousand in our pockets every week. We had no workers. We were the guys on the block hustling. I had taken that deal just when we were on the cusp of coming up. In exchange for me going down for them, they took the twenty-seven thousand that I had stashed in our parents' home and, over the last ten years, turned it into a million dollars' worth of assets, investments, and properties. We weren't drug lords with Bentleys in the driveway of estates. Yet, my brothers had made sure that the ten years I did for them was worth it and that all of our siblings were eating without slaving for it.

"I'm comfortable," I added. "Money and Shon know that nothing goes down without my say so. I might let them have their lane. They worked hard for it. They earned it. I'm proud of them niggas."

I was proud of all of my brothers. Money and Shon were running the drug aspect of the family business. The oldest brothers—Shon, Money, and I—refused to allow our younger brothers to go down this deadly path of the drug game, however. We had seen what it did to others and us. So, we'd purchased our twenty-one-year-old brother, Shamar, a tattoo shop. He was teaching our youngest twin brothers,

Every Love Story Is Beautiful, But Ours Is Hood
by *Jessica N. Watkins*

Jeremiah and Josiah, known as Mayhem and Kaos in the streets and to our family, the art of tattooing as well. So, when they graduated from high school, their bad asses would have a way to make money, instead of the drug game and gang life that they so desperately wanted to be a part of.

I was proud of my brothers. We all made the Savage name proud and spoiled our sisters, Yummy and Tanisha.

A boss not only balled out and told motherfuckers what to do; a boss was about putting people in position and changing their lives. That was exactly what I had done and planned to continue to do for the Savage family.

"You should be proud," my father assured me with another nod. "They've been doing a great job at running things."

"They've been doin' a *damn* good job."

"Nova has too."

I agreed. "She has."

"That girl is a piece of work. She hustles harder than a man. You should be proud of her too."

Shon and Money may have been the brains of our organization, but *Nova* was the heart. She had held my brothers down in my absence. She took care of the books. She risked her own freedom by involving herself heavily in our

EVERY LOVE STORY IS BEAUTIFUL, BUT OURS IS HOOD
by *Jessica N. Watkins*

drug business. She hid money, and there were a few spots in her name. She was a down-ass bitch, and I loved her for that, even though she'd been distant as fuck since I got out. She was there physically; making me feel at home, sucking a nigga's dick every night, and throwing my celebration party. She had been there to visit me every week for ten years, only missing a visit when a family emergency caused her to. She had been my eyes and ears on the streets. My rider was there, but my *girl* wasn't.

I just chopped it up to us never having an opportunity to have a real relationship. Our loyalty was very committed to each other. In the ten years that I spent behind bars depending on her every word, every letter, every call, I had time to fall in love with her, but she hadn't had the chance to fall in love with me. She had just fallen in the love with the name and the hustle.

EVERY LOVE STORY IS BEAUTIFUL, BUT OURS IS HOOD
by *Jessica N. Watkins*

SHAMAR SAVAGE

"Unt-uh. Don't move. This what you came in here for, right? Take this dick."

"I'm taking it, boy," Taraji fussed with a lustful giggle.

I smacked her phat, chocolate brown ass as I told her, "Then bend over...all the way over."

Out of all the chicks on my current roster, I loved fucking Taraji the most. Her mother was Haitian, and she had inherited her mother's smooth, dark, beautiful skin that covered a tall, slim-thick frame that had the nerve to house a big ol' ass. I mean, *literally*, she had average sized, perky titties, an invisible waist and stomach, and then bam! From that waist fell forty-five inches of ass and hips. Gawd damn, my dick got hard just looking at her. And when she was bent over in front of me butt-ass naked, my phat, long dick was hard as fucking concrete, and I could barely control my nut.

As I lustfully stared at her ass, I bit my lip, trying to keep from cumming before I was done punishing her with these long death strokes.

Taraji groaned seductively as I forced her back to a perfect arch on my tattoo table.

EVERY LOVE STORY IS BEAUTIFUL, BUT OURS IS HOOD
by *Jessica N. Watkins*

It was after eleven at night, almost closing time. Taraji had walked her pretty chocolate ass in here an hour ago. She claimed she wanted a new tattoo on her back, but by the time I was done with the 3-D roses on the back of her right shoulder, she was on her knees sucking my dick as usual.

Taraji wasn't just some thot, though. At the age of twenty-one and being a Savage brother, a nigga like me did indeed do his fucking thing out here. I was tied down to no bitch. But Taraji was like a friend, more than just a piece of ass, so this pussy felt a lil' bit different as it clung to my dick tightly.

As I admired her long leg as it dangled off of the table, my dick hardened inside of her even more, so much that it was painful. Most niggas would fantasize about her beautiful ass, but her track star long legs had a nigga melting like a bitch every time she showed up in something short or some tight jeans.

"Argh! Fuck!"

"Ssshhh!" she quickly hushed me. "Shut up before they hear you."

"Fuck, I can't help it. This pussy good, girl," I honestly told her. I watched in awe as my dick went in and out of her while she came all over the Magnum. The oozy white

Every Love Story Is Beautiful, But Ours Is Hood
by Jessica N. Watkins

substance was making that pussy look so pretty, making it impossible for me to hold on to this nut any longer.

With a hard grunt, I busted and held on to the condom as I slid out of her.

After throwing the rubber in the nearby trash can, I flopped down on the couch in my tattoo station and caught my breath as I buckled my pants back up. As I did, I caught the satisfied grin on Taraji's face while she put on her jeans.

"What you smiling at?" I asked her with a smirk across my big lips.

She looked so pretty when she smiled and the diamond in her small, delicate nose sparkled.

"You know what I'm smiling at."

Yeah, I did. No matter the time we spent apart between fuck sessions, whenever we got together, the sex was so fucking good.

Me and Taraji were strictly friends, though, despite our sexual chemistry. A nigga like me wasn't even looking for a girl, and I knew Taraji did her thing. She was the only chick that never tried to tie me down, so I figured she was as much of a playa as I was, which was all good with me.

"C'mon," I said as I stood. "I gotta close up and get the brats outta here. Let me walk you out."

Every Love Story Is Beautiful, But Ours Is Hood
by *Jessica N. Watkins*

"Thank you for the tattoo." She smiled as she stood on her tiptoes and wrapped her arms around me. "And the dick..."

Even though she was 5'7", she was short to a big nigga like me. I took after my brother, City, and father in size and height. So, at 6'3" and damn near two-seventy, she was still petite to me.

She gave me a slow peck on the lips and moaned.

I smacked her ass and spoke against her mouth, "Don't start, girl."

"I can't help it. You know I love those big pretty lips."

"Your soup coolers ain't short stoppin', nigga."

"Whatever. Bye. C'mon. Let's go."

I could barely walk. The nut had sucked the energy out of me. I was stumbling almost as I followed Taraji into the lobby of Savage Ink. I also followed her into a kush cloud.

"The fuck is y'all doing, man? Damn!" I barked.

Mayhem, Kaos, and Yummy looked at me like I was the one trippin'.

"What? We closed, ain't we?" Kaos shrugged as he pulled from the blunt.

Before he could inhale, I was on his ass, snatching the blunt out of his mouth and breaking it in half.

Every Love Story Is Beautiful, But Ours Is Hood
by *Jessica N. Watkins*

"Aye, man!" Kaos fussed, but this little motherfucker wouldn't dare square up with me. He and his twin, Mayhem, were some lil' niggas. They were tall like my pops but had slim athletic builds that I would crush, and they knew that.

"What the hell I say about smoking in my shit while customers are here?" I sneered.

"She ain't no customer." Yummy giggled. Her eyes were riding low as she said, "Hey, Taraji."

Mayhem chuckled. "Oh, that's Taraji? I thought that was that other chick."

I glared at him. "Shut the fuck up. You know who she is. Stop playing."

"I'm outta here, baby," Taraji said with a laugh and a shake of her head. "Talk to you later."

"Byyyyye, *Taraji*," Mayhem taunted.

Without turning around, she waved her hand in the air. "Bye, y'all!"

I just shook my head at these motherfuckers and followed Taraji to the door. After locking it behind her, I went in on these little bastards.

"I promise you, if I gotta tell you niggas again to respect my shit, I'm fuckin' y'all up, dead ass. Y'all may run shit in the streets, but in here, *I* run shit. Under-fucking-stood?"

They didn't want to, but they nodded.

Running my fingers over my smooth, silky waves in frustration, I stomped into my office to get ready to get outta there before those bad asses blew the good nut that I had just busted.

Mayhem and Kaos were trying hard to live up to their nicknames. As kids, they caused havoc in the hood; beating ass, robbing people, breaking into homes, and stealing cars. They didn't have to do any of that. If Deuce and their mother didn't make sure that they didn't want for anything, our big brothers most definitely did. Those little motherfuckers just wanted to make a name for themselves and went about it the wrong way.

That's why our big brothers bought this shop for me. They didn't want the rest of us to ever go through what they had in the streets. After I graduated from high school, they were on my ass about going to college. But my heart was art. I had a gift for drawing. And once I got my first tat at seventeen, I was determined to be one of the coldest tattoo artists in the Chi. I learned how to tattoo from homies that tatted out of their cribs. Then I practiced on my brothers. My

EVERY LOVE STORY IS BEAUTIFUL, BUT OURS IS HOOD
by Jessica N. Watkins

work was so cold that they bought me this shop. Even though they had bought it, Savage Ink was *my* baby. And now I was trying to teach Mayhem and Kaos the art so that we could build an empire outside of the drug kingdom that our big brothers had built. But Mayhem and Kaos wanted that street life so bad that they seemingly wanted it more than they wanted their own lives.

EVERY LOVE STORY IS BEAUTIFUL, BUT OURS IS HOOD
by *Jessica N. Watkins*

TARAJI GREEN

I slipped into my Camry with a satisfied smile on my face. I loved me some Shamar Savage. Not literally. I *liked* him, but I *loved* that dick! Most women would be totally in love with Shamar simply because of his looks and who he was. But not me. Fuck love.

I had given my heart to my high school sweetheart freshman year. We were together for four years. I thought that he was going to marry me. We had plans to go to the same college. Then I got pregnant, and it was like he didn't know me. Suddenly, he didn't want me or my baby. I was crushed. I was willing to miss out on college just to have my family. I couldn't convince him of that, though. He wouldn't even answer my calls. Then I found out why. He had met another bitch, and they were all over Facebook. I aborted my baby. It took me two years to get over that heartache. Now, I was to be damned if I let a man get so close to me that he could hurt me by his actions. I treated men like they treated me—like a hoe. And Shamar Savage was *definitely* a hoe.

Mind you, when me and Shamar hung out, he had the utmost respect for me and treated me good. Hell, we were

Every Love Story Is Beautiful, But Ours Is Hood
by *Jessica N. Watkins*

actually really good friends. Our conversations on the phone and in person lasted for hours, and they just flowed. Because of that, we learned so much about each other. The fact that he had good dick was a plus! But I wasn't stupid. After a year of fucking around, Shamar had never even tried to update me to a boo, let alone a girlfriend. I was cool with that, though, because I had a couple of guys that I was dating, and the last thing that I wanted or needed was to be somebody's woman.

Speaking of which, as I finally pulled out of the parking lot of Savage Ink, my phone rang. Just as I assumed, it was Reggie's name flashing on the phone.

"Urgh! Gawd damn!"

I just let it ring. Reggie was a guy that I had been fucking with for a little over a year as well. Then he kept trying to smother me, commit, and be my man; things that I wasn't at all interested in. So, I had to let him go. Soon as I did that a month ago, he went from zero to a hundred real quick. At first, I was answering his pleading calls and replying to his four-page text messages, but after weeks of dealing with that nagging shit, I had to put him on pause cold turkey.

I knew most twenty-one-year-old women were waiting impatiently to be wifed by a man like Reggie. He was attractive. He didn't have any kids. At twenty-five years old, he had a successful career as a manager at the Ford plant. He had his own home and car. That's why I couldn't understand why he just couldn't let go and get one of the chicks that wanted him... because I sure the fuck didn't!

CHAPTER FOUR

BLISS DAVIS

The last thing I wanted to do was move into Money's building. Swear to God, if I didn't have bad luck, I wouldn't have any luck at all. When my house burned down two weeks ago, it was bad enough that my son and I were spending our Christmas at the fucking Springhill Suites. I had put my son through enough by placing him in this fucked up love triangle. Then I lost our home by leaving a space heater too close to the curtains. Now, we had to live with Zoe's crazy ass above our heads.

"This is some bullshit," I muttered as I flounced on the bed.

I hated to be there, but I had to admit that I felt relief. Finally off my feet from moving what little me and my baby had left after the fire, I was happy to be out of that hotel and in a roomy condo. I just wished it was in a building that Zoe didn't live in.

"Explain to me again why you think this is a good idea," I told Money softly.

EVERY LOVE STORY IS BEAUTIFUL, BUT OURS IS HOOD
by *Jessica N. Watkins*

The last thing I wanted or needed was for Zoe to hear me and bring her wild ass downstairs, but this condo was so big that I could have been down here for months and she would have never known. But still she was here; Money's girl, the woman that he'd chosen over me, the woman who hated me and had said that she wished that my baby wasn't here. How was I supposed to live like this? This was the shit that was going to blow me; having to walk on eggshells where I slept because my baby's daddy's bitch was upstairs.

"It's not a good idea, but it is what it is."

I could barely look at Money as he sat on the couch in the bedroom playing with our son, Keandre. I had stopped fucking with him when I was six months pregnant because he wouldn't leave Zoe. But although I had stopped fucking with him over a year ago, my heart still skipped a beat whenever our eyes met.

Keandre 'Money' Savage had snatched my heart out of my chest when we first met, and he had never let go. We hadn't touched in so long, but I still got so nervous just being in his presence.

"You think you're slick," I told him while putting my eyes on the pile of clothes on the bed. I decided to fold them and put them in the drawers near the bed to give me something to put my attention on.

"What you mean?" he asked slyly.

"You just want me here because you want Keandre here."

When Money didn't respond, it forced me to look over at him. My eyes met his chinky, gorgeous eyes, his large, tall build, and those full juicy lips. When he licked his lips while smiling devilishly at me, I had to clench my thighs together to stop my clit from throbbing. I wanted to run over there, straddle him on the couch, grab a handful of his curly top fade, allow his beard to graze my skin right before letting him stuff his big dick inside of me.

I swallowed hard, forcing back the urge and gave him a fake attitude. "You can't make me stay here because you want to be with your son every day."

"Why not?"

"Because your fucking woman lives upstairs, Money, and she hates me."

He shrugged, showing me that he didn't give a fuck. "So."

"I know all you're thinking about is you and Keandre, but what about me? I can't live like this—"

"Live like what? Comfortably?"

I could only fold my arms across my chest and stare at him. He got on my nerves, but he was right. Nothing about the space that he had provided for me and Keandre was uncomfortable. The hotel had been nice, but I had to admit that it wasn't suitable for a one-year-old that wanted to throw this, drop that, and have his toys everywhere. Had this not been the condo in the same building that Zoe lived in, I would have been in love. Initially, this house was a three-unit building that Money had remodeled after purchasing it. He had turned the first two floors into a duplex condo. This basement condo was also remodeled, which he had rented out. It was currently vacant, however, and fully furnished.

As we stared at one another, he let his guard down; something I knew better than to take advantage of. Money was a savage in the streets and the bedroom. He never let his guard down. But I knew that no matter that hard exterior, he respected me because he let that guard down more than often with me.

"Look," he said with a sigh. "I know it's not the coolest situation to be in. I'll get you out of here as soon as I can. In the meantime, let me enjoy my son being with me like I want him to for once." Then he put his attention on Keandre. "Ain't that right, my dude? Don't you wanna be with daddy every day?"

When Keandre started to giggle uncontrollably as Money threw him in the air, I couldn't do anything but smile. Little did Money know, I would love for Keandre to be with him every day... and me too. I loved Money so much, but I had spent too many days crying and hurting. I refused to deal with him and his bitch any longer.

I didn't know about Zoe when I first met Money. I was eighteen at the time. I was young, dumb, and excited to have a Savage brother inside of me twice a week. I started to fall in love with him when I started to get to know *Keandre Savage*, when I got to know the man behind the money, swag, and bad bitches. And no matter how much of a dog he was, I knew that Money cared for me. With me, he was timid, caring and loving; the total opposite from the monster he had to be in the streets. He slowly started to take care of me with money, shopping sprees, paying my bills, and more. But I couldn't help but realize that he disappeared on the holidays and after a particular time on certain nights.

After weeks of pressing, he finally told me about Zoe. I had known about the women that constantly called his phone and knew better than to assume that he was only fucking me, but I had no idea that he had a whole woman of five years at a crib that he had never taken me to. I was hurt and ready to walk away from his ass, until I found out that I was pregnant. And when he begged me to have my baby, I thought that was him choosing me and my baby; our family. But nah. He had just always wanted a child and Zoe had never gotten pregnant. And after months of fighting with him and waiting and begging for him to choose me, I chose sanity, but my heart was still choosing Money.

EVERY LOVE STORY IS BEAUTIFUL, BUT OURS IS HOOD
by *Jessica N. Watkins*

ZOE MOORE

I had been crying for three days. I wasn't even mad at Money. This was the type of man he was. He had followed his own heart without considering the amount of hurt his decisions inflicted on anyone else's. And Bliss moving in was definitely something he wanted in his heart. I knew that as soon as he told me that she was moving in. Money wasn't filthy rich, but he could most definitely afford to get Bliss a condo, apartment, house, or whatever if he wanted to. He wanted her here, and that hurt like a motherfucker. I was hurt beyond repair. This was something I could never get over. I had already forgiven him for so much and now *this*?

I literally felt a horrific, sharp pain in my chest, but I still couldn't find the courage to leave this son of a bitch, and that made me furious with myself.

I lay in our bedroom with tears flowing from my eyes, knowing that Money was downstairs with *Bliss*. I was too afraid to creep down the stairs in order to try to hear anything in fear that it would hurt me even more. I wanted to go down there and whoop her ass, but I didn't want to put any more bullshit between Money and me with my actions.

EVERY LOVE STORY IS BEAUTIFUL, BUT OURS IS HOOD
by *Jessica N. Watkins*

Then I was mad at myself for even giving a fuck about that. My feelings were all over the place.

I was so fucked up that the pills weren't working. There was so much Xanax and Percocet in my system. Yet, I still felt this shit, even in my sleep. Because of the drugs, I had been like a zombie for three days; only waking up to use the bathroom and cry. I was barely even eating.

I snatched up the phone after one ring. "Hello?"

"You okay?"

I perked up when I heard his voice. I hadn't looked at the Caller ID before answering, but knowing that it was him gave me something, anything else to think about. I had honestly been waiting for his call or presence since Money told me this bullshit. If being high wouldn't take my mind away, I knew Shon could, if only for a lil' while.

"I'm good," I lied as I wiped my face and tried not to sound like I had been crying.

I doubted that Money had told his brothers about Bliss moving in. If he had, Nova would've called me by now, gagging. And since he hadn't said anything, I wouldn't either. I didn't need the embarrassment.

"You busy?"

EVERY LOVE STORY IS BEAUTIFUL, BUT OURS IS HOOD
by *Jessica N. Watkins*

"No," I quickly answered because I knew what Shon's call meant.

"Meet me at the Sheraton in an hour."

"Okay."

I hung up and got dressed quickly, opting to shower with Shon at the hotel. Then I went to my Uber app. I was way too fucking high to drive, but I was going to get to that dick one way or the other. I didn't even bother telling Money that I was leaving. He was downstairs with his bitch. If I had to go fuck his brother to make myself feel better with that, then so be it.

Before heading out, I slipped into Money's stash in the safe in the wall that he thought I didn't know the combination to. I took what looked to be a couple of hundred dollars. Shon had initiated this fuck session, but this room and dick was going to be on Money, since he wanted to play games. Hell, I was even planning on taking Shon to the finest restaurant and feeding him lobster and filet mignon since he treated me better than his brother did.

EVERY LOVE STORY IS BEAUTIFUL, BUT OURS IS HOOD
by *Jessica N. Watkins*

KEANDRE 'MONEY' SAVAGE

"Money, we need you at the spot out West."

I groaned. Chilling in the basement with Bliss and Keandre had been so peaceful that I had forgotten about this street shit for a minute. Bliss and Keandre had only been at my crib for a few hours, and a nigga already felt at peace.

"It's an emergency?" I asked Paul, one of my workers.

"Pretty much."

I groaned and sat my son down in his playpen. "A'ight. Be there in a minute."

I hung up and grabbed my Moncler coat off of the couch. Then I followed the sounds of pots and pans and saw Bliss' back toward me. After settling in, she had dressed down to some boy shorts and a cami. No matter the sour look on her face, Bliss was beautiful to me. Her hair was dyed this dope orangish-red color that made her peanut butter complexion pop, and it was in these deep waves that fell down her back. She had eyes that could make me hard just by staring at them. They weren't some exotic bright color, but they were so dark, and her lashes were so pretty that they looked exotic to me. She was a petite height, and like I said

90

Every Love Story Is Beautiful, But Ours Is Hood
by *Jessica N. Watkins*

before, I like my women cornbread thick. At a young nineteen years old, Bliss had a grown woman's body, which she hadn't let me touch in a long time. Unlike my other hoes, I actually cared about Bliss while we were fucking around. I hated that I had hurt her, so I respected her wishes of not wanting to fuck around with me anymore, but her chocolate curves were damn good to look at.

"I'm outta here," I told Bliss as I approached her.

She turned as I approached the island that separated the living room from the kitchen. I could see the anxiety in her eyes where I stood.

I sucked my teeth and told her, "You scared or something?"

"I already told you that I don't have time for your bitch."

"She doesn't have the keys to this unit. I told you that. I'm leaving out the back. Keep an eye on my son."

She smacked her lips and spat, "What the fuck you think I been doing for twelve months?"

"Whatever. You heard me."

"Bye, Money. And hurry up and find me some place to live!"

"I'll think about it."

EVERY LOVE STORY IS BEAUTIFUL, BUT OURS IS HOOD
by Jessica N. Watkins

She rolled her eyes and gave her attention back to the boiling pasta shells on the stove. I had an urge to run up behind her and feel on that phat-ass booty, but I kept it moving toward the back door, telling myself not to make this situation more fucked up than my selfish ways already had.

I think just because she was the one woman in this world that wouldn't fuck me, I wanted her so gawd damn bad. But as I spent time with Keandre that afternoon, I realized that maybe I wanted to do more than just fuck Bliss. I was feeling her before she stopped fucking with me, but I wasn't ready to give her what she wanted. I knew that if I had settled down with Bliss, I would have to commit myself to our family a lot more than I had with Zoe. With Bliss, I knew that I would have to commit myself to her to the fullest. At twenty-three years old, I wasn't ready for that type of commitment. The only thing that got my devotion on that level was the streets.

I knew that Bliss was the good woman that every man needed in his corner, but as I got into my car, I shook that thought off, though. Last thing I wanted was feelings for a woman.

My father had taught his sons that falling in love with some pussy would get you killed and advised us to fall in love with the money instead. And that's what I had to focus on and

Every Love Story Is Beautiful, But Ours Is Hood
by Jessica N. Watkins

not whatever soft-ass feelings that were trying to creep into my heart for Bliss.

****

"Where you been, motherfucka?" Tony flinched like a bitch as I nudged him in the forehead with my gun, urging him to answer. "We been looking for you."

Once I arrived at the spot out west, Paul led me to the basement and showed me that he had finally found this coward, Tony, who had been causing the Savage empire major trouble over the past three months. He was tied up to a chair as I pointed my gun to his head.

Tony used to be one of the few workers that I trusted in our organization. Being Nova's cousin, we had fronted him ten bricks so that he could get back on after getting out of prison from a three-year bid. This bitch-ass nigga had dipped off with the bricks and had never returned our bread. We had been looking for him for months. But I knew that he was somewhere living off of our money with hopes that, because he was Nova's cousin, we would spare his life. But not so.

EVERY LOVE STORY IS BEAUTIFUL, BUT OURS IS HOOD
by *Jessica N. Watkins*

I looked up at Nova, who was looking at Tony with eyes full of rage. Nova didn't play no motherfucking games when it came to this organization or its money.

I didn't take disloyalty lightly. As a matter of fact, I didn't accept it all. So, I was ready to take Tony's life and get back to my son, because I was that type of man. I had killed a man because of his disloyalty, but I'd paid for his funeral because he was my cousin.

Disloyalty was a death sentence because I had made everybody that worked up under me. I paid the crew's bills, bought them cars and got them fresh in order to control their loyalty to the Savage family. That gave me control of their minds. My father had taught me that if you have been taking care of a person for months, helping them feed their families, giving them the exact thing that they had always wanted in life, and then you tell that person about a beef and hand them a pistol, they will pop that nigga out of loyalty to you.

"Sis!" Tony called out to Nova.

"Fuck you, nigga!" Nova spat. "Don't ask me for help now! You're all out of help from me. I tried to help you off of the strength that you were my family, then you played me!"

Tears flowed from his eyes and landed on the concrete beneath him.

Every Love Story Is Beautiful, But Ours Is Hood
by *Jessica N. Watkins*

"Fuck these motherfuckers! I'm your family!" he spat to Nova.

"Fuck this bitch-ass nigga," I spat just before aiming at his head and pulling the trigger.

The shots ricocheted off of the concrete walls around us, but nobody flinched as we watched his brains spill out as he slumped over.

I could hear Nova's heels against the concrete as she walked toward me, watching him bleed out. Once standing beside me, she spit on her cousin's dying body. Then she told Paul, "Get rid of this motherfucka."

Once he nodded, I returned my gun to my waist and followed Nova out of the back door and into the wintery night air.

"City know you here?" I asked her.

"No. I wanted to give him some time to enjoy some peace before he had to start stressing over this drug shit."

"I feel you. Well, go home to my bro."

"See ya."

I made sure that Nova got into her BMW truck safely before I climbed into my own truck and made my way back to crib, telling myself that I had to go lay with my woman and not where my heart wanted to be downstairs.

HAPTER FIVE

AKIRA WHITE

Friday evening I was in the skybox at Soldier Field watching the Bears play against the Falcons.

"So, how are you and Davion doing, baby girl?"

I leaned into my father in order to hear him. The box was full of other family members and football wives and girlfriends. Because of the free drinks, everyone was loud and barely paying attention to the game, which we were losing anyway.

"We're fine, Daddy."

"When are you all going to get married?"

My eyes rolled into the back of my head with a smile. "Daddyyy," I whined with a warning tone.

He chuckled and gave me an admiring smile. "I just want to know when I need to get my tux ready."

I reminded him, "Daddy, we've only been engaged for a year."

"You all have been together for three years, though."

"I'm only twenty-four. What's the rush?"

Every Love Story Is Beautiful, But Ours Is Hood
by *Jessica N. Watkins*

My father looked at me curiously. "Why *not* the rush?"

I couldn't tell my daddy that I wasn't rushing to meet Davion at the altar because he couldn't fuck me. Mind you, I was content and was willing to meet the man at the altar, but if he wasn't rushing me to marry that whack dick, then I wasn't rushing either.

Before I could think of a good excuse, the door to the skybox opened. When City walked in, it was as if the entire Skybox stood still. He demanded attention in that way. Shon and Money were behind him.

Suddenly, the air in my lungs vanished, and I couldn't breathe. City's overt swag, gorgeousness, and presence were suffocating the hell outta me. My mouth was gaped open because I was shocked at how fine this man was. But I forced my mouth to close in order not to gain the attention of my father. I had succeeded, but City had definitely gotten my father's attention because he wouldn't take his fucking eyes off of me!

My heart started to beat like crazy as he walked through the crowd of people toward my father and me as we stood at the bar. I knew that City had probably seen that I had read his Facebook message. I prayed to God that he wasn't bold enough to attempt to have any type of conversation with me in front of my father. But what was I thinking? This was City motherfuckin' Savage. He would never let another man intimidate him.

His Gucci cologne draped over me as soon as he was inches away. Before I could attempt to play anything off, City closed the space between us and wrapped his arms around me as if the ten years between us had never existed.

"It's good to see you, Ma."

When his voice slowly and seductively swam into my ear, I couldn't stop my body from shivering. For a second, I forgot where I was. I was back ten years ago, in City's apartment, in his arms with a throbbing virgin bud, trying desperately to hold on to my virginity.

Then I heard my father clear his throat roughly.

I quickly tore away from City's arms and swallowed hard to get rid of the sexual tension in my own throat.

I quickly spoke to his brothers. "Hey, Shon. Hey, Money."

They were about to say something to embarrass me or piss my father off. I knew it. I saw it in their taunting smirks and grins.

"This is my father," I quickly told them. "Mr. White."

City's eyes bucked, and he stared at me. He knew from our many talks back in the day that I didn't know my father. The concern and interest in his eyes made me realize just how deep our connection was back then.

They told him hello respectfully, and I was relieved.

My father didn't return their gestures, however. He simply looked at them sternly and nodded barely.

City being the man that he was, chuckled at my father's attitude and gave his attention back to me. "Let's talk *soon.*"

Those slanted dark eyes seemed to twinkle as he stared at me. To cut the tension, I simply replied, "Good to see you." Then I gave my attention back to my father. But I shouldn't have. His eyes were burning a hole into City's back as he and his brothers walked away.

"Who is that motherfucker?" my father barked.

"They are related to Neko, Davion's teammate. You remember him, right? You guys met at my engagement party."

Daddy wasn't paying me any attention. His eyes were still behind me; I assumed on City. I touched his arm to get his attention. "Daddy?"

He looked at me, glaring. "I don't like that motherfucker."

I shook my head with a smile. My daddy didn't like anybody that looked at me twice. He had only approved of Davion, but little did he know, my heart had only ever approved of City.

TAYE 'CITY' SAVAGE

"Damn, bruh. Akira is lookin' good as fuck."

I glared at Shon's smirk as he lustfully stared at Akira. I spat, "Eyes off, nigga."

Of course, these goofy-ass niggas got a kick out of that.

"Really, motherfucka? That's how you feel?" Money fucked with me.

I hated to say it, but I did anyway. "Yeah, that's how I feel."

"Fuck you mean, my dude?" Shon asked with wide eyes.

"Means stop looking at her," I answered, but as I felt Akira's presence in that skybox, I knew that I meant more.

When I first saw Akira at my party, I was caught off guard. I never expected to see her again, and when I did, my natural instinct was to start where we had left off. But I figured that I needed to focus on my own woman before I tried to get in touch with somebody else's. Yet, my own woman hadn't been acting like she was my woman since I had been home. All she wanted to talk about was the business. When we fucked, she acted like she was finishing a chore just

EVERY LOVE STORY IS BEAUTIFUL, BUT OURS IS HOOD
by *Jessica N. Watkins*

so she could check it off of her to-do list. I wasn't a soft man, but ten years in prison leaves a man wanting some passion from his woman. I wasn't getting that from Nova. I was getting a business partner instead of my woman.

Nova was no longer the loving woman that had begged to be with me ten years ago. I was finally realizing that the letters and visits were all just because she was doing what she had to do to keep the title of being City Savage's woman. She had done what she had to do to keep her spot. But now that I was back at home, it was like she was used to me being gone and continued to live her life like a nigga wasn't there.

So, of course I started to think about the last woman I had in my arms before I got locked up—Akira. Then I found her on Facebook and lost myself in the few pictures that were public. Even though I had committed myself to Nova for ten years, it wasn't physically. The last girl that physically had my heart was Akira. The more I looked at her Facebook page over the last couple of days, the more I remembered what her presence had done to me back then. I couldn't believe that it was pissing me off that she wouldn't reply to my message. I knew that I had hurt her back then. I wanted to fix it, when I shouldn't have given a fuck. But I had sense enough to know that what Akira and I had was ten years ago, and no matter what we had back then, time had changed a lot. We weren't teenagers anymore. We had obligations and families. But now that she was in my eyesight again, I couldn't push away the memory of the little girl that I held until she stopped crying. It touched a nigga's heart that she had found her father after not knowing him for so long. I couldn't help but want to talk to her about that, to hug her with congratulations and love.

"For real, bro," Money said as I looked at the ground. I was fighting hard not to look at Akira even though she had her back to me. "What's up? You sure you just came to this game for the free tickets from cuzzo?"

I put on a front. "Why else would I have come?"

"To bump into Akira," Shon answered sarcastically.

I just shrugged and gave my attention to the game. "Maybe... maybe not."

CHAPTER SIX

TAYE 'CITY' SAVAGE

"Where are you going?"

I stood in the doorway of the bedroom, thrown the fuck off that Nova was fully dressed. She was wrapped in a brown mink bomber, skinny jeans, red bottom boots; the whole nine and ten.

Definitely not a graveyard outfit.

Nova looked at me how she'd been looking at me since I got out of the joint; like she didn't know what the fuck I expected from her. "I'm going to meet my girls for lunch. What's the problem?"

"The problem? You forgot we were goin' to my mother's grave today?"

"Oh," she said more nonchalantly than I liked. "I have a reservation for lunch with my girls downtown. Sorry."

She avoided my eyes. She gave her attention to a two-thousand-dollar purse that she was filling with so much shit that it was obvious that she would be gone all day. She was avoiding me, so I avoided her. I left the doorway and made

104

Every Love Story Is Beautiful, But Ours Is Hood
by Jessica N. Watkins

my way downstairs and toward the door. On my way through the halls, I frowned at all the fancy shit on the walls. When I went to prison, I was living in the projects in a one bedroom, seven hundred square foot space that I shared with my niggas whenever they wanted to come over. I was happy with that. I loved money, but I didn't need all of this fancy-ass shit that Nova had put my money into. The fuck did I need with a four-thousand square foot crib? Shit, that was too much room for somebody to sneak up on a nigga.

Once out of the door, I marched through the snow toward the brand new truck that my brothers had waiting for me the day that I got out. I let it warm up as I rolled a blunt. I needed to smoke in order to keep me from going back into the crib, snatching that fucking mink off of Nova, and putting my hands on her conceited, self-absorbed ass.

She was so into herself that she forgot the most important day of my life. My mother had died five years ago. She was dying when I was in prison, so I couldn't even tell her that I loved her one more time. I couldn't touch her. I couldn't kiss her face. I couldn't attend her funeral. I had all kinds of plans for when I got out of that prison, but the most important one had always been to visit my mother's grave.

Nova knew that, but this bitch felt like eating with stuck up bitches was more important.

I smoked all the way to the cemetery. I tried my best to keep it gangsta as I roamed the graves, looking for the headstone that read "Valerie Savage." I couldn't remember the last time I'd cried. I didn't even shed tears when the judge gave me my sentence. The streets had taken my closest niggas. I had taken lives with my own hands. Death hadn't hurt me until it came to my favorite girl, so when I finally saw her headstone, a lone tear fell down my dark skin. The icy winds froze it before I could even wipe it away. When I saw the thirty-nine years between her birth date and death, I felt like there was a massive gut punch to my stomach. Breast cancer had stolen my mother at such a young age. She should have had time to see me and my brothers shine. I should have had the chance to allow me to take care of her.

"*Fuck!*" left my throat in a loud boom that bounced off of the trees that surrounded me. "I miss you, Mama," I croaked. I swallowed hard, refusing to let more tears fall.

For thirty minutes, I talked to her, wishing to God that she would talk back. But I never heard her sweet voice. All I heard was the sound of harsh winds and then eventually the dinging sound of the notification on my phone.

EVERY LOVE STORY IS BEAUTIFUL, BUT OURS IS HOOD
by *Jessica N. Watkins*

I was tired of sulking like a bitch, so I bent over and kissed my mother's headstone. "I love you, Mama."

Then I made my way through the snow toward my truck as I checked my phone.

My footsteps staggered a bit as I saw that it was Akira finally responding to my instant message. The simple words, "It was really nice seeing you again," brought a grin on my face at the most awkward moment. It made my dick jump, surprisingly. I was excited, as I trudged through the snow. It was a feeling over me that I had looked forward to experiencing while I was in prison. It was the feeling that I was expecting to feel when I got home to Nova, but quickly realized that I didn't.

Despite Nova being feared by many, bitches had been throwing pussy at me left and right since I got home. When usually a nigga would be shoveling through those pussies, I was trying to show Nova how much respect I had for her loyalty to my family, but nobody... *nobody* had my interest like Akira.

BLISS DAVIS

See? This was exactly what I didn't have time for. I should have known that I couldn't live here without bumping into this bitch at some point!

"I told him!" I spat as I collected my purse and keys. "I fucking told this nigga!"

My blood was boiling as I grabbed my purse and phone out of the driver's side seat of my Challenger. As I climbed out of the car, I could hear Zoe's footsteps against the pavement as she walked toward her car that was parked a few feet in front of mine in the double car driveway. I silently thanked God that my son wasn't with me. I just wanted to get to that door, get in the house, and tell Money that I couldn't do this shit and that I wanted outta here today! This shit was weird!

"Umm, could you not park in my driveway?" The sound of her nagging attitude made my skin crawl.

I looked at her and wondered why Money was so committed to this bitch. Zoe was pretty with a body that any nigga would want to fuck, but the bitch's bad attitude just made her look so ugly! She actually looked like she had lost some weight from the last pictures I had seen of her while stalking her and Money's Facebook pages. I guess Money was stressing that ass out.

I chuckled and looked at her like she was crazy. "Money told me that I can park wherever I want to." I knew that would piss her off; that's why I said it.

She started fuming! Her head started spinning like Poltergeist.

"Bitch, this is *my* house!" she shrieked as she started charging toward me.

"Actually, this is *Money's* house," I taunted her, not backing down. "And I wouldn't be in this motherfucka unless he wanted me here!"

That made her charge toward me even faster. She threw her purse to the ground. I knew this bitch was ready to fight and so be it. I knew this fight was coming one day. Once Money told her about Keandre, she threatened me in every way that she could over the phone and on social media. The bitch basically stalked my life. She hated me, no matter how many times both Money and I told her that I had no idea that she even existed until after I was messing around with him for quite some time. She didn't care about any of that. She swore she would beat my ass the moment she saw me, but Money had never allowed us to cross paths until now.

I had no beef with her, however. I wasn't even mad at her. Money was the one that had lied to me and hurt me. But if I had to whoop this bitch's ass in her own front yard, then so be it. I was willing to show her that I had hands and they did work.

I didn't have to, though. As soon as this bitch tried to swing on me, her goofy ass slipped on some black ice and busted her shit!

"Ahhh!" she screamed as her face hit the pavement.

"Ha!" I started cracking up and left her goofy ass on the pavement while running toward the security gate with tears of laughter running down my face.

She looked up at me with her eyes fuming with anger, but I died laughing as I saw the way her lip was leaking blood.

I walked away cracking the fuck up. "Hell nah! Hilarious!"

I hurried to get through the security gate and door. Then I ran up the few stairs to my front door and rushed inside.

EVERY LOVE STORY IS BEAUTIFUL, BUT OURS IS HOOD
by *Jessica N. Watkins*

"Money! Moneyyyy!" I called for him as loud as I could while trying to keep my voice down because I was hoping that Keandre was still asleep.

"What?"

Luckily, Money was still downstairs with Keandre, where he had been when I left to run to the store to get Keandre some diapers.

"Go get your, girl," I told him, still laughing.

He looked at me with questions all over his face. He couldn't understand why I was so tickled. "What happened?"

"Go get Zoe and see if she's okay. She done busted her ass outside trying to fight me."

"She what?!" he asked with a chuckle.

"I told you this wasn't a good idea! What the fuck made you think that the two of us could live under the same roof? You had a baby on her with me!"

When Money didn't have an answer, I told him, "I'm leaving." And I meant it. I was laughing now, but I wasn't about to live every day wondering what was going to happen every time I bumped into that crazy bitch.

I was making my way toward the bedroom to pack my shit yet again.

"You ain't goin' nowhere! Where you gon' go, Bliss?"

EVERY LOVE STORY IS BEAUTIFUL, BUT OURS IS HOOD
by *Jessica N. Watkins*

Now I was done laughing. Fuck he thought? "I don't care where I go! I will sleep in the fucking car before I go through this shit every fucking day! Fuck this!"

"Stop playin' with me, man!" he threatened.

Then I felt a hard grip on my arm as I was snatched around to face Money. I thought he was going to argue with me, tell me what to do, and curse me out. When he didn't, I was completely caught off guard. His eyes were soft. His touch was tender. His eyes were loving.

"Don't go. I like yo...um...I like *Keandre* being here."

Was he about to say what I think he was about to say?

Suddenly, I was weak. I wanted to leave, but now I couldn't. My feet were planted to the floor. But the tension between Money and I was so thick that I couldn't say any of that before loud banging started on the front door.

"*Money*! Let me in! Fuck you and that bitch! I'm beating that bitch's ass! Money! *Money*!"

Money bit his bottom lip, and his eyes rolled into the back of his head. His nostrils started to flare. Just as the gentle Keandre had appeared, Money, the savage, was back.

"Let me go take care of this shit. Don't leave."

by *Jessica N. Watkins*

The bargaining started again. I cringed as her irritating voice could be heard outside. "I'm killing that hoe! Get her the fuck out of my house! Let me in!"

I just looked at him, so Money reiterated, "Do *not* leave."

KEANDRE 'MONEY' SAVAGE

Fucked up as it was, I meant it. I did not want Bliss to leave. I had put her in a fucked up situation, but it was for the best. I had never brought Keandre around Zoe, and I never would. So, even though they were only a few thousand square feet apart, when I wanted to see my son, I would go downstairs. And I wanted to see him all the time. The more time that I spent with him and Bliss, the more I realized that I liked the feeling of a family. It was how my mother and father had raised us. No matter how fucked up my father was with all of his cheating and kids outside of his marriage, we had a family: a mother and father who loved us. I had always wanted that. I knew that I wasn't giving my son that when I begged Bliss to have him knowing that I was in a relationship with Zoe. But having Bliss in my home was showing me how much Zoe wasn't doing to please me and what Bliss was willing to do. Every time I went down to spend time with my shorty, she was feeding a nigga and not stressing me out with an attitude and ten thousand questions. I knew that she wasn't doing it to lure me because it was obvious that she was done with me. She did it because outside of the hurt, I looked out for her, I took care of her, and she respected me for that more than Zoe's crazy ass ever has. Those were qualities of a real woman who loves you unconditionally and a down-ass bitch.

"I'll take care of her," I promised Bliss. "Okay?"

She looked down at the floor. She didn't want to be here. She didn't trust me. I knew all of that. But for my own sanity, for me to have some joy to come home to when I was leaving those dirty-ass, ruthless streets, I needed her to stay.

I lifted her chin tenderly to make her look into my eyes. "*Okay?*" I asked her again.

"*Moneyyyy!*" The sound of Zoe's rage banging on the door again made Bliss jump.

Irritation was all over her face as she spat, "*Okay.* Just go shut her up before she wakes up Keandre."

When the banging started again, I hit a light jog toward the door and swung it open. Zoe immediately tried to rush by me, but I stopped her ass by snatching her up by the arm.

I slammed her against the wall, hemming her up in a corner.

"Ow, Money! You're hurting me! Let me the fuck go!"

"Shut up before you wake up my son," I told her through gritted teeth.

"*Your son*? Fuck your son!"

"Shut the fuck up!" I threatened as I used my body weight to press her back into the corner. "Don't make me shut you the fuck up myself, Zoe."

"Fuck you, Money," she cried, blood still spilling from her lip. "I fucking hate you! How could you do this me?!"

"You did this to yourself, trying to fight that girl. She didn't do shit to you—"

Her mouth dropped as tears fell. "You're defending her?!"

"Man, she didn't do shit. She didn't even know about you. I did it. I lied. You wanna fight somebody? Fight me!"

My eyes dared her to, but she wasn't about to get her ass whooped with Bliss a few feet away.

"I hate you," she barked through gritted teeth. She used all of her strength to push past me. That shit felt like a pinch, but I let her walk away. "Y'all can have this motherfuckin' house! I'm gone!"

I chuckled sarcastically. "Don't bust yo' ass on the way out."

"*Fuck you, Money!*"

116

AKIRA WHITE

City and I had been talking all day on Facebook. I only wanted to tell him that it was good to see him, in order to at least acknowledge his attempts to speak to me. But when he told me that he had just visited his mother's grave, our conversation went on for hours. It broke my heart to hear that his mother had died. I had witnessed for myself how close they were. He was her first born. Being only fourteen years apart, they grew up like sister and brother, rather than mother and son.

For hours, he went on and on in the inbox about her, expressing how much he missed her and how much he hated himself for not being there when she was dying. It seemed like he really needed to talk, so I allowed him to and consoled him. Instead of grieving with him, I started to share good memories of his mother that I recalled from our days in the Dearborns. So, he went from grieving to laughing along with our funny memories.

We chatted for hours, and then suddenly he went inactive. So, imagine my surprise when he, Neko, and Money came walking through my front door!

EVERY LOVE STORY IS BEAUTIFUL, BUT OURS IS HOOD
by *Jessica N. Watkins*

"Davion! My nigga!" Neko greeted.

Davion walked toward them with a big grin on his face. He was too busy shaking up with Neko and then City and Money to see the stupefied look on my face as I stood in the middle of the living room floor. Davion had told me that he was expecting Neko, but he said nothing about City and Money coming too.

"Hope you don't mind me bringing my people with me," Neko told Davion.

"Hell nah, it's cool. Hope ya'll enjoyed the game the other night."

"Yeah, that skybox is ill, but ya'll sucked," Money spat jokingly.

They all laughed while I attempted to walk out unseen, but of course City or Money's asses weren't going to let me get away with that.

"What's up, Akira?" I heard Money say with a hint of sarcasm in his voice.

I turned around, smiled, and waved. "Hi, Money. Hey, City."

My heart was beating so hard that I thought they all could see it. I was fidgeting under City's eyesight as he stared

Every Love Story Is Beautiful, But Ours Is Hood
by Jessica N. Watkins

a hole through me. I wondered if he was actually staring at me that intensely or if it was just my imagination.

It must have been just my paranoia because he just waved and turned back to the boys who were already on their way toward the bar in the living room.

Three hours later, they were all slapped. I was a little tipsy myself because I had to drink to knock the edge off. I hated what City's presence did to me, especially because I didn't know what the feeling meant.

"What you doin'?"

The sound of his voice made me jump out of my skin. I looked toward the doorway of the den where I had been hiding out clutching a homemade Long Island iced tea while pretending like I was watching reruns of Love and Hip Hop New York. But really I was listening to City's smooth, hypnotizing voice a few feet away the entire time. When our eyes met, I had to snatch mine away because my stomach was doing flips and my heart was beating out my chest again. I didn't want him to see the effect that his presence was having on me.

"Don't worry. Your boy is up there drunk as fuck and passed out," he rushed to say.

I giggled, but I kept my eyes away from his and on Yandy and JuJu. "Already?"

"Probably my fault."

"*Probably?*"

"Most definitely. I wanted that nigga to pass out so I could get back here and get close to you."

My heart skipped a beat. My breath became short. I hated that. I didn't like how City made me feel. I ignored it all and asked, "What are you doing here?"

"Neko invited us. That nigga's been on our bumper since I got out."

I smirked. "And you just agreed to come, huh?"

"Yeah. I wanted to see you."

I heard his footsteps coming into the room, and I swear to God, I couldn't breathe. Why the fuck was I having this goofy-ass high school crush reaction from some nigga that I was with ten years ago? It was so annoying!

When he sat down next to me on the couch, my eyes actually closed for two seconds. During that two seconds, I enjoyed him being the closest he'd been to me in a decade. I enjoyed his scent, his presence...just *him*.

"Thank you for talking to me today. I needed that. I didn't have anybody else to talk to."

EVERY LOVE STORY IS BEAUTIFUL, BUT OURS IS HOOD
by Jessica N. Watkins

"You didn't? Where was *Nova*? Why couldn't you talk to her?"

I heard him sigh heavily and then felt him sit back on the couch. His muscular arm extended, draping the back of the couch, which encased me in his presence. The fact that he was getting relaxed was driving me insane because I wanted to get comfortable as well and lay under him.

Even though my life had changed for the better in the last ten years since I'd seen him, I could secretly admit that I had not been as comfortable since I was lying in City's arms. I knew that it was because he was the one man, the only person who knew every single thing about me and still loved me.

"Let's just say Nova was more of my woman when I was locked up than she is now that I'm out."

I finally looked back at him. He tried to mask the disappointment, but I saw it. I knew that City had seen way too much and done too much in his lifetime for a woman to break his heart. But he was definitely hurt.

"You're not happy," I told him.

Of course, he didn't answer that. He just replied, "Who is really happy in their relationship?"

"Many people are."

His eyebrow raised, giving him the most adorable curious expression. "Are *you*?"

"Yes." I couldn't tell whether I was telling the truth or a lie.

"Have you been made love to yet?"

Goosebumps covered my body. I shivered from the sensation. To play if off, I laughed. "Stop playing."

"You may have been penetrated before, but has he *made love* to you?"

Again, I shuddered under his intense gaze. I struggled with what to say. The last thing I wanted to do was admit to the love of my life that my fiancé couldn't satisfy me sexually. But I knew better than to lie to him because I knew that he saw the truth in my eyes. No matter how long it had been, he was still that nineteen-year-old boy that knew everything about me before I could tell him.

I didn't have to say anything. He sat up just a bit, those slanted bedroom eyes still staring at me. His locs were styled into a manly up do, making me feel like I was in the presence of royalty.

"You're a queen," he told me. "Never let a man half fuck you."

EVERY LOVE STORY IS BEAUTIFUL, BUT OURS IS HOOD
by *Jessica N. Watkins*

I was stuck. I swallowed hard, trying to get rid of the huge lump in my throat that wouldn't allow me to speak past the throbbing in my sensitive bud.

"You held on to that body for so long. I can't believe you're with somebody who don't treat that pussy right."

Speechless, I stared at him, knowing that he would treat this pussy right. He had never fucked me, but the way that he used to kiss me and eat my pussy back then made me know that he would. I just knew that he would fuck me in ways that I only imagined, while Davion was humping on me like a fucking puppy.

I don't know whether it was City's presence, the alcohol, or both, but, suddenly, I wanted him. I wanted him on me and in my arms. Gawd, I wanted those big, suckable lips on me so fucking bad. And I don't know what I was thinking when I began to slowly lean over or why I was so happy when it didn't look like he was going to stop...

"Yo', City!" Neko's voice shot through the air and scared the fuck out of me.

I literally jumped out of my dark brown skin.

"Where you at, man?!"

I quickly scooted away from City. I was both relieved and disappointed, but I saw the disappointment in City's eyes as he rolled them into the ceiling. He groaned, stood up, and reluctantly walked out.

I squeezed my thighs together tightly, trying to smother the pulsating feeling between them, grabbed my glass and gulped down the rest of the Long Island, groaning to myself, "*Fuuuck.*"

CHAPTER SEVEN

ZYSHONNE 'SHON' SAVAGE

I watched as Zoe switched over to the table in the suite. She was butt-ass naked. Through the opened blinds, the multi-colored lights from the stores on Michigan Avenue were bouncing off of her yellow skin. When she bent over, her big-ass booty fell open, exposing that pretty, pink pussy. I could hear as she snorted the line of Xanax into her nose.

I shook my head, sitting on the chaise lounge with my dick in my hand. I was waiting for her to finish getting her high so that I could get this head and third nut out.

The moment that I first saw Zoe, I thought she was beautiful. I felt like Money didn't deserve her. I knew my brother, so I knew from the beginning that he would hurt her. I also knew that I could never go against my brother by taking his girl, but I eventually got her time because he was never around. Then I got the pussy. I didn't feel bad for fucking her because Money didn't love this girl, but I would never defy our brotherhood by doing anything more than sticking my dick in her.

Every Love Story Is Beautiful, But Ours Is Hood
by *Jessica N. Watkins*

At the moment, it was three in the morning. Zoe and I had been at the hotel all day, laid up and fucking. It was obvious to me that she and Money had gotten into it because this was the first time that she had spent the night out.

"You ain't goin' home?"

She finally turned around. My mouth watered at how perky those big, plump, milky titties sat up and her nipples looked straight at me. She had lost some weight, so her stomach was smaller, emphasizing how wide her hips were. My dick jumped a little and hit my belly button. She didn't see that, though, because her eyes were rolling to the ceiling as she wiped her nose. Then she grabbed her glass of 1738 and finished it off.

"Fuck your brother," she finally replied.

"What did he do this time?"

She folded her arms across her chest and looked at me like I was playing games.

"What?" I asked her.

"Don't act like you don't know."

"I don't."

She huffed and puffed before she said, "He moved Bliss into our building."

EVERY LOVE STORY IS BEAUTIFUL, BUT OURS IS HOOD
by *Jessica N. Watkins*

My eyes bucked as a loud laugh left my throat. "Helllll nah! Heckie nah, Joe!"

"It ain't funny!" Zoe pouted.

I knew I was bogus for laughing so hard, but I couldn't help it. Money was in rare form. "That nigga, Money, is crazy!"

I was laughing so fucking hard that I doubled over. I heard Zoe eventually start laughing as well. I knew that she could only laugh now because she had made her feelings so numb with pill after pill after pill.

"He didn't tell you for real?"

"Hell nah. I'm sure he will, though." I finally stopped laughing and looked at Zoe sincerely, knowing that behind the drugs and alcohol, she was hurt. "Come here," I demanded.

Zoe walked toward me and straddled me on the chaise. I grabbed the back of her neck gently and told her, "You gon' be all right."

She smiled and kissed me. I wanted some head, but I knew that she needed to be loved, so I gave her what she needed. This may have been my brother's girl, but I knew the hell that he had put her through. And though I would never disrespect the family by wifing her, over this last year of fucking her, I had grown a liking to this pussy and her. I hated that she was so weak that she couldn't walk away from this nigga back then, but now I was proud that she finally had. So, I was about to give her a prize of this good dick.

"Get up," I demanded.

She did, looking curiously at me as I stood. I lightly pushed her back. Then I grabbed her knees, held them to her chest with one arm and wet her center with my mouth, sucking her clit softly and quickly until my slob, mixed with her juices, rolled down the crack of her ass.

"Mmmm!"

I knew that her moans were exaggerated because pills made sex feel so fucking amazing. But I didn't pop pills, so as I stood and dove into that slippery middle, I knew that it felt good to me just because it was that good. It was tight around my phat, long dick and it fit around it like a rubber.

With each of her legs dangling in the crevice of my arms, I forced myself deep into that pussy, pulled out slowly and forced my way back in.

"Oh gaaaaaawd! Fuuuuck!" she squealed.

"That's it, baby. Take this dick. Take all of this dick."

I could feel her nails digging into the back of my legs as my strokes became long, fast, and hard. I was hitting that pussy so right and deep that she was squirting all over this dick.

"Ahhh! Shit! Nigga, damn!"

Her wetness caused the loudest smacking sound as my pelvis connected with that pussy. That shit turned me the fuck on and made me even harder.

"Gawd, it's so fucking hard! Yes, give me that big dick! Yes, Shon!"

ZOE MOORE

I woke up the next day.

"Urgh," I groaned as I pried my heavy eyes open.

I felt like a fucking CTA bus had hit me. I don't know what had me feeling like complete shit more; the drowsiness from the Xanax in my system or the recollection of what had happened yesterday. I wanted to beat that bitch's ass. I had already let her slide by getting knocked up by my man, because I believed that she didn't know about me at first. But I'd be damned if the homeless bitch didn't know her place in my fucking house!

I frowned at the sunlight beaming through the windows. I looked at the clock on the nightstand next to the bed, wondering how long I had been asleep. It was four o'clock in the afternoon. Then I realized that I was still in a hotel.

"Fuck," I moaned.

I looked over, saw the indent on the pillow and remembered that Shon was with me last night. I listened for sounds of him and heard nothing. Then I realized that Shon had left without waking me.

Every Love Story Is Beautiful, But Ours Is Hood
by *Jessica N. Watkins*

I looked at my phone, wondering if he had at least sent a text, and expecting that Money must've been blowing my phone up. But there wasn't one fucking notification from a missed call or text from either one of them niggas.

"What the fuck was I thinking?"

Being in this hotel wasn't fixing anything. I was twenty years old with no job experience and only a high school diploma. Money had provided everything for me. Even his money had financed this hotel room. While I was running away from my man, I didn't know of another one who would provide for me like Money did, especially not his fucking brother. Even though Shon liked this pussy, he didn't like it more than he loved his brother, so he damn sure wasn't gonna wife me.

I got my broke ass up, put some clothes on, and took my ass home. I was mad because that bitch was downstairs, but I'd be damned if Bliss was able to move *upstairs* because I walked away and didn't put up a fight for my man!

KEANDRE 'MONEY' SAVAGE

I chuckled to myself as I heard the security system chirp, alerting me that the front door was open.

Knew this bitch was gonna come home eventually.

I knew she would return, and I was disappointed as hell. This house had been so peaceful since Zoe left that I had actually opted to chill in the crib all day with my son. It was cool as fuck to finally have my son in my crib without worrying about Zoe being in her feelings. My lil' nigga was finally able to sleep with his pops. For most of the day, I had been downstairs enjoying the fuck outta my son because I figured Zoe would be home at some point that day. The only reason I was home to witness her return was because Bliss had taken Keandre to her mother's house for dinner.

This wasn't a game that Zoe wanted to play with me. She was still in this house by respect alone. I wasn't attracted to her nagging, junkie ass no more. I was tired of her stealing from me and getting high. The only reason I hadn't kicked her out was because I had enough respect for our history not to put her broke ass out on the street. Plus, I at least wanted a mouth in the crib that sucked my dick every now and then

EVERY LOVE STORY IS BEAUTIFUL, BUT OURS IS HOOD
by *Jessica N. Watkins*

that I didn't have to pay for or sweet talk into it. Lucky for Zoe, I wasn't trying to wife no chicks right now, because I would have replaced her ass last year when our shit started going bad. Lucky for her, the only move I would be willing to make would be to get the peace that I got downstairs on a regular basis, but I knew Bliss wasn't goin' at gunpoint.

"What's up?"

Even the sound of her voice irritated me. I didn't even take my eyes away from the flat screen on the wall in the den. I just repeated sarcastically, "What up?"

I heard her huff and puff. "That's all you got to say to me?"

Reluctantly, I looked at her. My disgust with her stupidity was evident. "Fuck else am I supposed to say? You the one actin' a fool."

"You don't think I *should* act a fool? You moved your baby mama in here!"

"So be mad at me, because that girl ain't do shit to you."

She was fuming. Her nostrils flared, and tears filled her eyes.

I knew that she hated me taking up for Bliss, but fuck that. Bliss wasn't in the wrong; *I* was. But I felt bad for Bliss because I had lied to her. I had put her in a fucked up situation. But time and time again, Zoe chose to stay in this shit knowing what was up, so fuck her tears. Obviously, she liked this shit.

"Do you even still want to be with me?"

I could hear her broken heart all over her words, but I wasn't fazed. If she wasn't willing to put up with my shit, she wouldn't have come back home.

I wasn't about to get into this with her, though. We'd had this conversation so many times. If she wanted to fuck up her day with the same bullshit, she could do that. I wasn't, though.

"What that got to do with anything?" I spat. "What does her being downstairs have anything to do with me still wanting to be with you? I moved her in, but I didn't kick you out, so why the fuck are you tripping?"

"You think I'm stupid? It's been a week! Money, she wouldn't be here unless you wanted her here."

"I want my *son* here."

"Bullshit!" she spat as she punched the doorway.

"You're so busy worried about me wanting her that you done talked yourself into believing that shit. This shit is about my son; some shit that you would never fucking get

Every Love Story Is Beautiful, But Ours Is Hood
by *Jessica N. Watkins*

because you don't even give a fuck about me enough to have my fucking kids!"

Zoe's eyes bucked. She looked as if she had swallowed her own shit.

"So, that's why you like her? Because she cared enough about you to have a fucking baby?"

My jaws clenched instantly. "Zoe, shut the fuck up—"

"Answer this question, Money. Do you still love me?"

Women are like the police; they can have all of the evidence in the world but still want a confession.

I stood up, stepping into my Balmain boots. She was still watching me, waiting for an answer with tears in her eyes. As I grabbed my coat from the couch, I noticed that her bright skin was turning red. This shit was sad as fuck. I was a young, rich nigga. The last thing that I *had* to do was deal with this bullshit.

I walked toward the doorway, watching her tears, not believing that she was still waiting for an answer. I did feel bad for the old her, the Zoe Moore that used to make my dick hard on sight and the Zoe Moore that used to make me laugh.

Once I was inches from her, I bent down and kissed her cheek, telling her, "If you got to ask me that, baby girl, then maybe not."

Every Love Story Is Beautiful, But Ours Is Hood
by *Jessica N. Watkins*

I heard her inhale sharply, but I kept walking toward the front door. That answer had finally shut her the fuck up. That's what she'd kept asking for, so that's what she got.

On the way out of the front door, my cell started to ring. I saw that it was Shon calling, so I answered, despite my irritation.

"What up?"

"What up, bro? Can you talk?"

"It ain't nothing that's gon' piss me off, is it?"

Shon chuckled deeply. "Nah."

"What's the word then?" I asked as I hopped into my ride.

"Now that City is out, we need to talk about expanding the business."

My eyes rolled as I bit my bottom lip with irritation. "You motherfucker, this *is* gonna piss me off," I barked.

"Why?"

"You know why. You keep asking me this shit, and I keep telling you that I ain't down."

"But why wouldn't you be down?"

"We good."

"Yeah, we are good, but we aren't good enough," he tried to get me to believe. "We're riding around in BMW's

Every Love Story Is Beautiful, But Ours Is Hood
by *Jessica N. Watkins*

when we could be riding around in Bentleys. We're living good, but if we just put more product out in the streets, we could be living like fucking kings."

"And we could also be living in a fucking prison because we have caught the attention of the Feds. Do you want that shit too? City just got out. He did not do ten years just for us to go to fucking prison anyway or, worse, get killed because we in the street flaunting in three-hundred-thousand-dollar cars—"

"Ain't no nigga gon' kill me, bro."

"Maybe not, but yo' tough ass can't stop the Feds."

Shon sucked his teeth. "Whatever, bro. Fuck the Feds. We're smarter than them."

Shaking my head, I stared out of the window. My eyes landed on the living room window in Bliss' condo. Thinking of my son, I knew that there was no way that I would attract the attention of the police by putting more product in these streets. No, we weren't rich, but we were living better than most. Our family was straight, and our women were comfortable. I didn't need Bentleys and mansions to feel like the man. I *was* the fucking man. All that other shit attracted was thieving, trigger-happy niggas and the police. The last thing I would do was leave my son alone in this world because I was dead or in prison.

Shon didn't give a fuck about any of that, though. He was greedy. He had enough, but he wanted more. He had diamonds, but he wanted bigger ones. He had foreign cars, but he wanted more expensive ones. I feared that my brother's greed would get him locked up or in a grave one day.

"Look," I told him. "You done come at me with this shit before, and I tell you no every time. Stop asking me." Then, I hung up on his ass.

I cuffed my forehead trying to stop an oncoming headache. Then I grabbed my blunt from the ashtray. I needed to smoke this stress away before Zoe and my brother killed me.

Every Love Story Is Beautiful, But Ours Is Hood
by *Jessica N. Watkins*

TARAJI GREEN

"Daddy," I answered my phone with a smile.

I heard Shamar chuckle deeply. Even the seduction in his laugh made me wet.

"Stop playin' with me, girl."

"You know this pussy calls you Daddy," I teased.

Again, he chuckled seductively. "Now my dick is hard."

"Good," I purred.

Shyly, he snickered again, and I loved the fact that I had made him speechless. There was nothing more attractive than making a thug blush.

"What's up? What are you doing tonight?" I asked, hoping that this was a booty call.

"Me and my brothers are about to hit a few spots tonight. I was calling to see if you wanted to pop out with me."

My eyes bucked, but I didn't let him hear how surprised I was. "That's cool," I simply replied.

"Bet. I'll pick you up in like two hours. Is that long enough for you to get dressed?"

"Fuck you." I giggled. "It will not take me that long."

"Well, take your time. Look good for me tonight."

EVERY LOVE STORY IS BEAUTIFUL, BUT OURS IS HOOD
by *Jessica N. Watkins*

I was so confused. I answered, "Okay," with the most bewildered look on my face.

"A'ight. See you in a minute."

I hung up, asking myself, "What the fuck?"

Mind you, me and Shamar had been fucking around for about a year, but he had never, ever taken me out. Usually, we met up after he had already kicked it or on some Netflix and chill type shit. He most definitely had never invited me out with his brothers. I had only met the few of them that I had in passing.

"Is this a date?" I asked myself. I didn't know what to think. But as I jumped out of bed, I was ready to make sure that I was going to be cute either way.

"Wait! Whoa." I stood in the middle of my bedroom floor, taking a deep breath. "Calm down, bitch." I didn't like this; being excited over some shit a man was doing. Like... I was smiling; cheesing and shit. Shamar had made me happy...like not just with dick; with his actions. This was weird.

I got myself together emotionally, but I still walked toward my closet ready to *slay*. I was about to hang out with the Savage brothers, so a bitch had to look more than good.

EVERY LOVE STORY IS BEAUTIFUL, BUT OURS IS HOOD
by Jessica N. Watkins

On my way to my closet, my phone rang, and I actually got disappointed. I instantly assumed that it was Shamar calling back to change his mind.

And that was the exactly what I did not like about doing more than just fucking a guy; the anticipation and the disappointment.

But it wasn't Shamar, thankfully. I saw Reggie's name on the Caller ID and instantly groaned, "Urrgh! Creep ass," as I threw the phone on my bed and marched toward the closet.

Reggie had been calling me non-fucking-stop. The more I ignored him, the more and more he called and sent me these long-ass text messages. He was turning into a real-life creep. I would literally send him text messages telling him that I didn't want to be with him anymore, and he would reply with love letters. Like, literally, the other day he sent me a poem. A *poem*! Who the fuck does that?

Fucking creep.

Anyway, Shamar ended up being right; it took me the full two hours to perfect my look. I chose a bandaged pink two piece that popped great off of my smooth, brown Haitian skin. The tube top stopped right at my belly button, so I was able to show off my naturally flat stomach and small waist. The tight skirt hugged my massive hips and ass, but it fell down

Every Love Story Is Beautiful, But Ours Is Hood
by Jessica N. Watkins

past my knees so that I wasn't showing off too much skin. I barrel curled my long, twenty-six-inch weave, which didn't look as long because I was 5'7" and 5'11" with my silver, four-inch pumps on. With my smooth skin, high cheek bones, full, long lashes, naturally high arched thick eyebrows, and full lips, I barely wore makeup. So, I only applied tinted moisturizer, lip gloss, eyeliner, mascara, and a little blush.

After applying Ralph Lauren Romance all over my body, I was ready as soon as my doorbell rang. I lived alone, so I hurried toward the door, through my condo on the lake front.

After a year of working as a stylist in one of the most popular shops in Chicago, I had been able to move out of my parents' house about six months ago. My goal was to be a celebrity stylist with my own shop one day, though. I was nice with the scissors and could slay a weave. I was good with customizing lace frontals and wigs too. I had over ten thousand followers on Instagram and other social media outlets, so my clientele was nice, which included a few local artists, models, and dope boys' girlfriends. I even did Nova and Zoe's hair from time to time. That's how Shamar and I met; when he and Money were meeting Nova at the shop one day.

Every Love Story Is Beautiful, But Ours Is Hood
by *Jessica N. Watkins*

Anyway, I took a moment to perfect my curls and smooth out my clothes before opening the door. But as soon as I did, I lost my composure. Gawd damn, this nigga was *fine!* Shat! It was so hard to find the perfect big, tall, and attractive man, but Shamar Savage was that and then some! He looked so fucking good that night. His wide, big build was wrapped in Givenchy from head to toe. One of the things that attracted me to Shamar was that even though he was a big guy, he did not wear his clothes big and hanging off of him. His tee and jeans fit his football build nicely, I also liked that unlike most men, he did not have dreads. He had a waved out silky black fade, but he did have the signature full beard and goatee that accented those pretty, big, juicy lips.

The way that I'd stopped and stared at him made his caramel skin blush. "What you lookin' at?"

His sexy, flirtatious smirk made me blush my damn self. "You, *Daddy*."

"Stop callin' me that, man. Gonna make me fuck you right now, and then we won't make it out."

I giggled at his lustful threats.

He continued, "Come here." Without permission, he stepped into the doorway, took me into his big arms, and wrapped them around me. "You look so damn good. Good job."

"Thank you."

Fuck. I discreetly exhaled as his masculine cologne took over me and made me feel so safe. *Don't wake a bitch, 'cause I must be dreaming.* But, as he let me go, and I went to grab my coat, I told myself to relax, not to get excited, and just treat this night as just what it was—*some dick.*

****

The night ended up being way more than that, however.

Shamar and I ended up only a few minutes from my place at R Lounge. It was a cool bar that had a poppin' Monday deejay, so the party was crackin'. However, it was small, so even from the VIP section that Shamar, his brothers, and I were sitting in, I could see Reggie's stalking ass leaning against the bar staring at me!

Oh my God! I was freaking out.

After months and months of just fucking Shamar, we were finally *out...together... with his family...*having a good-ass time. And here this creep go! I could *not* believe my fucking luck!

I was able to play it off, however. There were so many people packed into this small space that I was only able to notice Reggie because I knew him. Shamar wasn't playing his weird ass no mind. He was so busy drinking and chilling with his brothers that he wasn't paying any attention to me as I tried my best to avoid Reggie's eyes that were staring a fucking hole through me. Even though Shamar was drinking with his brothers, he surprisingly missed no opportunity to make it known that I was with him by placing his hand on my thigh or leaning into me, whispering nasty things that he wanted to do to me. That shit made me blush and Reggie fume.

Reggie wasn't that crazy, though, because no matter what, he stayed where he was. I was surrounded by four goons, so he dared not approach me. Yet, I feared the repercussions that I would face the next day.

CHAPTER EIGHT

SHAMAR SAVAGE

'Cause I eat it up for a while, let me through

Got you shakin', screaming aloud, I'ma fool

Make my face your chair, leakin' everywhere

Ride it out, I don't care what you do

Every time I lick it, you be losing it

These young boys didn't know what to do with it

You got it all on my face, I love the way that it tastes

When you got it all on my plate

It won't go to waste

That's what you get everyday

When you fuckin' with me

"*Fuckin' wit me. That's what you get every day when you fuckin' with me.*" When Taraji caught me looking at her, she licked her lips and gave me this smile that made my dick solid as concrete. She knew it too as she continued to roll slowly in the passenger's seat. "Ayeee! That's my shit!"

Every Love Story Is Beautiful, But Ours Is Hood
by *Jessica N. Watkins*

I had asked Taraji to step out with me because I was tired of being around these hard legs. The Savage family was so tight that it was like I was around these niggas every day. I wanted something soft and pretty to look at and rub on if I had to be with my brothers all night, so I called Taraji, and she was the perfect choice. Not only was she beautiful, but she was cool as fuck and vibed with me and my brothers perfectly all night, surprisingly.

Any other female would have embarrassed me, been extra, or started some shit. But not Taraji. She was cool as shit.

"You're cool as fuck, man," I admitted before I realized it. That was a slip of the tongue like a motherfucker. The Ducce had me trippin'.

One rule of mine was *never* to let a woman know how I felt about her. All that a woman got from me was a hard dick, a smile, and maybe a meal. But it seemed like Taraji was able to make me break all of my rules without me knowing it.

Taraji looked over at me from the passenger's side of my Charger. The diamond in her nose sparkled amongst the darkness in my ride. "You say that like you didn't know it already."

Every Love Story Is Beautiful, But Ours Is Hood
by *Jessica N. Watkins*

Fuck it, I thought, trying to encourage myself to be honest. "I did know it, but you're *really* cool. I can kick it with you all night with no issues. That's rare as fuck."

At the moment, the way that we were looking at each other was different. It wasn't just lust between us anymore. This night had been confirmation that beyond our intense sexual chemistry being real, our spiritual and emotional chemistry was equally real. I had kind of known that when I found myself talking to her for hours at a time; another one of my rules that I broke often with her. However, tonight was definitely confirmation.

EVERY LOVE STORY IS BEAUTIFUL, BUT OURS IS HOOD
by *Jessica N. Watkins*

TAYE 'CITY' SAVAGE

After leaving the R Lounge, a nigga was drunk as fuck, and my dick was rock hard. I sat in my ride staring at that big house and hated to go in that motherfucker. I found myself wishing that I was still living in the Dearborns. That was home to me, not this three-hundred-thousand-dollar bullshit.

I just sat there, pissed as fuck that my only option for some pussy was Nova's stank ass. That bitch had really been in her own ass since I got home. I had thought highly of her for what she had done for my family while I was in prison. Now, it was obvious that I had made a big mistake by giving her the title and the boss status that I had. She really thought that I owed her something just because she had held down what I gave her.

"Fuck that bitch," left my lips in a drunk slur as I turned off the engine and regretfully left the car.

The night air was so cold that it was biting a nigga in the ass and sobering me up. I hurried up and got in the crib, whether I wanted to or not. I slowly went upstairs, wishing that I didn't have to lay with this thoughtless bitch. But after

Every Love Story Is Beautiful, But Ours Is Hood
by *Jessica N. Watkins*

sleeping on a cot for ten years, I would be damned if I slept on a couch.

Suddenly, thoughts of Akira entered my drunk mind. I remembered her being ready to kiss me before Neko's goofy ass came and fucked shit up. The memories of her getting ready to finally submit to me made my dick jump in my Rag and Bone jeans.

Sitting on that couch with Akira, with her legs crossed, watching me with the same sexual innocence that she had when she was fourteen, I felt the familiarity of what I used to know. When I was with Akira, a nigga felt like he was truly at home. This shit wasn't home; these fancy cars, lobster dinners, minks, and foreign cars. I was a true hood nigga. I knew the streets, the hustle, and *Akira*. I wanted that shit back...all of it. That's why I had been instant messaging Akira ever since the night that I was at her crib. We talked for hours every day about everything and nothing. It was fucked up that there was more passion in her words for me than Nova had shown me since I'd been home.

I wanted to get Akira alone again so bad that I thought about that shit every day and all day. But she was still too scared of her attraction to me to give me her number, let alone meet up with me.

EVERY LOVE STORY IS BEAUTIFUL, BUT OURS IS HOOD
by *Jessica N. Watkins*

"Where the fuck you been?"

Soon as I stepped into my bedroom, Nova's nagging pierced the darkness.

I snarled as I kicked off my boots. "Fuck you mean where I been? Didn't I tell you I was going out with my brothers?"

"Yeah, but—"

"Then that's where the fuck I been," I barked.

"I'm just making sure you wasn't with *Akira*."

That threw me off, but I tried to play it off. I cut the light on and casually asked, "What are you talking about?"

Nova jumped out of bed. She was dressed in a lacy, black panties and bra set. No matter how much of a bitch she was, nobody could deny her beauty. If the bitch acted like she cared about a nigga and not just my money, I probably would have grabbed her ass up and quieted her with this dick. But nah. Fuck this bitch. All she gave a fuck about was cash and her reputation of being the woman of a Savage nigga.

"Don't fucking play with me, City!" she fussed as she walked up on me like she was as tough as a gangsta on the street. "I heard you were over at Davion and Akira's spot the other day!"

"How you know where I been?"

Every Love Story Is Beautiful, But Ours Is Hood
by *Jessica N. Watkins*

"Don't fucking worry about it. Don't play with me, nigga," she spat just as she muffed the shit outta me.

Soon as she did that shit, I spazzed. I had been in prison for ten years, not no fucking day camp! Nobody could run up on me suddenly. Before I knew it, I grabbed her wrist and twisted that motherfucker until she was wincing and collapsing to the floor in pain. "*You* don't play with *me!*" I warned.

"Aw, City! Stop!" she whimpered.

I let her go with a push, and she fell further back on the floor. I didn't feel bad for hurting her. She needed to be brought down to her level and *quick*.

"Yo' head done got too big," I fussed. "Remember who the fuck I am."

She slowly stood from the floor, nostrils flaring and eyes full of rage. But she fucking knew not to try me again.

"*I'm* City Savage. You remember that shit!" Then I left her to sleep alone since she thought she did everything herself anyway.

Nova had helped build this family, but it was time that I taught her who had started this shit.

TARAJI GREEN

I have to be the luckiest bitch in the world.

I had to be. As I lifted my head slightly and saw Shamar's waves in between my legs, I knew that I clearly was the luckiest girl in the world.

I fought to wake up from the deep, drunken stupor that I had been in while enjoying the feeling of his big, juicy lips sucking on my clit. In all of the times that I had given him some, he had never tasted it, so I fought not to cum too fast from the excitement.

But I couldn't help it. During the night before, Shamar had been blowing my mind. He was looking at me in a different way. He held me differently. He fucked me differently. I was trying my best not to get excited and start thinking too much of his passion and efforts, but fuck! It was so hard not to let my guard down for him.

"Mmmm, yes," I moaned. "Right there. Don't stop."

He listened to me. He didn't stop sucking my clit softly. In fact, he added a twist. He took his big, long finger, pushed into my wetness, found my G-spot, and started playing with it.

Every Love Story Is Beautiful, But Ours Is Hood
by *Jessica N. Watkins*

My mouth fell open. No words could come out, although I had so much to say.

What is he doing to me? I couldn't wrap my head around why Shamar was eating my pussy so ferociously. He was talking to this pussy like he had a point to prove. But why was he doing me like this when he clearly didn't want a woman? Why was he eating my pussy to the point that I wanted to look for him in the daylight with a flashlight when he clearly did not want to be attached?

"Aaahhh shit!" I squealed as I felt my orgasm coming.

I started to rotate my hips against his face. It turned me on even more that he welcomed me riding those big lips.

"Fuck, I'm cummin'!"

"Mmmm humph," he moaned cockily into my pussy.

And that was it! That's all I could take! Shamar was already snacking on this pussy, but he moaned in it too?! I was cummin' all over his face. "Shiiiiiiiiiiiiiiiiiiiit!"

But he kept sucking me and fucking me his fingers.

"Stop, stop, stop, stop, stooooop!" I shrieked.

But he wouldn't. So, I used my foot to lightly push his shoulders in order to free myself from his lips.

Every Love Story Is Beautiful, But Ours Is Hood
by *Jessica N. Watkins*

He fell back giggling. I just fell back, unable to catch one damn breath, looking at the ceiling, stuck like what the fuck?

Then I felt him leave the bed. I looked over to see him dressing.

I guess he saw me staring at him because he told me, "I got a client meeting me at the shop in an hour."

Why is he explaining himself to me? He never did that! As a matter of fact, he never spent the night. Even if he was drunk and it was four in the morning, he made sure to leave.

He was blowing me!

"You don't have any clients today?" he asked.

"Yeah," I forced out. Shit, I was still barely able to talk. I cleared my throat and forced out, "Not until this afternoon, though."

As he pulled up his jeans, he looked into my eyes. Swear to God, my soul cried. *Cried*! As our eyes locked, I felt how I was losing my cool. I realized that I couldn't find the right words to say. I realized that I even gave a fuck if I said the right thing or not. I didn't like that. Nope, not all...

"You...uh..."

Every Love Story Is Beautiful, But Ours Is Hood
by *Jessica N. Watkins*

I watched him, waiting for him to say whatever it was that he was trying to say, and wondering why he couldn't just spit it out.

"You wanna grab something to eat before you go to the shop? This tat should only take about an hour to finish."

I couldn't help it. I looked at this dude like he was crazy.

He chuckled. "What, man?"

"What's up with you?" I finally asked.

"What you mean?" He had this funny look on his face, so I knew that he knew exactly what I meant.

"I mean you took me out, you spent the night, and now you wanna go on another date?"

He laughed at himself because he knew I was right. He knew he was acting different.

"What's wrong with that?" he asked, trying to seem nonchalant.

"Nothing," I answered with a shrug. I figured I would shut up and not fuck up a free meal with my mouth.

He shrugged as he grabbed his keys. "Yeah, a'ight. Just text me when you're ready."

Every Love Story Is Beautiful, But Ours Is Hood
by *Jessica N. Watkins*

I ignored the butterflies in my stomach and replied, "Okay." Then I told him, "Just lock the bottom lock on your way out."

Fuck that! I wasn't walking him to the door. No more awkward moments.

"Nut got you stuck, huh?" he taunted me as he walked out of my bedroom.

"Whatever, nigga," I replied, fighting myself.

I was so busy staring at the ceiling in wonder that I didn't know that Shamar was still in the room until I felt his lips on mine.

My eyes bucked open, but they fell on his closed eyes. I felt his hands wrap softly around my neck as his tongue softly made love to my mouth. I stopped fighting. I closed my eyes and kissed him back, tasting my pussy on his breath. Just as I was getting wet again, his mouth left mine.

He stared down on me as he simply said, "See you later." Then he left.

I stared with bucked eyes into the ceiling in pleasant surprise until the door closing snapped me out of my trance. I pulled the covers over me. I bit my lip as my pussy began to pulsate. My legs squeezed together underneath the blanket.

EVERY LOVE STORY IS BEAUTIFUL, BUT OURS IS HOOD
by *Jessica N. Watkins*

Shamar wasn't even in the car yet, and I wanted him to come back already.

This was exactly what I did *not* want! This was exactly what I did *not* have time for! No!

Suddenly, there was a round of knocks on the door. I jumped out of bed. I grabbed a T-shirt from a pile of clothes on my way out and slipped it on. My hair was all over my head from getting sucked and fucked all night and morning. But I didn't care. Figuring it was Shamar coming back for something he left, I opened the door without asking who it was.

I gasped when I saw Reggie. "What are you doing here?!" I snapped.

"I brought you something."

I hadn't even noticed the flowers in his hand until he shoved the bouquet into my arms.

"Um...uhhh...," I stuttered. "Thank you."

"You're welcome."

Then there was awkward silence between us. I just stared at him, waiting for him to explain his presence.

"Who was that nigga you were with last night?" he finally spat.

Every Love Story Is Beautiful, But Ours Is Hood
by *Jessica N. Watkins*

My eyes darted toward his. "What?" I asked, not believing his audacity.

And just like that, I remembered. Shamar's odd behavior had taken my mind off of it, but I quickly remembered through my lustful fog how Reggie's weird ass was staring at me all night at the club. I anticipated him coming over and embarrassing the fuck out of me at any moment, but he never did. He just stared all night. When the lights came and on and the deejay announced last call, he disappeared, and I was relieved.

But now that relief had been replaced with anxiety. Reggie had the weirdest look in his eyes. He had given me the flowers with sincerity, and now suddenly, the longer I took to answer his question, it seemed the angrier his eyes got.

"That nigga..." he reiterated. "Who the fuck was—"

"None of your business," I spat.

"Is he why you don't wanna be with me no more?"

"Be with you no more?" I laughed sarcastically. "*We were never together.*"

When his nostrils flared, I got scared. I slammed the tulips back into his hands. "Reggie, I told you, I don't want to date you anymore. And this is why. You are too pushy. I am no longer interested in you-"

EVERY LOVE STORY IS BEAUTIFUL, BUT OURS IS HOOD
by *Jessica N. Watkins*

"Just give me a chance to—"

"No. I am single, and I want to stay that way. I am not committed to anyone, and I do not want to be, which means that I can date whoever I want to. So, please leave me alone. Please?"

I was trying to be as sincere as possible. Reggie and I shared a good past. He had the perfect chocolate skin with pretty, brown eyes. He was average height. We stood eye to eye. He made up for it by staying in the gym and having a bomb-ass body, though. He was a good-looking dude. He did everything right. He had courted me, taken me on dates, and cherished me. But I didn't want that shit! And the more I didn't want it, the more he was obsessed with making me accept it!

Finally, he nodded and spat, "Cool." Then, he turned on his heels and went down the stairs.

I slammed the door with a frown. "Eww. That short motherfucker got some nerve."

But something told me that, against my hopes, that wouldn't be the last time that I saw Reggie.

CHAPTER NINE

AKIRA WHITE

"Ooooh! You ain't shit!" Lola squealed through the phone.

I giggled. "Shut up, girl."

But she didn't. Lola kept on teasing me. "Yoooou ain't shiiiiit!" she nearly sang. "I knew you liked him!"

"I do not!" But if I didn't, why was I smiling like a little girl?

"Yes, you do!" Lola replied as if she could see my smile. "You are meeting him for lunch! That's a date!"

"No, it's not."

"Yes, it is! Y'all have been chatting all week, and now you are about to meet him for lunch. That's a damn date."

"A man like City Savage doesn't date."

"Well, he's taking *you* on a damn date."

I sucked my teeth. "Lies."

"*Truth.* Where are y'all eating at?'

I cringed and hesitantly answered, "III Forks."

"Tuh! That's a date!"

EVERY LOVE STORY IS BEAUTIFUL, BUT OURS IS HOOD
by *Jessica N. Watkins*

I shook my head, trying to hide my blushing, even though Lola wasn't in my presence to see me.

However, as I sat at the table for two, I did wonder if this was a date or not. After days of chatting with City on Facebook, I finally got the courage to meet him because he'd asked me literally every day.

Just as I suspected, my knees got weak when I saw City coming. He had just appeared in the doorway of the restaurant like black Jesus, looking all royal.

Staring at City, I told Lola, "I gotta go." Then I hung up before she could continue the conversation.

City was like a god. He demanded the attention of everyone in the restaurant. His walk was so effortless and slow that it appeared as if he were floating above us all. And considering how massively tall he was, he definitely was floating over everyone in the restaurant. I felt privileged that I was the one who had his attention. I was honored that his presence was because of me.

"Akira," he said with satisfaction as he smiled down on me.

I stood on my weak knees, but I fought it and wrapped my arms around his massive body. I was unsuccessful, however. My arms could hardly hug his huge frame. I

EVERY LOVE STORY IS BEAUTIFUL, BUT OURS IS HOOD
by *Jessica N. Watkins*

hesitated, taking a moment to inhale deeply and drown in his masculine scent of black currant, French apples, Italian bergamot and royal pineapple.

"Hey you," I greeted as I finally let him go.

"Did you order yet?"

"No, I was waiting for you."

After we sat down and started looking over the menus, I was disappointed in myself. I could feel the sexual energy still lingering between us that started the night that he was sitting on the couch next to me. On my way here, I'd told myself just to have a friendly lunch with City and to ignore the pulsating between my legs. If I didn't, it would only start a snowball of bullshit. My man didn't satisfy me sexually, but he loved me, and he had chosen me. City had never done that. Even as he sat across from me looking like a sexy, lump of bad boy swag, he was still a taken man, with me on the side lusting after him, just like it had been when I was fourteen. Nothing had changed.

"What you thinkin' about?"

When he spoke, I realized that I had been staring at him. I refocused on the menu, saying, "You make me think of my mama and things that happened back then."

EVERY LOVE STORY IS BEAUTIFUL, BUT OURS IS HOOD
by *Jessica N. Watkins*

That wasn't a complete lie. It may not have been what I was thinking at that very moment, but for the past couple of days and ever since I saw City again, my mother had been at the forefront of my mind for once in the past ten years.

"You don't still feel bad for what you did, do you?"

I shifted in my seat. Anxiety rushed through my entire body. I couldn't breathe. This is what happened every time I allowed myself to remember that I was the person who'd taken my mother's life. Regardless of her being a whore and a drug addict, I hated the fact that I was the person who took her life. The guilt washed over me with such a force that my eyes began to well with tears. City was used to this. This happened every time we talked about it as I lived with him after I had murdered my mama. And just like he did back then, he took my hand into his. Reaching across the table, his simple touch calmed my anxiety as he looked into my eyes with confidence.

"You have nothing to feel bad about. You were defending yourself. You did what you had to do." When the anxiety was still in my eyes, he pushed, "You hear me? You don't know what she was going to do to you that night. For all you know, she was going to kill you or make you sleep with that motherfucker. You did what you had to do."

My voice cracked as the tears finally started to fall. "But she was my *mother*."

"But she didn't act like one. No *real* mother would ever sell her daughter for some crack or do anything else to hurt her child. You have nothing to feel guilty about, you understand?"

I quickly nodded and wiped away the tears that had fallen from my eyes.

When he flashed a genuine smile at me, I hated him for making me feel like that vulnerable fourteen-year-old girl who was madly in love with him.

"What are you smiling about?" I asked.

"*You*. You haven't changed. You look the same. Still my little pretty virgin girl, scared to give that pussy up."

I laughed, appreciating that he had smoothly changed the subject. "I ain't no virgin," I told him, trying to sound confident.

Yet, he quickly dismissed me. "You still are."

I tilted my head, silently asking him what he meant.

"That nigga ain't fuckin' you right. You haven't been fucked right yet. I can see it in your eyes. So, you're still a virgin to me."

Every Love Story Is Beautiful, But Ours Is Hood
by *Jessica N. Watkins*

I swallowed hard, trying desperately for the truth not to be seen in my eyes. To ensure that it didn't, I looked back down at my menu. I was relieved when the waiter walked up just in time. I quickly rambled off my order. Then I attempted to look busy, looking in my phone as City talked with the waiter over what entrée he should choose. His words made me so nervous that my fingers were shaking as I browsed through Instagram. I was so happy that City was engaged in such deep conversation with the waiter that he didn't notice. I hated that what he'd said to me was right. Davion was not at all fucking me right. He was perfect in every way, except in the bedroom. I felt like a terrible person for allowing sex to outweigh all of the good he had done.

Yet, honestly, I wanted nothing more than to feel City's body on top of mine and allow him to cure years of dissatisfaction in the bedroom. But I couldn't allow that to ruin the contentment that I had at home. Davion was my 80, and City was 20. Davion gave me 80% of what I wanted in a man. He satisfied me in every way, but I had to admit that there was no passion or true lust in my heart for him. But all City was willing to give me was the 20% that I was missing from Davion, while he was at his own home giving his 100% to Nova.

EVERY LOVE STORY IS BEAUTIFUL, BUT OURS IS HOOD
by Jessica N. Watkins

BLISS DAVIS

I was sitting on the couch in my living room watching Money play with Keandre as he sat in the middle of the floor. Money had been spending so much time with his son, and it was driving me crazy. I hated it. Before I moved in, I had been unsuccessfully trying to get over the love that I felt for Money. Having to see him every day like this was driving me insane.

I couldn't take watching the man that I loved spend all this quality time with me and my son and then go back home upstairs to that crazy-ass bitch!

"When are you going to find me a new place, Money?"

Just as he had done every time I asked that question over the last week, he ignored me. He continued to play with Keandre as if I hadn't said anything.

"*Money*," I pressed.

He kept ignoring me.

I picked up the nearest throw pillow and lunged it at his head.

He caught it, cursed with a grin, "I'mma fuck you up if you hit my son."

Every Love Story Is Beautiful, But Ours Is Hood
by *Jessica N. Watkins*

"Then answer the fucking question!" He just continued to look at me with that sexy-ass grin, but I ignored him and how my sex throbbed just watching him. "When are you going to get my place?"

"Soon. But I like y'all being here, real talk."

I was swooning! *Swooning*! Yaaasss, bitch! Yaaasss! Hearing him say that made the love in my heart for him just bubble over. But I quickly had to check that love. It had gotten me in so much trouble before. It had gotten me in the position of a side bitch, and I refused to be in that position ever again. I couldn't. It hurt too fucking bad. It hurt not having him, but it hurt way more having him part time while another bitch had him all the time who didn't fucking deserve it.

"You like *us* being here?" I needed clarification. I wanted to know if I had heard him right.

"Yeah. It just... feels *right*."

Unt-uh. "Money don't do that."

"It's the truth. Don't act like I wasn't feeling you. *You* left *me*, remember?"

I stared at him with cautionary eyes. "I don't want to go there. You chose Zoe. You have a woman that you obviously want to be with."

"How is that obvious?" he asked nonchalantly.

EVERY LOVE STORY IS BEAUTIFUL, BUT OURS IS HOOD
by *Jessica N. Watkins*

"She's still here."

"But who do I spend my time with? You don't even fuck me and I *still* spend my time with you."

"You spend your time with *your son*."

"And you."

I shook my head. I was shaking off his effect on me, the tremors, the love. "I'm not getting in the middle of you and Zoe again. I am in the middle enough. Get me a place, or I'm moving out of state to my mom's house." Before he could argue with me, I got up, stomped into my bedroom and closed the door behind me.

I had to put my foot down before things got out of hand. If I had to move out of state to keep Money from breaking my heart again, I would.

I had finally reached a place in my life that I could function without him. Finally, I wasn't crying every day because I missed him. For once, I felt like I was worthy of a man choosing me. At nineteen years old, I deserved to be young, wild, and free; not waiting for a man to choose me. And now he was sitting in the middle of the floor playing with his son, looking like the ultimate great father and man, but at the same time, he was telling me that he liked having a family with me when I could still hear this bitch walking upstairs above my head.

No, I could not get back in bed with Money.

KEANDRE 'MONEY' SAVAGE

I walked straight into the hole-in-the-wall and slapped some money on the bar.

"Give me a shot of 1738 stat," I barked at Jo, the bartender.

Jo knew me well, so she wasn't taken aback by my attitude. She took my hundred-dollar bill and poured me up.

"Damn, bro, you straight?" City asked as he watched me gulp down the shot.

"Hell nah," I spat. Then I told Jo, "Run that shit back and give my brothers a round of whatever they're drinking."

"What's the word, bro?" Shon asked.

"Maaaaan, these chicks are driving me fucking crazy."

"What happened?" City asked.

I sat in the bar stool between my brothers. I figured that it was time that I told them about the bullshit going on in my crib. With City getting out, at first, I didn't want to fuck up his good time with my bullshit, but now I figured he should be well adjusted to being home.

"I moved Bliss into the vacant unit in my building."

EVERY LOVE STORY IS BEAUTIFUL, BUT OURS IS HOOD
by *Jessica N. Watkins*

Shon started cracking up so hard that this fool was hollering. "*You what*?!"

City nearly choked on the beer that he was sipping on. "Nigga, do you wanna die?" he asked. "You done lost your mind!"

I grimaced and shook my head. "I know. It was stupid. But I had to. I didn't want Bliss to take my son out of state."

"I know Zoe is spazzing," City replied.

"Spazzing ain't the word. She wanna argue every fucking day. She hate that Bliss is there, but she isn't doing shit that a woman should do. She don't cook. Half the time, she ain't there. When she is there, she's doped up, zoned out, or sleep. She ain't fucking or suck—"

"Whoa," Shon stopped me. "She ain't *what*?"

"She ain't fucking or sucking." I had no problem admitting that to my brother. "But I don't want to fuck her either. I haven't hit that pussy since New Year's. She nags too much, and she's high all the gawd damn time on pills like a dope fiend. My dick don't even get hard no more."

"Shit, even chicks who nag want the dick. You think she's cheating?" Shon asked.

"Hell nah. I wish she would, though. I *want* her to give another nigga these problems."

172

Every Love Story Is Beautiful, But Ours Is Hood
by *Jessica N. Watkins*

Shon and City laughed hard as hell, but I was serious as fuck. Maybe if Zoe fell for a new nigga that could take care of her, I could get her off my hands.

"I'll be back. I'm going to the bathroom," Shon excused himself.

"Man, it ain't even Zoe that got my head fucked up, though, big bro," I confessed to City after Shon walked away. "It's *Bliss*. When I moved her in, it was strictly because of my son. I didn't think that I would start to like her like—"

"You *like* her?"

"Hell yeah. No matter what kind of nigga Pops was, he was always a family man. We had both of our parents, and I like that I've been able to give that to my son. It don't hurt that his mama is sweet as pie with a phat ass and has a hot meal on the stove whenever a nigga shows his face. That girl got me rethinking some shit."

I didn't like the taunting look that City was giving me. "Don't look at me like that, bro."

This dude had the biggest shit-eating grin on his face. "My little brother is growing the fuck up," he teased.

"Shut up, nigga."

"I'm proud of you."

"Don't be proud yet. That girl is in love with me. I see it in her eyes. And I care about her enough not to keep toying with her. I can't make that move unless I'm ready. I've been with Zoe for years, but it ain't been real. I still did my thing. I've hurt Bliss enough, so if I get with her, a nigga gotta settle down and be a family man. And I don't know if I'm ready."

City nodded. "I feel that."

When I saw Shon emerging from the bathroom, I cut the conversation. "Let's change the subject. You know Shon and Zoe is buddies. I don't want that nigga repeating anything to her."

"I feel you," City agreed. "I gotta holla at y'all about something anyway."

"What's the word?" I asked.

As soon as Shon returned to his seat, City got to it. "Nova is out of the picture. Her head done got too big, and she thinks she's running shit. For the past week, I have been transferring whatever is in her name out of it. Whatever positions she had in our organization and whatever decisions she made, dead that shit. *I'm* the head nigga in charge."

Money's eyes widened. "Straight up?"

City nodded confidently. I saw a stern, fuming look in his eyes that told me that he was seconds away from walking away from Nova altogether.

"Okay, bro," Shon told him. "Understood. I gotta holla at you too."

I immediately cut my eyes at Shon. When City noticed the tension between us, he pressed, "What's going on?"

"Look, bro, I'm ready to get this money," Shon told City.

I just shook my head and took a shot as City told Shon, "We *are* getting money."

"But we can be getting *more* money. I have buyers lined up ready to get up to a total of fifty bricks right now. We can stop selling a few bricks here and there and up our team to working with buyers that are out here moving real weight and—"

Like I knew he would, City cut him off. "And we can get real prison time too. I just got out."

"Ex-fucking-actly," I cut in.

"Shon, I ain't no money-hungry motherfucker," City added. "You like all the glitz and glamor, not me. Shit, I'm a project nigga. I don't even like standing out amongst the rest."

I chuckled. "Right. Real shit."

Shon grimaced and quieted. I was glad that City was on my side. Without me and City behind him, Shon couldn't make these unnecessary moves. There was no way that any connects would work with him alone because we were known as a team. Whether he wanted to realize it or not, we were essentially saving his life.

CHAPTER TEN

TARAJI GREEN

I hung up the phone with a sigh. I was crushed.

I hadn't talked to Shamar since he had left that morning, and I had no idea why. As he'd told me to, I called him when I was ready for lunch. He never answered, and I hadn't heard from him since.

Tears actually fell down my face as I sat in my car. I had taken a break from working to get some lunch, but I was so upset that I didn't have an appetite. I looked at the greasy bag of Five Guys, wishing that I wanted to eat it because I hadn't eaten all day, but my appetite just wasn't there.

This was why I avoided treating a man like anything more than dick; it hurt too bad when they made painful, bold moves like this. This pain reminded of the hurt that I felt when my ex chose another bitch over me and my unborn child. This hurt like a motherfucker, and I was not willing to go through it again; not even for a man like Shamar Savage.

I jumped out of my skin when my cell began to ring. When my heart anticipated that it was Shamar, I felt so

EVERY LOVE STORY IS BEAUTIFUL, BUT OURS IS HOOD
by *Jessica N. Watkins*

stupid. I felt weak. This was why I had never given up
control. This was why I played men like they always played
me.

Despite me knowing better, I was still hurt. Despite
me knowing that I wasn't a weak bitch, I felt lost without
Shamar, my friend, my lover.

The tears continued to leak when I saw that it was
not Shamar calling me back. It was one of my clients,
Kennedy. She was one of the dope boy's wives who was a
regular client of mine. She tipped well, and no service was
too expensive for her, so I answered despite the sadness
evident in my voice.

"Hello?"

"Whoa, baby girl, what's wrong with you?"

Since I saw Kennedy every two weeks, we had grown
to get to know each other. You know how it is when you are
sitting in your hairstylist's chair for hours. So, we had more
than just a professional relationship.

At the time, I was so vulnerable that I didn't mind
telling her the truth. I needed to vent to somebody, and I
would rather it be Kennedy than those gossiping chicks in
the shop.

EVERY LOVE STORY IS BEAUTIFUL, BUT OURS IS HOOD
by *Jessica N. Watkins*

"Girl," I sighed. "I done got myself in some shit with this guy."

"*What?!*" she asked, her voice full of surprise. "You've let a man make you sound like this? You let yourself get this close to a man?"

"I have. No matter how hard I tried to stop it, but it's hard when a man starts to be your friend and fucks you good."

"You ain't lyin'."

"Then we finally went on a real date. We had such a good time. I was so happy...like *genuinely* happy; that once in a lifetime happy. Then he just disappeared. I haven't heard from him; no call and no text message. We've been knowing each other for a year. Even if we don't fuck all the time, we talk often, so I don't understand why he is doing this to me."

"You miss him," she told me.

"Yeah," I admitted as tears flowed. "I do."

"Girl, these men be trippin'. They are so bipolar. Don't let him piss you off. He'll be back."

"I don't want him to now. I don't like this feeling."

"But do you want him?"

EVERY LOVE STORY IS BEAUTIFUL, BUT OURS IS HOOD
by *Jessica N. Watkins*

When I thought about it, I really didn't know. I enjoyed Shamar, but I preferred death than willingly being in any situation that would have me feeling this pain on a regular basis.

"I don't know," I admitted.

"Well, now is the time to think about it because being with a man is no cake walk. No person is perfect. You gotta be willing to take the good with the bad."

Kennedy was right. No person was perfect. Yet, I had nothing to think about because, apparently, Shamar had considered the same thing and already made his decision.

EVERY LOVE STORY IS BEAUTIFUL, BUT OURS IS HOOD
by *Jessica N. Watkins*

ZOE MOORE

Once I heard knocks on the bathroom door, I quickly snorted my last line. I dusted the residue off of the tissue holder, wiped my nose and darted out of the bathroom, not even paying attention to who was waiting to get in. I took a deep breath, happily awaiting the coke to hit my system. I had left the Percs and Xans at home. I was tired of being sleepy and floating through my bullshit. I wanted to party tonight!

This was the second time that I had tried coke. The first time had been earlier that day when I needed energy to get out of bed. I had spent the last week in a complete fog. I was numb, and that was the only way that I could deal with Money basically admitting that he didn't love me anymore. I didn't want to feel the realization that my relationship with Money was over. I wanted to get so high that I was unconscious of the fact that he spent more time downstairs with "his family" than he did with me.

I needed to get out of the house. When Nova sent me an invite via text to come hang out with the girls, I figured it was the perfect excuse to get cute and show Money that I was the bitch to chase. But I had no energy. I had heard that coke was a party drug that gave you so much liveliness. So, I went into Money's stash, grabbed me a bag and went into the bathroom. I came out with the most exhilarating, and intense high. I hadn't felt that alive since before Money started breaking my heart. But the effects were short lived. By the time I got to Zoe's, I needed another line.

"You ready, heffa?" Nova spat as I walked into her bedroom. She was standing in the mirror fixing her Hermes bandage dress. Her ass was so fucking big and fake. But, hey, if she liked it. I loved it.

"Awww shit! You look so fuckin' pretty, bitch!" Before I knew it, I ran up to her and smacked her ass.

She turned around, laughing at my antics. Then she zeroed in on my face. Suddenly, she took her finger and ran it under my nostrils. Then she held her finger up. White residue sparkled on it.

"Really, bitch?" Nova snapped. "Money said you were getting high. I thought he was lying. What the fuck is wrong with you? You snorting lines and shit?" She frowned at me as she looked at me with disgust.

I lightly smacked her finger out of my face and laughed. "Fuck Money."

EVERY LOVE STORY IS BEAUTIFUL, BUT OURS IS HOOD
by *Jessica N. Watkins*

"Look, you're my girl and all. You're damn near like a sister to me, so I won't say anything to Money, but you better stop using that shit."

I sucked my teeth. "A'ight."

This bitch was about to blow my high with this bullshit. I ignored her judgmental eyes. The effects of the coke were kicking in. Just that fast, the euphoria was returning. I just smiled and started twerking in the middle of the floor. "Let's go biiiiiitch! I'm ready to fuckin' kick it!"

"Hype-ass bitch," Nova muttered. "Let's go. I can't deal with you."

I giggled uncontrollably as she pushed past me. I knew that she was disappointed in me. But at the time, I didn't give two shits. I felt alive. I felt like me again. I was *that bitch* again!

Who the fuck was Nova to judge me? If she were in my shoes, she would do what the fuck she had to do too. This wasn't about Money. This was about me, and I had to win over Bliss.   Money had to choose me. Bliss couldn't have him. I was going to wait that bitch out just like I did every other bitch. I would be the last one standing *again*. I may have been fucking myself up while doing so, but I was going to fight Bliss for my man.

AKIRA WHITE

Three days after my lunch with City, I still couldn't get that man off of my mind. He was stalking my thoughts and *me.*

"Oh God," I muttered as I turned my back toward the door of the skybox.

I wanted to fucking kill Neko for steadily inviting the Savage brothers to the games. Neko was being so corny, hanging off of City's dick now that he was out. They had never been to games before City was released, and now he had seemingly given these motherfuckers season passes or some shit!

"You okay, sweetie?"

I looked up into my father's stern expression and smiled to soothe him. "Yeah, I'm good. Why?"

He didn't answer, but he did glance across the suite at City, who was the one man in the room who my father did not intimidate. He looked past my father's eyes and into my soul.

"Why is that motherfucker staring at you?" he barked.

"Daddy," I warned. "I already told you that he is related to Neko."

EVERY LOVE STORY IS BEAUTIFUL, BUT OURS IS HOOD
by *Jessica N. Watkins*

"So why is he staring at you like he knows you?"

"He does. I have gotten to know him while he attended some of the team's functions."

My father didn't need to know about City's history at the Dearborns. That would only lead him to do a background check on City. Once he found out that City's father was the pimp that turned out my mother, there was no telling how my father would use his power in law enforcement to destroy the Savage family.

The less he knew, the better for City and me.

It was a wonder that my father had even heard me. His eyes were burning a hole through the side of City's head. City was paying him no mind, however. That dark chocolate piece of perfection was staring directly at me. I found it hard to hide the blushing smile that wanted to escape my red matte lips.

I found it desperately sexy that he didn't give a fuck about my father's warning glares. He was that hard and dangerous bad boy that Davion could *never* be. Davion cowered under my father's threatening glares, when they seemed to give City more confidence to do him.

When I wondered if City was as intense and aggressive in the bedroom, I felt my pussy leak. Nervously, I began to fidget with the denim, knee-length, high-waist skirt that I was wearing. I forced my eyes on someone else. They fell on Money, who was watching my father with a glare.

I reached for my father's arm and gently turned him toward me. "Would you please stop, Daddy? That is so embarrassing. I am twenty-four, and I am a pretty girl. Men are going to stare."

When he saw the sincerity in my embarrassment, he sighed and kissed my forehead. "Okay. I apologize, sweetie."

"Good. Now, let's the watch the game. Half time is over."

I guided him toward the seats near the window that allowed a clear view of the field. Along the way, I felt City's eyes on me, and when I dared to look at him, I damn near lost my balance.

Gawd damn. What is this man doing to me?

****

After a surprising win by the Bears, I waited until City and his brothers were so immersed in their conversation that they wouldn't notice me rushing my father out of the suite.

Every Love Story Is Beautiful, But Ours Is Hood
by *Jessica N. Watkins*

Although I had successfully kept my father's attention on the game for the second half, it was as if I could still feel City's eyes on me. I wondered if he could feel that my thoughts were on him. Just knowing that his cocky ass was a few feet away from me had my imagination on some real porno-type shit. Getting the mediocre dick from Davion while City was in my ear all day was making me a fucking whore. I hadn't physically cheated on Davion and hadn't planned to. However, my heart and mind were with City. They stayed on Taye 'City' Savage because I was obsessed with him.

Just as I received a text from Davion saying that he was on his way out, I told myself to stop obsessing over City. There was no way that I could risk the comfortable and committed love that I had with Davion for some possibly good dick that was still committed to the woman that he'd chosen over me in the first place.

No way.

Davion emerged from the locker room, and I watched him with a smile. He was missing one thing, but he had everything else that many women were praying for... that any woman would kill me and anyone else to have.

Once close enough, he grabbed the back of my head softly and kissed my forehead.

I smiled at the weariness in his eyes. "Good game, baby."

In the third quarter, Davion had gone in the game and made a record-setting amount of sacks in the second half. He had killed the competition.

"Thank you, baby."

"Tired?"

"Hell yeah. I gotta get some sleep. We hit the road tomorrow early as hell for the game next Sunday. You coming?"

If the Bears won on that Sunday, they were going to be one step closer to the Super Bowl. It was a crucial game that I couldn't miss.

"Of course," I assured him with a smile.

"Cool. Let's go."

Davion grabbed my hand. As we walked through the stadium toward the parking lot, I noticed all of the female fans lusting over Davion's status, tattoos, and perfectly light brown skin. I smiled at them while holding his hand tighter.

Once he had walked me to my BMW, he opened the door for me and then planned to see me at our home, which was only about fifteen minutes away from the stadium. But

EVERY LOVE STORY IS BEAUTIFUL, BUT OURS IS HOOD
by *Jessica N. Watkins*

as he walked toward his truck, my Facebook messenger app notification rang through the car.

After starting my car, I checked the message, and my damn heart started to flutter when I saw that it was City.

City: *Come have a drink with your boy.*

Everything that I had just said to myself immediately flew out of the window.

"Urrrgh!"

I wanted to say no, but my body was saying, "Hell yeah, biiiiiitch."

****

Of course, I met him for drinks! Who could say no to Taye 'City' Savage? I clearly couldn't. I had told Davion via text that I was stopping to have drinks with friends, knowing that he wouldn't argue with that. And just like I thought, he didn't. That weak shit only made me feel better about meeting City. But just a little better. No matter how whack

Davion's dick was, I had respected his love for me enough to never entertain another man. Even the conversations with City had made me feel guilty, and that lunch made me feel like I was doing too much. But lying to Davion and meeting with City this late at night was doing the complete most.

However, as soon as I walked into the bar inside the Godfrey hotel and spotted that big, sexy motherfucka sitting at the bar, staring at me lustfully with those slanted eyes, all of my guilt and resistance disappeared. As it always was when I was in the presence of this king, thoughts of Davion disappeared. It was as if he no longer existed.

I switched toward City, slowly unzipping my bomber jacket and revealing the denim bustier that matched my skirt. I saw those beautiful eyes squint even tighter in lust as they found my cleavage.

"Mmmm," he moaned as he hugged me. "It's so fucking good to see you."

I giggled like a school girl as he stood and helped me into my bar stool.

"What are you drinking?" his deep voice rumbled.

I fought hard not to allow his rich voice to seduce me because he was just asking me a simple question. But, damn, anything this man said or did was sexy as fuck. "Whatever you're drinking."

His eyes narrowed at my heroism. "Straight up? You're a big girl now?"

"I keep telling you that I'm a grown-ass woman, City."

His smirk was so handsome as he nodded. "A'ight then. Bet."

Why the fuck did I say that?

Mind you, I was a drinker, but I usually drank cute drinks like Tequila Sunrises and Long Islands. I had already had a few Tequila Sunrises at the game, so I felt nice already. But City was drinking 1738 straight up! After two drinks, I was tipsy as hell! I tried my best to hide it, but City saw it anyway because, no matter the amount of years that we had been apart, he knew me. He saw that I was feeling that liquor and started fucking with me.

"How're you and *your man*? That nigga fucking you right yet?"

I laughed him off and tried to confidently say, "Yeah."

I think he knew I was lying. With his barstool facing mine, he was able to place his hands on my thighs. It was the closest we had ever been, so my clit started to instantly throb, and my heart started fluttering.

EVERY LOVE STORY IS BEAUTIFUL, BUT OURS IS HOOD
by *Jessica N. Watkins*

Staring deeply into my eyes, he asked me, "How many times does he make you cum?"

Hell, *never*, gawd damn it! But I didn't say that. "That's none of your business."

"Why not? I thought we were friends."

"How many times does Nova make you cum?" I retorted.

"Recently?" he asked, then immediately shook his head. "She hasn't been."

Hummm. Interesting. "Why is that?"

"My mind has been on somebody else that deserves this dick way more than she does."

I wanted to ignore that. I *needed* to ignore that. I wasn't about to play these games with this sexy-ass motherfucker. No!

I smiled bashfully and checked the time on my cell. Realizing how late it was, I sighed and told City. "I think it's time for me to get home."

It was time, clearly. I had given City about an hour of my time. I needed to get back home while I was sober enough to drive and was still committed to my fiancé.

Thankfully, City didn't argue with me. He stood, left a few hundred dollar bills on the bar and assisted me into my

EVERY LOVE STORY IS BEAUTIFUL, BUT OURS IS HOOD
by *Jessica N. Watkins*

jacket. He threw me off when he took my hand before he guided me out of the bar. All eyes were on us, and my conscience feared that people were staring at us, but they weren't. In all actuality, they were staring at City. His eyes pierced through his dark skin like a feline. The epicness of his sexiness was so jarring that women could not hide the fact that they were staring lustfully. His beard was so lustrous that he must've moisturized it with shea butter. Next to his massive size, I looked very much like the scared little girl that he was pursuing when he was nineteen.

I was so relieved, though. I had made it through yet another intense, sexual encounter with City. I was walking toward the door full of relief.

Then I felt a tug on my hand. City had stopped walking. We were in front of the elevators. I looked back at him questionably, and he simply said, "Come up to my room with me."

Fuck!

I wanted to say no. I was prepared to say no. My lips formed the word no. My eyes looked toward the heavens. I was waiting for God to send a sign or some powerful force that would push me toward the door.

But God must have been busy with more serious issues because the exit slowly became the furthest thing from me. Despite me not giving City a response, he was walking toward the elevators, and I was following him without reluctance.

I guess *yes* was my answer.

CHAPTER ELEVEN

TAYE 'CITY' SAVAGE

Nova's body had been sculptured to perfection. Literally, she had paid some doctor to take a knife and make her perfect. She looked good. No man could deny that. But there was something about the simplicity and naturalness of Akira's curves that had my dick hard as a fucking rock the moment that I saw her in the suite at the game. My dick hadn't been treated right since I'd left prison. Nova's nonchalant head and pussy were minuscule compared to the passion in Akira's eyes for me. I couldn't ignore that shit anymore.

Akira stood with her hands in the pockets of her jacket. Her brown eyes were staring widely around the suite that I had gotten for the night. "Why did you get a room?"

I dropped the key card down on the end table and honestly told her, "Hoping that I could get some more alone time with you."

I watched her body shiver. She thought she was hiding it. But she was twenty-four and ripe with little experience

Every Love Story Is Beautiful, But Ours Is Hood
by *Jessica N. Watkins*

with men. Whatever the projects had taught her about the streets, it had taught her nothing about men. But me? I was twenty-nine with the soul of an old nigga. I knew a woman who needed and wanted to be fucked and sucked in the rightest way.

Since linking up with Akira again, it was obvious that I still had the same feelings for her that I had when we were shorties. Yet, I forced myself to bottle those feelings up because it was clear that she was happy with her lame ass fiancé and I had a woman at home. But it was also clear that he was making her happy in every way, *except* the bedroom. I couldn't take her from him if I still had a woman, but, tonight, I would take what I could get.

I wasn't about to keep beating around the bush with this pussy. I had been trying to be subliminal with my intentions, but it was apparent that I wanted her. And since she had been trying to ignore all of my subtle advances, I had to take it.

As she stared out of the picture window, I walked up behind her and started to remove her coat. I was able to take it off without protest from her. My hands took the opportunity to finally rest on her ass. I hoped that she wouldn't reject me. When she didn't, my dick got harder than

Every Love Story Is Beautiful, But Ours Is Hood
by *Jessica N. Watkins*

it had ever been during the days that I was in prison praying for the opportunity to be in a woman.

"I missed this," I confessed.

And that was the God's honest truth. I had been committed to Nova, but for ten years many of my lustful thoughts went to Akira, the woman that this dick had always wanted to be inside of us.

Her heavy breath was all that could be heard in the suite. Then, I felt her body relax against mine. The last thing that I wanted to do was scar her innocence with this hard ass dick, but this monster was fighting its way out of my jeans.

As soon as she felt that motherfucker poking her in the back, she jumped slightly, turned, and those light brown eyes bore into mine. I was hoping that I now didn't see or hear any reluctance.

I still didn't.

All I heard was silence, so I took my chance. I took that pretty mouth with mine and made more love to hers than I ever had anyone else's. That's when I knew that it was confirmed that she was the woman that deserved this dick.

When I took her tongue, I finally felt a little resistance, but I persuaded it to go away by pulling her closer to me so that she felt this big dick against her. That little resistance faded. She started to fall into me fucking her mouth with mine and even started to fuck mine back with hers.

"Mmmm."

As soon as I heard that moan, it was a wrap! I used my massive size to swoop her body up into the air. She instantly wrapped her legs around my waist as I carried her to the bedroom.

I looked into her eyes, searching for a sign to stop, which I was going to fucking ignore anyway, but there wasn't one. Her eyes said keep fucking going and please don't ask her anything that would bring her back to reality. I was more than cool with that.

Once inside of the bedroom, I laid her on top of the bed and didn't hesitate or pause for one second. I removed her clothes before she could comprehend what the fuck was going on; first her heels, and then her skirt, top, and her bra and thong last.

And that's when *I* hesitated. Ten years ago, she was still a scared virgin. She gave me head and let me play with that pussy, but we had never been so sexual that I saw her butt-ass naked as I saw her at this moment. Her body was fucking beautiful. My massive form stood over her, casting a dark fog over her shadowy brown body as I stood over her in the darkness that was only slightly lit by the streetlights streaming in from the window.

"Gawd damn, you're beautiful."

She hadn't said anything since she'd entered the suite, and she still had no response. Her body only stirred under my intense gaze. So, I stripped before she could change her mind about what was about to go down. I threw off my Armani tee, trying to ignore how she started to play with her pussy as soon as my massive chest was exposed. I ripped the matching jeans off fast as fuck. Watching her play with her glistening middle was making me want to burst, when I hadn't even been inside of her yet.

Once I stripped off my briefs, her eyes bulged at this monster-ass dick that was so hard that it was running toward her and already leaking precum.

I raced toward that sweet, dripping pussy. I probably should have strapped up, but fuck that. I had waited for this moment for over ten years. I wanted to feel and taste every inch of her.

I saw so many questions in her eyes. The answers would fuck up the mood so I climbed on top of that beautiful brown body, brought this beast of a dick to her core and was about to quickly ease my way in, until the opening damn near snatched the cum out of this dick as it sucked me in.

"Fuck," rose from my throat in a husky groan. I had to come outside of my cocky self-confidence and let her know how good this pussy was feeling before I had got in it good.

I found her eyes and looked deep into them. I wanted her to see me as I entered her for the very first time.

EVERY LOVE STORY IS BEAUTIFUL, BUT OURS IS HOOD
by *Jessica N. Watkins*

AKIRA WHITE

Okay, so I *thought* I could assume what City would do to me. I *thought* I could imagine it. I *thought* I was a grown-ass woman.

But, clearly, I wasn't! *Clearly*!

On the way up to the suite, I knew what I was agreeing to. That's why I just couldn't say much. I wanted it. But behind my intoxication, I knew I was bogus, so I just wanted to do it with no words so that I could get through the moment with as little guilt as possible.

It didn't matter that I wasn't saying anything, though. City could read me. And it fucked me up that this man had spent a minimal amount of time with me, compared to Davion, and he could still read me in my silence; some shit that Davion could never fucking do on his best day.

So, when the tip of City's dick found my center, I was prepared... I thought. I was a grown-ass woman... I thought. I had had his dick in my hands and in my mouth before, so I knew how big it was... *I thought*. I had fucked before, so I knew what this was gonna be... I thought.

Every Love Story Is Beautiful, But Ours Is Hood
by Jessica N. Watkins

Girl, bye! I thought I knew, but I was wrong as two left Louboutin shoes.

Once he tried to force himself inside of me the first time, he hesitated. So, I was thinking like, *Yeah, nigga, this tight pussy got something on your grown ass.* I was feeling cocky. I watched him swallow hard to get his bearings together. I had gotten the big head for two seconds until he forced himself past my wet opening.

First of all, his dick was massive. But beyond that, his dick felt like it belonged in this motherfucker! It's a difference between good and bad dick, but it's a *huge* difference when the dick, no matter the size, feels like it belongs inside of you. His dick hit spots that I knew I had, forgot I had, and never even fucking fathomed I had.

"Fuuuuck...City...Oh my God!" My eyes were bucked toward the ceiling as he delivered strokes that I couldn't wrap my head around. My mouth was stuck agape. My eyes squinted in curiosity as I wondered how this man could fuck me so good the very first time that he was in the pussy.

In response, I felt his deep breathing on my neck as his face cradled in it. I heard the surprise in how good this sex was to him as well, despite no words of approval leaving his throat. However, these strokes were approval enough.

EVERY LOVE STORY IS BEAUTIFUL, BUT OURS IS HOOD
by Jessica N. Watkins

Yet, after his seconds of silence, he moaned, "Gawd damn, it feels just like I thought it would."

That made me leak more as I marinated in every stroke.

Then, before I could wrap my head around the dick, he rose up on his knees. He was so big and so strong that he was able to flip my curves around effortlessly. It took milliseconds for him to put me on my side, straddle my leg, throw the other over his shoulder, hold my waist tightly, and start hammering this pussy.

"Ahhh! Oh my God!" Tears of pleasure and pain filled my eyes as I attempted to bury my face in the pillow. "Shit, City! Yes! Yessss!"

City was pounding away in the middle of my legs, which formed like opened scissors. I was too ashamed for him to see my inexperience in such good dick to look at him, but I could feel his sweat dripping down on my perspiring skin. This dick was so good that I just wanted to bathe in his perspiration.

"Shit, City!" I squealed.

His dick was so immense that it hurt, but it felt fucking amazing.

EVERY LOVE STORY IS BEAUTIFUL, BUT OURS IS HOOD
by *Jessica N. Watkins*

"You were right, baby," he groaned. "You are a big girl."

No, no, I'm not! my mind screamed.

I bit my lip, attempting to push past the pressure in order to enjoy the pleasure surrounding it.

"Oohhh!" I screamed. "I'm about to—"

"Unt uh," he stopped me. "Not yet."

My eyes whipped toward him, wondering why he had stopped my orgasm. I wanted that motherfucker like I wanted my next breath. He answered the question in my eyes by flipping me effortlessly again. He put me on my knees. I gladly arched my back and buried my face in the pillow, both anticipating and fearing his rough and dynamic strokes.

＊＊＊＊

My eyes squinted open.

Then I realized that I had fallen asleep.

I gasped as I sat straight up so fast that I gave myself a headache. I felt around the bed in a rush, in a desperate attempt to find my phone. While doing so, City started to stir in his sleep.

His eyes looked heavenly as the moonlight shone down on them. However, I couldn't bask in his beauty like I wanted to. I had to find my phone. And when I finally did, my heart sank when I saw the thirty-two missed calls from Davion and the time.

"Shit!" I cursed as I scrolled through my phone.

"What?"

"It's four in the morning."

I jumped out of the bed and started scrambling around for my clothes that had been thrown everywhere around the room. As I bent down for my shirt, I caught a glimpse of City's epic perfection standing on the other side of the bed dressing slowly. I damn near tripped over my shoe staring at him.

The silence was so thick as we got dressed. The memories of our sex were loud as hell in mind, however. The visions of him riding the fuck outta this pussy doggie style made me shiver as I stepped into my shoes.

City had proven that he was right; I had never been fucked right... but, now, I had. Oh, God, I had.

I peered at his back as he silently put on his shirt. I watched him step into his shoes, wondering if this was it. I

EVERY LOVE STORY IS BEAUTIFUL, BUT OURS IS HOOD
by *Jessica N. Watkins*

tore my eyes away, forcing myself not to stare. I focused on fastening my skirt as my mind still wondered. I wondered if this was all City had wanted. I wondered if I had been some fantasy that he'd had while he was locked up. I wondered if, now that he had fulfilled it, if this would be it for us. I wondered why I cared. I wondered why I hated the fact that I was leaving him to go home to my loving fiancé, knowing that City was leaving also willingly to go home to his woman.

I wondered if this was it and if that was a good or bad thing, until I felt a dark shadow over me. Before I could look up, I felt his hand on my chin, forcing my eyes on him. My knees weakened as he smiled at my uncertainty. My pussy leaked as he slowly kissed it away, his tongue making as good love to my mouth as he had done to my body with his dick.

What we had experienced in this bed for three, long, unforgiving hours was not fucking. City had made love to me. For the first time in my life, my body had been pampered with pleasure, and it was by the man that I had always wanted it to be by anyway.

Suddenly, a bright light pierced the darkness of the room. City attempted to let me go, but I fought to keep his lips on mine.

He chuckled. "You know you need to get that."

EVERY LOVE STORY IS BEAUTIFUL, BUT OURS IS HOOD
by Jessica N. Watkins

I looked toward the light and saw that it was my phone ringing, but it was on silent. No wonder Davion's calls hadn't been heard in my sleep. I groaned, left City's arms, and snatched it from the bed. But I didn't answer. I knew that it was Davion. Unfortunately, I had more respect for City than Davion to answer his call in front of City. So, I locked the screen and slid it into my purse.

"Ready?" he asked me.

I pouted. "No."

He chuckled again. "Me either. We can stay if you want."

I looked at him. My knees weakened at the sight of the sincerity in his eyes. I struggled with the decision, and the fact that I was struggling was fucked up.

City knew it too. "But you shouldn't. C'mon."

He took my hand, and I regretfully followed him out of the bedroom. My feet were so heavy. I didn't want to leave. I wanted to be in his arms more than I wanted my next breath. I had thought about this moment more in the last ten years than I had inhaled a breath. But I had to leave.

EVERY LOVE STORY IS BEAUTIFUL, BUT OURS IS HOOD
by *Jessica N. Watkins*

****

"Fuck!"

For the second time that day, I was waking up out of my sleep in a panic. Only this time, I was in my own bed. Again, I searched around my bed for my cell phone. When I found it, my heart dropped.

"Shit," I groaned as I fell back on my pillow.

It was almost one in the afternoon. Lack of sleep and the liquor from last night had me so knocked out that I had missed my alarms and my flight to Green Bay.

"Fuuuuck!" I kicked and screamed.

I was fucking up for real. Davion had already left to hit the road with the team by the time that I had got home. I finally decided to call him since I had my story together. I was ready to tell him that I had gotten too drunk while having dinner with the girls from my spin class and had fallen asleep on one of their couches until I was sober enough to drive. But he didn't answer. That's when I knew he was pissed for real. I fell asleep wondering if he somehow knew what I had done. Then the realization of the possibility of him being so pissed that he would leave me entered my mind.

EVERY LOVE STORY IS BEAUTIFUL, BUT OURS IS HOOD
by *Jessica N. Watkins*

That scared the fuck outta me. City had shown me that he felt for me last night, but he still wasn't with me. Davion couldn't fuck me, but he had chosen me, and I was risking that over some dick.

And now I had missed my flight to a crucial game.

I hopped out of bed and started to frantically get dressed. Green Bay was four hours away, but I would make it there in three considering how I was about to drive.

"Stupid, bitch. Stupid, stupid, stupid."

I was straight tripping. I was letting some dick mess me all up...some good dick... damn good dick.... A-1 dick... but still! I needed to get my shit together quick. No matter how I felt for City, he had a woman of ten long years that he was choosing over me. I needed to smarten up and choose my man too... before I lost him.

BLISS DAVIS

So far, my threat to Money had gone unanswered. He still hadn't gotten me a place. He was also becoming more and more comfortable in my space.

This evening, he was taking me out to dinner. When he offered, I was reluctant. Money needed to be finding Keandre and me a place to live, not wining and dining me. However, I had been so wrapped up in fixing my situation, that I hadn't been out in a long time, nor had I had a meal that I hadn't cooked myself.

"You look nice."

Money was grinning at me from across the table at Sixteen, a French-inspired restaurant on the sixteen floor of the Trump Tower.

I looked down at the fitted, long sleeved cotton dress that hugged my curves. I nervously smoothed it over and then more nervously ran my fingers through my red waves. Looking at his smile, I couldn't help but blush. Having a man like Money stare at you with admiration was humbling and made you feel like a princess.

"Thank you, Money. You don't look too bad yourself."

Every Love Story Is Beautiful, But Ours Is Hood
by *Jessica N. Watkins*

He sure didn't. He had actually stripped off the tees and gym shoes. He was wearing a fitted button up, slightly fitted black jeans, and Giuseppe loafers. I was impressed and amazed at how gorgeous he looked when he had come downstairs to pick me up.

"Not as good as you. You look good enough to eat, Ma." Then, to add more pressure to this moment for me, he licked those big-ass lips.

"Stop it, Money," I told him. "Just because I came to dinner with you doesn't mean that I am going to fuck you. This is an *innocent* dinner between two parents."

Money held up his hands in defense. "I was just saying you looked good enough to eat. If you don't want me to eat it, then that's on you. I understand."

He knew what he was doing to me. He bit his lip seductively as I gave him a warning glare. Under my glare were juices flowing onto the crotch of my thong. I wondered if Money even knew how much I loved him or how much I would give to be able to have him eat this pussy under the right circumstances. If he didn't know, I wasn't going to tell him. He didn't deserve to know. He'd had that privilege before and played with it.

He saw my serious look and gave up. "Okay, let me quit playing. But I can't lie, I want to taste you. I haven't done it in a long time, but I understand why you don't want me to. I get it."

"Do you really understand?" I pressed.

"I really do. I understand that I hurt you when I didn't leave Zoe. I feel like shit that it took me so long to realize what was important. I had to grow up. I just wish that you would give me the chance to make it right."

"You really want the chance to make it right? Honestly, Money?"

He nodded slightly. "I do."

"Why? Why all of a sudden?"

"Because having you so close makes me realize what I don't have and what's important. It makes me realize what I risked losing you and my family for. You're a beautiful woman. You love me right. You deserve to be loved right. And I owe it to you to give you that."

"But you're still with Zoe."

He nodded. "I am."

"And that's the bullshit. I can't give you the chance to do anything until you leave your woman. I can't go down that road with you and Zoe again. I can't survive it. I can't be

Zoe. I am ride or die, but I will not ride with you until you kill me."

Money slightly nodded again. "I know. That's why I'm not pressing you. You're right; you shouldn't be with me until I leave Zoe. We are family, so I would never play you again. I know that when it comes to you, I am going to have to man up. I know what I have to do. But while I'm trying to do it, at least just let me show you the best way that I can that I want you."

This was the most vulnerable I had ever seen Money. Clearly, he was letting his guard down and trying to be the best man that he could. He wasn't a perfect man, but at least he was trying. If all he wanted to do was dote on me, then great, because I fucking deserved it.

CHAPTER TWELVE

ZYSHONNE 'SHON' SAVAGE

"That's it, baby. Yes..."

Zoe didn't have to encourage this dick to cum. I was already about to burst.

"Urrrgh!" I growled as my nails dug into her sides. I braced myself. No matter how many times I had felt this pussy, regardless of the fact that I knew that she was so in love with my brother, the pussy still felt fucking excellent.

With a thrust, I pulled out of her and rolled over onto my back, breathing heavily. Zoe left the bed and went into the master bathroom. This was one of the few times that I had let her come to my crib because Money had had a key to my spot for years, as I did his. But he had told me and City that he would be tied up tonight. I knew that that was code for him being tied up with one of his bitches, so I was free to be with his.

Zoe came back to the bed with a wet towel. I watched her as she cleaned me with the hot, soapy rag, thinking that it was too bad that she was a pill head that belonged to my brother. Otherwise, she would have made a good girl for me for sure. She was attentive and so loving, so much so that she was too devoted to the wrong man and she was shoving the hurt up her nose now.

She had done the pills in front of me. And when she started to snort the Xanax, I figured that harder drugs were to follow. But when I saw the evidence of her doing coke, that shit actually broke a nigga's heart. Zoe was literally letting Money kill her slowly. That wasn't the girl that I had met years ago. She had been stronger than that, but Money had chipped that strength away inch by inch with every bitch he had cheated on Zoe with and every lie he'd told.

I couldn't wife Zoe, but besides being my dip, she had become a good friend over the years. That's why I hated to see her disappearing like this. But it was also why I felt comfortable readying myself to confide in her.

"I gotta tell you something."

She placed the towel on the nightstand, lay beside me and rested her head on my chest. "What's up?"

"I'm thinking about leaving the family business to start my own."

Zoe quickly lifted her head and frowned at me. "Why?"

Every Love Story Is Beautiful, But Ours Is Hood
by *Jessica N. Watkins*

"It's simple. I wanna be my own boss." I ignored the way that Zoe was looking at me and continued, "I got a supply connect. Some Columbian dude. He's giving me a better deal than that Mexican motherfucker we've been using. I'm going to link up with him in order to get on by myself."

"The money you're making with your brothers isn't enough?"

"It's enough, but people are out here making more than enough. I've been trying to talk Money into making bigger moves, but he ain't hearing me. So, I'm gon' do that shit myself."

Zoe didn't say anything, and I had expected that. Me, Money, and City had gotten money together for years. There was not one of us without the other. But I had spent years getting the next man on. If my brothers didn't want to hear me out and get this money, then I had to get it myself.

SHAMAR SAVAGE

"Grrrrr," I groaned and threw my phone into my lap. That was the second call that Taraji had ignored, and it was blowing me.

Sure, she had her reasons to ignore me. It had been a week since we had hooked up last, and today was my first time calling her. She probably thought that I was playing games. I could totally see how it would seem that way.

Taraji blew my phone up last Saturday. I had told her that I wanted to take her to lunch, but once I was back at the crib and had time to realize how I had been acting with her, I decided to stand her up. I couldn't even answer her calls. I just didn't know what to say to her then. Luckily, she stopped calling. I had been cool with not hearing from her for a few days because I needed the space.

I didn't like how I felt with Taraji. I was uncomfortable with how I didn't want to leave her. I had spent the night, ate the pussy, and then I wanted to see her later! Who the fuck was I turning into? I didn't like how, after I left her place, I wondered if she was with the next nigga or not. That girl was doing something to me that I couldn't handle, so I avoided her like a punk-ass bitch.

Now, after a week of not hearing her voice, I was missing the hell out of shorty. I actually jumped when my phone rang, like some broad waiting for a nigga to call her back. I had to laugh at myself.

"Aw man," I moaned with a chuckle. This girl had me shook. I knew it when I saw that it wasn't her calling and was disappointed. "What up, Tiffany?" I answered reluctantly.

Tiffany was a chick that I had been fucking on and off for months.

"What you on tonight?"

When she asked me that in a sexy voice, I felt nothing. I knew then that I was feeling Taraji way more than I wanted to. My mind was telling me to stay clear of these feelings, to stop this drama before it started. I had seen how this relationship shit went. Money was just existing in his relationship with Zoe. After ten years of being emotionally invested in a woman, City was barely speaking to Nova. I didn't want to exist in anything like that. Yeah, things were always cool in the beginning, but that honeymoon phase seemed to fade fast as hell. I was straight on moving through life with a tumor on my side that I didn't even wanna fuck, let

EVERY LOVE STORY IS BEAUTIFUL, BUT OURS IS HOOD
by *Jessica N. Watkins*

alone love. My life wasn't like that. I was good. I was happy. And I wanted to stay that way.

"I'm on you," I told Tiffany. "Where you at?"

"My mama's house."

"I'll be there in an hour."

AKIRA WHITE

"Don't move. I'm cummin'."

My face contorted into a frown that met the pillow. *Don't move? Nigga, I ain't moved since you started fucking me!*

Like, seriously, I had been so still in the doggy style position that I needed to check my own damn pulse. Davion was too busy humping like a rabbit and sweating to even notice that I hadn't even moaned, let alone gotten wet.

"Mummmph! Fuck!" he groaned as he came.

I rolled my eyes to the back of my head as he fell over next to me. He caught his breath and then sat up on the side of the bed. I just lay there staring at the ceiling, thinking about City, as I had been since I left him a few days ago.

Although sex with City was off the chain, I felt like shit for cheating. Davion was no City, but he was the one man that I knew for sure was faithful to me. So, I had been playing the faithful fiancée, especially after driving ninety miles an hour to get to that game just for the Bears to lose. I was not only disappointed that they had lost their opportunity to play for the Super Bowl; I was also pissed that I now had to deal with Davion on a regular basis. Now that the season was over, he

EVERY LOVE STORY IS BEAUTIFUL, BUT OURS IS HOOD
by *Jessica N. Watkins*

was home more to torture me with his whack sex, and I was so over it!

Minus his NFL career, the games, the clout, status, parties, and celebs, our relationship was so dull. Our fire had lost its flame a long time ago. I'd tried to change that; God knows I did. But Davion had no passion. He didn't even have enough passion to be mad at me for ignoring his calls that night. With no argument, he accepted my excuse of being too drunk with girls. I wanted a man with a spine! I had tried to teach Davion how to be spontaneous, how to be fun, and how to fuck me right. But he thought he knew it all. He didn't even try to do the things that made me happy, which made me think about City more and more, despite wanting with all my heart to be faithful to my man.

"I'll be back. Me and Neko about to hang out."

Of course you are.

That's *all* he did. You would think that now that the season was over, he would want to be under me, romancing me, and loving on me. But his young-minded ass just wanted to be under Neko, and I let him. But that only gave me more time to obsess over City and his potential, which City had taken every chance to show me since the moment we left the Trump.

221

EVERY LOVE STORY IS BEAUTIFUL, BUT OURS IS HOOD
by *Jessica N. Watkins*

That night, I wondered if that sex would be it. Yet ever since, City had shown me that it was only the beginning. Obviously, after that dick session, he deserved my number. I had given it to him before leaving the room, and he used it every chance he got. When Davion was away, City and I talked for hours. I wondered why he was able to lay up on the phone with me for so long. I wondered where his girl was. But I dared not ask about Nova because City never asked about Davion. We had managed to hook up once on a Monday just for lunch, but the whole time I imagined him in this pussy.

As soon as I heard Davion leave, I called City. And it was pathetic how my heart sank when he didn't answer. I left the bed hoping that he would call back so I could take this opportunity to spend more time with him. We didn't even have to have sex; his voice in my ear would be enough verbal penetration to soothe me until City was able to give me that dope dick again. Yet, if he was able to sneak off, I would be willing to meet him anywhere. I would meet that man on the damn moon.

Just as I started to run my bath water, the doorbell rang. Since the doorman had let someone up without calling, I figured it was a delivery of one of the many orders that I had placed online shopping that week. I slipped on a robe and

Every Love Story Is Beautiful, But Ours Is Hood
by *Jessica N. Watkins*

hurried toward the front door. Peering through the peephole, I couldn't see a thing. It was blocked, and all I could see was red. I slowly opened the door and gasped at the sight of an abundance of roses. There were so many of them that the delivery man struggled to hold them.

"Are you Akira White?"

"Yes," I answered with a smile. "Come in. You can set them there." I pointed to the dining room table, and the delivery man hurried to set them down. Eyeing them, I counted that there had to be one hundred red roses.

"Thank you."

"Have a good day, ma'am." He nodded and then left out of the door, closing it behind him.

With a smile, I began to feel bad for silently talking so much shit about Davion. I looked through the bouquet for the card and saw a box rather than the usual card. I ripped open the box and squealed when my eyes fell on the Blue Nile Signature Diamond floating three-stone pendant, platinum necklace.

This was why I had to remember that no matter his lackluster dick and immaturity, I had to be patient with Davion because he was a good catch. I finally found the card and read with wide, excited eyes.

Every Love Story Is Beautiful, But Ours Is Hood
by Jessica N. Watkins

The other night was everything that I had imagined it would be. You might be his, but I own your heart, body, and mind. You're still that little fourteen-year-old girl that I waited patiently for. I thank God that I finally got to have you. I won't let it be the last time.

City

My eyes closed as both excitement and fear rushed through my body. "Damn!"

Every time I tried to devote myself to Davion, City came along, convincing me that my heart was where it should be. With a heavy sigh, I eyed the roses, taking in their beauty. Then I took them into my hands, left the condo, and walked down the hall. Once in front of the garbage shoot, I took in their beauty one last time and dropped them. There was no way that I could explain all of those flowers to Davion. Yet, once back into the condo, I took the necklace and tucked it and the card under a drawer in my jewelry box.

Then I returned to my phone and bath.

EVERY LOVE STORY IS BEAUTIFUL, BUT OURS IS HOOD
by Jessica N. Watkins

Just as I sank into the hot, soothing water, my phone rang. I excitedly scooped it up and hurriedly answered when I saw that it was City.

"Hey you," I purred.

"What up?"

"You and all of your roses. Thank you so much. The necklace is beautiful, but that card was even better. Thank you."

"You don't have to thank me. You deserve shit like that every day."

I was grinning like a little kid as I sank down in the bubbles. "You're trying to get me in trouble. What if Davion had been here when the flowers came?"

"Fuck that lame-ass nigga," he barked. "You're *mine*."

My thighs tightened. Despite my attempts to stop it, my pussy creamed and my heart exhaled. Fuck it. I might as well had stopped trying to fight it. This was it! I was falling out of love with my fiancé and in love with a Savage.

TARAJI GREEN

I know this nigga didn't just walk up in here with a bitch!

I was fuming! Ooooh, I was pissed!

"You cool, baby?"

I smiled at Corleon, some guy that had been in my DM's for weeks. I had finally met him for a drink because I was tired of being at home sulking over this motherfucka that had just walked his big ass in the bar with a bitch on his arm!

I played it off, though. I forced my smile to look genuine as I told Corleon, "I'm good. Just enjoying being here with you."

Luckily, I was looking good and was with a real nigga. Corleon was a local rapper who was on his way to the top. He was well known and nobody to sneeze at. He looked good, smelled amazing, and he had money and fans. He was the total opposite of whoever this busted bitch was that Shamar was with.

Look at that bitch's frontal. Eew. I could see that hoes unbleached knots from here.

"You want another drink?" Corleon asked.

Every Love Story Is Beautiful, But Ours Is Hood
by *Jessica N. Watkins*

I tore my eyes away from Shamar, who hadn't even noticed me yet. "Yes, please."

While he ordered my drink, my eyes drifted toward Shamar again. I wanted him to see me. I wanted him to know that I had hoes too. I had been in the house sulking, crying and missing the hell out of him, but he didn't need to know any of that.

He wanted to play this game? Cool. Well, this was a two-player game.

Just as I figured, when ol' girl saw me staring at Shamar, she brought his attention to me. I could see that she had an issue with me staring at him, but fuck that bitch. When his eyes finally met mine, I simply looked away. Corleon returned right on time with my drink. For a Friday night, Lamelle's wasn't as packed as it usually was, so Shamar had a clear view of Corleon kissing my cheek before he handed me my double shot of D'usse.

I was satisfied with that, so I gave my full attention back to Corleon. If Shamar wanted to be with that heffa with the busted weave, cool. I wasn't about to play these fucking games with him. This was exactly why I didn't want a man and played them just how I wanted to.

EVERY LOVE STORY IS BEAUTIFUL, BUT OURS IS HOOD
by *Jessica N. Watkins*

Just then, some guy walked up to Corleon. It sounded like they knew each other from the music industry, so I took the opportunity to check my phone.

I had missed a few phone calls from Reggie. I quickly searched the club to see if he was somewhere lurking. I was relieved when I didn't spot his crazy ass, but my chest got tight when my eyes fell on Shamar's. He was staring right at me. I couldn't tell whether he was happy to see me or pissed because there was a mixture of both in his expression.

I quickly turned my head and blocked Reggie's number. It was about time that I had. That dude just did not get the fucking picture, and I was done pacifying him.

Then a text message came through.

Shamar: *So that's why you couldn't answer the phone? Because you with this goofy nigga?*

"Tuh," I grunted under my breath. "*This* nigga is funny."

I peeked over at Corleon before I responded to Shamar. Corleon was still talking to his friend, so I hurried and replied to Shamar.

Every Love Story Is Beautiful, But Ours Is Hood
by *Jessica N. Watkins*

Me: *Don't worry about why I didn't answer the phone. I'm not your business. That busted bitch is. Fuck you and lose my number.*

I wanted to mean that too. I wanted to ignore Shamar and focus on Corleon. I didn't want a man, but I wanted a strong lineup. I needed to get my team built back up. This wasn't me; mad about some dude and hurt that he was with another woman. This wasn't me! This was why I didn't get feelings and lay up with niggas. And fuck Shamar for making me let my guard down. But since I had only let it down a little, I was able to easily put it back up. I was back like I'd never left.

I stood from the barstool and tapped Corleon on the shoulder. Once I had his attention, I told him, "I'm going to the bathroom."

"Okay, baby."

On my way to the bathroom, I smoothed out my dress. It was a long sleeve, fitted, maxi dress. For it to be nearly February, the weather was unseasonably high for Chicago; forty degrees, so the dress was perfect. I had matched it with a pair of five-inch boots to dress it up.

EVERY LOVE STORY IS BEAUTIFUL, BUT OURS IS HOOD
by *Jessica N. Watkins*

Once inside of the bathroom, I looked at myself and wondered why Shamar could leave my bed after a good night like we'd had and then ignore me. *Me!* I wasn't a conceited chick by no means, but I was an attractive girl, and I had my shit together.

"Fuck him," I groaned as I sat my purse on the sink counter. I reached into my purse for my gloss, with plans to strut out of that bathroom and shit on Shamar.

Just as I was about to apply my MAC lip gloss, the doorknob turned.

"Somebody is in here," I spat.

The door opened anyway. I freaked out, realizing that I hadn't locked the door. I squared up, ready to push whoever it was out. But I lost my cool when I saw that it was Shamar.

I instantly gave him an attitude. "What the f–"

His lips against mine stopped me. I wanted to pull away, but his hand on the back of my neck kept me from doing so. But he didn't need to hold me in place. I wanted to pull away, but I never even tried to. Fuck being hard. Having him there, on me, kissing me, was what I had been fantasizing about underneath my anger toward him. Despite my anger, I knew that I felt something for Shamar that had only started to boil over, the longer that we were apart.

EVERY LOVE STORY IS BEAUTIFUL, BUT OURS IS HOOD
by *Jessica N. Watkins*

I let him kiss me feverishly. I let his large frame lift me a few inches from the floor and sit me on the sink counter. He continued to fuck my mouth with his as he hurriedly gathered my dress around my waist. I began to help him. I lifted my ass up until I felt the cold granite on my bare skin. Shamar tore my thong off my body and threw it over his head. He didn't have to pull his dick out; I started doing it for him. I yanked and pulled at his belt. I tore at the button on his jeans, all while we breathed heavily into one another's mouths while sucking each other's tongues.

As soon as I felt his stiff, pulsating dick in my hand, I became weak. Gone was the bitch that was just talking shit. I had turned into a wet, soppy mess. The moment I felt his dick against my opening, I melted all over him and that sink. He was taking too fucking long to plunge into me.

"Fuck me," I demanded, begging with a whine that tried to come out strong but failed miserably.

Either way, it turned Shamar on. His hands gripped my thighs as he finally rushed into this pussy. This shit was so hot that all we could do was breath desperately into each other's mouths as he continued to kiss my soul.

I was cumming over and over again. He forced my back against the mirror, threw my legs over his shoulders and

231

fucked me compulsively, still kissing me deeply. The dick was so good and deep that I bit his lip in delight.

"Oh gawd," I whined as another orgasm came.

"Give it to me. Give me that nut."

"Ooooh gawd!" Tears filled my eyes as my pussy seeped all over his dick.

"Grrrrr. That's it. I feel that pussy cumming."

In minutes, I had cum three times. In minutes, he had exhausted me. My legs sat on his shoulders limply as he bore into my pussy over and over again, until his dick was so stiff that it was banging against my wet walls.

"Urrrrrrrrrrrrrrrrrgh!"

Thankfully, the music was so loud in the bar that no one heard Shamar's thunderous roar as he pulled out and nutted into the toilet. I sat on the sink, looking at nothing in particular, trying to catch my breath and figure out what the fuck had just happened and what it meant.

I watched as Shamar fixed his pants in silence while he continued breathing hard. I shook off the weakness and slid off the sink, fixing my dress. I felt him walk by me and his scent and presence made me tremor.

"Now...," he said as he opened the door. "Go back to that nigga."

EVERY LOVE STORY IS BEAUTIFUL, BUT OURS IS HOOD
by *Jessica N. Watkins*

I sneered behind his back and quickly spat, "Yeah, and you go back to that bitch. Fuck you!"

CHAPTER THIRTEEN

TAYE 'CITY' SAVAGE

"You got a lot of nerve, motherfucka! *I* built this shit!"

My eyebrow raised to my forehead. My blood was boiling, but I stayed calm as I sat on the couch in the den watching Nova huff and puff in front of me with her arms folded. She had finally pulled her head out of her ass long enough to realize that she didn't have any more power. She had finally realized that every business, property, and account had been transferred to Yummy's name. Now, all Nova had was the money in her accounts. She no longer had access to this empire.

"*You* built this shit?" I asked calmly. Fuck giving this bitch any more energy. I had allowed my loyalty to convince me to be so caring toward her that she clearly had forgotten who the fuck I was. "I could swear *I* was the nigga in the streets getting this money, not you."

"I been out here for ten years mak—"

Every Love Story Is Beautiful, But Ours Is Hood
by *Jessica N. Watkins*

"You've been a fucking *secretary* for ten years... a runner," I corrected her and then waved my hand dismissively.

Her eyes bucked. "All of this because I ain't kissing your ass like you want me to? Because I'm not playing the good wifey role that you want me to?"

"Hell motherfuckin' yeah! This ain't no business partnership. My brothers are my partners. You were supposed to be my *woman*! But you were too busy trying to be a fucking boss to fuck with the boss of all bosses properly."

Nova turned her nose up, as she had every time I mentioned her being my woman more than my fucking business associate. "Fuck that shit! Fuck a relationship! We are building an empire and getting this money!"

"*We*? You and I ain't doin' shit. *We* never were. You were supposed to hold me down and—"

"*I did!*" she screamed as her arms flailed. "Look at this shit! Look around you! You didn't have this when you went in!"

She had just proved my point. She didn't give a fuck about *me*. All she cared about was money, this house, and the street clout. And if it was that fucking important to her, she could have it. I didn't need this shit. Last time I remembered, I had survived with less - *much less* - and I was much happier.

I stood slowly, gathered my keys and phone, and walked out as I shot over my shoulder. "And you can have this shit. Thank you for your services."

TARAJI GREEN

"Urgh!" I cringed. "What are you doing here, Reggie?"

"Why haven't you answered my calls or messages?"

My eyes bucked. I couldn't believe that this fool was here. I tried to walk faster up the sidewalk toward my building, but I was carrying five plastic bags of groceries. "Because I don't want to talk to you anymore!" Attempting to walk fast, I fucked up and dropped one of the bags.

Reggie quickly picked it up and then took the rest of the bags from me. "Let me help you."

I sighed and gave up because, clearly, Reggie was intent on being here at this moment. I didn't have the energy to argue with another man. Shamar and I had been texting messaging each other since the night before. He was mad that after giving me that dick, I'd had the audacity to sit at the bar smiling in Corleon's face. And I was pissed that he'd had the nerve to still sit in that raggedy bitch's face. All the while, my feelings for him were burning on the inside, so I was mad at myself too—mad at myself for falling.

Reggie quietly accompanied me into the building and on the elevator. The ride was silent to the third floor as I

Every Love Story Is Beautiful, But Ours Is Hood
by Jessica N. Watkins

wondered how I could get rid of this dude quickly. I just wanted to fry my chicken, drink, and go to bed after a long day in the shop of trying to focus on laying hair while thoughts of Shamar molested me.

"Thank you, Reggie." I took the bags from him without looking into his eyes. As I walked into the kitchen with them, I felt a shadow over me. He was following me.

With a huff, I sat the bags on the floor in the kitchen and turned to Reggie.

"Look, Reggie." I cupped my hands together and attempted to be calm. I wasn't mad at him. I was mad at myself for falling for Shamar, for wanting Shamar, and for obsessing over Shamar. My irritation had nothing to do with Reggie, so I tried very hard not to take it out on him. "I know that I have been ignoring your calls, but it's for a good reason. I've told you many times that I am no longer interested in you, so—"

"But if you give me a chance to—"

"I am not interested in giving you a chance, Reggie," I interjected softly. "I'm sorry, but I'm just not interested. And it's not personal. I just don't want what you want."

He took a step back and nodded slowly. "Okay."

Every Love Story Is Beautiful, But Ours Is Hood
by *Jessica N. Watkins*

"You've said okay before, but you keep trying to change my mind and—"

"I get it," he cut me off. "I get it. I'm outta here. Just... Can I use the bathroom first?"

"Sure."

When he went down the hall to the bathroom, I was relieved. I took my phone from my purse and went to my blocked call list to see how many of his calls I had missed. He had called me over ten times since last night. Then I checked my blocked text messages list.

Reggie: *From the little time that we did spend together, I know that I love you and feel that you are for me.*

Reggie: *I want to know everything about you. I want to know your likes, your dislikes, the things that make you cry, that make you happy.*

Reggie: *Hello??*

Reggie: *Good morning, beautiful.*

Every Love Story Is Beautiful, But Ours Is Hood
by *Jessica N. Watkins*

Reggie: *Just one more date, and if it doesn't go right, if you're not feeling me, I promise I won't contact you anymore.*

And there were more.

"Oh my God," I muttered as I continued to scroll through the dozens of messages that lasted up until the moment that he'd walked up on me outside. "This nigga is crazy."

As soon as I heard the toilet flush, I rushed toward the counter and acted like I was diligently putting away my groceries.

After a few moments, I heard him coming down the hall.

"I'm out, Taraji," was all that I heard. By the time I spun around and followed behind him, the front door was closing behind him.

"What the fuck?" I questioned myself as I secured the front door.

I was so weirded out, but I was happy as hell that Reggie had gone quietly. However, I realized that I had to watch my back because he was popping up out of nowhere now that I wasn't answering his calls or text messages.

Every Love Story Is Beautiful, But Ours Is Hood
by *Jessica N. Watkins*

With a deep sigh, I went for the bottle of wine that I had just bought. I needed the whole damn bottle. It was Saturday night. Usually, I would be out with my girls or on a date, but forget all that. I needed to de-stress from all of the goings on in my life.

Just as I found my corkscrew, I smelled something. I couldn't put my finger on what it was, but it was strong. I went to the stove to make sure that all of the burners were off, and they were. But the smell was so strong that it was starting to suffocate me. I followed it, and it led to the hall. To my surprise, the hall was filled with smoke. Against my better judgment, I ran down the hall toward the source of the smoke.

"*Ahhhh!*" I let out a deafening scream when I saw flames fighting their way out of one of the guest bedrooms. I ran like a cheetah back up the hallway and into the kitchen where I'd left my phone. I hurriedly grabbed my purse and keys while sprinting towards the door and dialing 911 with tears in my eyes.

"9-1-1, what is your emergency?"

"I need help! Send the fire department! My ex set my condo on fire!"

ZYSHONNE 'SHON' SAVAGE

"Hey, Mama." I kissed her cheek and then she let me into her small townhouse on the Westside of Chicago.

"Hey, baby," she greeted as she lightly touched the side of my face.

I cringed feeling how hard and cold her skin was. I walked into the overcrowded house. My mother was a hoarder. There were way too many decorations, pictures, clothes, and bullshit. I made my way to the couch, pushing clothes and beer cans to the side before sitting down. I eyed my mother's appearance as she slowly walked toward me. No matter how hard I tried to get her out of it, the streets were still killing my mother slowly. At forty-one years old, my mother's light skin was dirty with infection and disease. Her long, wavy, dark hair was turning grey and falling out. They young body that she used to sell for Deuce had failed her a long time ago.

My mother's father was white and black. Her mother was a fair-skinned black woman. My mother's genes were strong. That's why the twins, Yummy, and I were much

EVERY LOVE STORY IS BEAUTIFUL, BUT OURS IS HOOD
by *Jessica N. Watkins*

brighter than the rest of our siblings and had dark, wavy hair. We couldn't dodge those signature, big, Savage lips, though.

Once the Dearborns were torn down, my mother used a Section 8 voucher to move into this townhouse. No matter the money or places that I offered her once I started getting money, she refused to move out. She just used the money that I gave her to support habits that never died no matter how much older she got. Unlike many in the projects, my mother wasn't a drug addict. Alcohol addiction and poor health were killing her slowly but surely.

When I was young, I knew that she was just drinking to deal with life. As a teenager, she was a prostitute in love with her pimp. Deuce loved my mother. I knew that because I saw him in our house loving on my mother just as much as I saw him in Valerie's. But my mother was the secret not so well kept. She was the side bitch never good enough to graduate to the level of Deuce's main bitch, and that fucked with my mother heavily. With every one of Deuce's babies that she birthed and every trick that she turned for him, she drank to ease the pain of him never choosing her, not even once Valerie died.

Sitting down next to me, she asked, "What brings you over on this side of town?"

EVERY LOVE STORY IS BEAUTIFUL, BUT OURS IS HOOD
by Jessica N. Watkins

"I just came to holla at you before my meeting tonight."

My mother was a street chick. Even though she had sold pussy instead of drugs, I knew that she knew the streets, so I ran every move that I made past her.

"I'm meeting with the connect tonight." Saying that made this step that I was about to take real. Even though it was something that had been a hood dream of mine, the reality of going against my brothers fucked with me.

I guess it was written all over my face because my mother then asked me, "What's that look on your face about?"

The look on my face was uncertainty, but I was too much of a man to admit that shit. Working alongside my brothers was all that I had known. But if these niggas weren't willing to take this risk, then I wasn't about to let this money pass me by.

Despite me attempting to act cool and collective, my mother saw the uncertainty anyway. She had given birth to me, so she could read me like a book. "Don't you feel no disloyalty to those motherfuckers. Don't let them make you feel like you owe them anything." She grunted and shook her head. "Those motherfuckers always got their asses on some high ass pedestal. That's how their mama was. She thought she was better than everybody while she laid on her ass, while I was out there making Deuce's money—"

"Mama," I called, trying to bring her back to the present.

No matter how long it had been, my mama felt like she and her kids had to prove something to Valerie, even though she was dead and gone.

Despite my warning, my mama kept pressing. She was already in a full rant. "Look, stop thinking about your brothers and think about yourself. Loving another motherfucka more than myself ain't got me nowhere in life but here. Don't be like your mama, baby. Be better than me."

****

I wasn't pressed about meeting with the connect. Sitting across from him at Shaw's Crab House was like another day hustling. Money and I had done it for years. This time it was only different because I was finally taking the steps to start my own empire and become the billionaire that I had always dreamed of being.

Every Love Story Is Beautiful, But Ours Is Hood
by *Jessica N. Watkins*

"So, tell me, Shon. I hear that your organization has a great relationship with the Mexicans. Why are you looking for another distributor?" Juan dropped his spoon into his bowl of lobster bisque. His sharp, green eyes peered into mine as if he knew I was about to lie.

"We're looking for a new connect. We're shopping for a better deal for the amount of weight we can guarantee to sell every month."

Though I was breaking out on my own, in the streets, my brothers and I were more trusted as a team because we had built all of our relationships that way. Juan had to be under the impression that I was making this deal on behalf of all of us so that he would trust that I already had trustworthy clientele in place. If he knew that I was working alone and with new buyers that I'd had set up on my own, he would be hesitant to work with me.

I hated to start off a new business relationship by lying, but once I moved these bricks for him, he would trust me. I had to do what I had to do. This motherfucker was sitting across from me dressed in hundreds of thousands of dollars' worth of labels and diamonds. Yet, he was only thirty, which was seven years older than me. This motherfucker was rich; not on, not paid, but *rich*. That's what I wanted for myself.

"And how much can you guarantee that you all can move?"

"We can get rid of fifty bricks easy."

His eyebrows rose, showing that he was impressed. "And you want me to front this product, I assume."

"Correct."

When he nodded slowly, my chest started to pound with anticipation. This deal would put me in control over a lot of dope. It would be worth over a million in street value. If Juan gave me a good deal on it, I would most definitely be on my way on the road to riches.

CHAPTER FOURTEEN

AKIRA WHITE

It was crazy how every time my eyes laid upon City, I felt like a school girl. I would blush so hard that it was almost foolish. My brown skin felt like it was flushing red and my hands got sweaty. I had known this man all of my life, it seemed. He knew me in and out. I had already fucked him, he had already sucked my pussy. Yet I was so nervous in his presence.

As he closed the door of the suite, I felt his eyes on me. Nervously, I locked eyes with him, something I always feared doing because it made me so weak.

He looked me up and down and licked those massive, pretty lips. "You look good."

Still swooning, I replied, "Thank you."

I admired his scent, black skin, and his smile; all of which made him look richer and more expensive than all of the brands and labels that he was wearing.

Every Love Story Is Beautiful, But Ours Is Hood
by *Jessica N. Watkins*

As I stared at him, I saw a bunch of suitcases behind him against the wall. My heart sank. "What's up with all of the suitcases? Are you going out of town?"

"Nah, I've been living here for a few days."

"You've been what?" I asked, trying to ignore the excitement in my heart. "You've been living here? Why?"

I dropped my purse down slowly on the coffee table in the suite's living room. Once again, I was in a hotel with City. I had finally been able to get away since Davion was on an annual trip with the team. They went to some exotic island at the end of every season. No women were allowed. Most of the team members' fiancées and girlfriends hated that, but I loved the freedom, especially now that City and I were.... were...

Shit, I don't know what to call what City and I were doing. It was more than fucking. The love that was in my heart when I was fourteen was slowly maturing with every conversation, every embrace, and every stroke of his dick. But I was also mature enough not to fall too hard too fast. I was engaged and he had a woman—*had*.

"You left Nova?" I asked as I sat next to him on the loveseat. I tried real hard not to sound too excited.

Even with a stern look, he was so sexy, and gorgeous as he replied, "Yeah."

"Why?"

It took him some time to get the words out.

When I noticed him struggling to answer me, I quickly said, "We don't have to talk about it if you don't want to."

"I don't mind talking about it." His big hand cuffed my thigh, and he squeezed gently. "I don't mind talking about it at all with you."

My skin underneath the high-waist skinny jeans warmed from his touch. I clinched my thighs together as if that would stop my clit from pounding.

It didn't work, however.

"When I got out of prison, nothing was the same," City started. "Nova had helped transform our street hustle to an empire. We went from moving nickels and dimes to major weight. She had a lot to do with that. She bagged work, cooked it, moved it, and hid our money under her name. We ain't millionaires, but my family eats good, and Nova had a lot to do with that. But I just know what I loved when I went to prison: the projects, the hustle and *you*."

EVERY LOVE STORY IS BEAUTIFUL, BUT OURS IS HOOD
by *Jessica N. Watkins*

Fuck. Why was he doing this to me? His words wrapped around my throat and choked me. I couldn't take it. I felt fourteen, in love, and naïve all over again.

"All of those things made me happy," City continued. "Not the fancy shit, the labels, or poppin' bottles. I just want back everything that made me happy."

"You want *everything* back? Do you want *me* back?"

Don't ask me why I asked him that. As soon as the question left my lips, I regretted it. My heart seemed to stop as I waited with smothering anticipation for him to answer. In mere seconds, so much ran through my mind. If he said yes, what would I do? If he said no, how would I put my heart back together? How would I nurse it back to health?

"I want you. But I want you to be happy; whatever that means to you."

What the fuck does that mean? Men! They always gotta be so damn difficult!

I sat there staring at the genuineness in those slanted eyes in silence, but my mind was racing. I wondered what happiness was to me. It had only been weeks since City returned, but he had already made me happier than Davion had in years. Even with ten years between us, he knew me better than the man that slept beside me every night.

Every Love Story Is Beautiful, But Ours Is Hood
by *Jessica N. Watkins*

City was right. What we had back then was what had made me the happiest. With Davion, I was simply content, but my heart only felt like it was really at home whenever I was in City's arms.

Davion was good to me. But could I honestly say that he was good enough? My heart was telling me to do right and stay with Davion because he was what I knew and he was safe. I wanted to stay with who had never inflicted the pain on me that many others had, including City. But he was unable to satisfy me physically. I wanted to stay with Davion where it was safe, but my heart, if I stopped to listen to it, was telling me to leave and run into City's arm.

Part of me wanted to do just that, and the other half remembered the rein that Nova had always had on City's life. He was claiming that she was gone, but the posttraumatic stress from me and City's heartbroken past had me fearing her return. I knew that she would come back. She always did.

SHAMAR SAVAGAE

"Why are you looking at me like that?"

I was playing dumb. I knew why Taraji was sitting on that bed staring at me with a blank stare. She was doing that because she didn't know what she was feeling. I knew it because I didn't know what the fuck I was feeling either.

When I walked in that club and saw that dude sitting next to her, I felt like he was sitting next to what was mine, touching what was mine, and making mine smile. I didn't like that shit. I wanted to run up on her, take her from that nigga, and put her in my pocket. But instead, I ran up on her ass in that bathroom and took that pussy. I walked out afterwards because I was too ornery to tell her that I was jealous.

But, afterwards, she was all that I could think about.

We had argued back and forth via text all night and day. I was pissed that she hadn't walked away from that nigga after I gave her that dick. I was cursing her out and acting like an ass, but what I really wanted to tell her was that she was mine and she could never be with another man again. Of course, I didn't do that. Then that crazy-ass motherfucker, Reggie, set her house on fire, so I had to be a friend and not the jealous lover. But for the past three days, I had been feigning for shorty.

So, yeah, I knew what she was feeling.

"Looking at you," she said flirtatiously.

I felt myself about to blush, but men weren't supposed to blush, so I tried to ignore her. Sitting on that bed, she was so pretty. Her long legs were bare and her chocolate brown thighs were shiny. Her phat-ass booty hung out of boy shorts. Her ass spread across the bed as she sat with her legs crossed. Her nipples plunged through the cami that she was wearing. She looked so feminine effortlessly as the spaghetti straps hung slightly off of her shoulders.

My dick was hard as fuck. I had to look away before I tried to fuck her and appear inconsiderate in light of what she was going through.

"Have the police found Reggie yet?" I asked, ignoring her flirtation.

She shook her head and replied, "No. He probably left town for a while."

I chuckled sarcastically and shook my head. "Lame ass running from a punk-ass arson charge. He is soft as fuck."

"He is *crazy*."

Every Love Story Is Beautiful, But Ours Is Hood
by *Jessica N. Watkins*

"What did your landlord say? How long do you have to stay here?"

She sadly shrugged and softly answered, "They couldn't tell me for sure. They said the renovations could take a while because there was smoke, fire, and water damage."

When Taraji called me crying three days ago, I couldn't believe what I heard when she said that her ex had set her crib on fire. But considering how good that pussy was, I wasn't surprised that it had a weaker man doing stunts like that.

"How much damage was there?'

"The fire department got there fast, but by the time that they arrived, there was damage to the walls and carpet in the bedroom. The bed was completely destroyed because that's where he started the fire. There was some smoke damage in the halls."

"Why do you even want to move back in there? Just get you a new place. If you need some help, I got you."

She giggled. "I don't need your help, but thank you. I'm a big girl. I can afford my own new place, which I might just get. I don't know. I just... I just need a few days to get my mind right."

"I feel you," I agreed with a nod.

EVERY LOVE STORY IS BEAUTIFUL, BUT OURS IS HOOD
by *Jessica N. Watkins*

She smiled, looking into my eyes devilishly. "You can help me with something else, though."

I knew what the lust in her eyes meant, but I wanted to hear her say it. "What can I help you with, Taraji?"

Every Love Story Is Beautiful, But Ours Is Hood
by *Jessica N. Watkins*

TARAJI GREEN

What can you help me with? This pussy!

But, nah, I didn't say that. I just smiled pretty, scooted back on the bed, and took off my boy shorts. That was answer enough. Then, as I removed my cami, causing these big milky titties to bounce, I saw that Shamar had left his seat and was walking toward the bed licking those big-ass lips.

As I fell back on the bed, it felt symbolic to me. It portrayed me falling *emotionally* for Shamar. There was no more fighting it. I couldn't fight it because it had already happened to me. I knew it when, even in the midst of all the chaos of Reggie and the fire, I wanted Shamar. I wanted him to protect me. It was crazy because Shamar hadn't even committed himself to me, but I still wanted him. And that's why I fought it, the urge to ask him to come visit me, for three days until I couldn't take it anymore.

I heard Shamar's Giuseppe boots hit the floor. When he straddled me and took off his Ralph Lauren tee, I got wet. Literally, I felt my juices spilling down my thighs and onto the sheets underneath me. He surprised me when he disappeared between my legs and licked me dry, only for more juices to replace the pool that he had slurped away.

"Mmmmm," my throat sang.

He had never eaten my pussy before the other day. But he must've been eating somebody's pussy before because his technique was perfect. Those big lips were skilled. He was eating this pussy so good that he was licking my soul.

"Fuck," I squealed with regret. I didn't want to cum yet. It was too fast. I wasn't ready for this to end.

I squirmed and twisted, but I didn't make it anywhere. He used his massive arms to wrap around my legs and hold my pussy in place.

"Ahhh! Shit!" I could feel those lips sucking my clit into his mouth. Sucking the orgasm out of me. I felt his beard tickling my ass as his face moved in slow circles. "Fuuuuck!"

EVERY LOVE STORY IS BEAUTIFUL, BUT OURS IS HOOD
by *Jessica N. Watkins*

ZOE MOORE

Tears welled in my eyes, but I tried not to let them fall. I was tired of crying over Money, but the tears fell anyway. One by one, every time I heard Money's thunderous laugh downstairs, the hurt was so bad that I couldn't help but wail and cry.

He was downstairs "with his son", where he always was. He tried to make it seem like he was just enjoying his child. But that was a fucking lie. Money was enjoying that bitch too. I knew it. He had cheated on me with her behind my back, and now he was doing it right under my nose. Every day, he spent less and less time in his own home and in our bed. We hadn't even had sex since the New Year. If he wasn't fucking me, then who was he fucking?

I wanted to leave him. I wanted to say fuck him and run. This man was ruining me. I was only twenty years old. I was too young to be this stressed. I wanted to be the pretty, secure girl that I was when I met him. I wanted to be the woman that had a lineup of niggas, a team of candidates that wanted nothing but to feed, take care of, and fuck this pussy. I used to be that bitch. I wanted to be her again so bad. I wanted to be strong again. I didn't want to be this weak woman, but I didn't know how to climb my way out of this deep funk. And it pissed me off that I didn't know how! It pissed me off that I could hear this motherfucker downstairs laughing as if I wasn't hurting like a motherfucker, and yet I still could not find the courage to leave his ass.

"Zoe."

I jumped when I heard his voice. I hurried and wiped my tears, but I knew that my eyes would still appear red and puffy. I peered from over the covers I was wrapped in and saw Shon slowly entering the room.

"Money is downstairs," I told him.

"Oh..."

Shon came toward me and sat on the bed. He pulled the cover back and admired the bra and panties that I had been lying in all day. He licked his massive, pretty lips as he cupped one of my breasts and squeezed the nipple. Even in my anguish, I wasn't too sad to appreciate that Shon's fine ass was touching me, so I got wet.

"Shon, Money is right downstairs."

He shrugged, "That ain't never mattered to me before."

EVERY LOVE STORY IS BEAUTIFUL, BUT OURS IS HOOD
by *Jessica N. Watkins*

It seemed like my fear only turned him on even more. He pulled the cover all the way back, took my legs and drug me to the edge of the bed.

"Shon," I protested weakly.

He knew I wanted this dick no matter where Money was. It made me feel slightly better. If Money had been where he was supposed to be, Shon wouldn't be able to get away with this so much.

Shon wasn't romantic, patient, or kind with this pussy. He pulled his dick out of his jeans, moved my panties to the side, and dove in. My legs were dangling in his arms as he held on tightly, diving in and out of this pussy that was now leaking onto the bed. His dick was so good that it was healing. Just like that, for the few moments that he plunged in and out of me, the sadness and pain melted away. I was that bitch again, even if for a moment.

As I felt his dick begin to throb, I began to return his strokes, fucking him back. We were panting like animals and allowing our moans to fill the room. Shit, Money was still so busy laughing that I knew he couldn't even hear his brother making this pussy cum.

But before I could cum, Shon was, loud, hard and rough as he started to beat me to it. "Arrrrrrrgh! Shit!"

EVERY LOVE STORY IS BEAUTIFUL, BUT OURS IS HOOD
by *Jessica N. Watkins*

"Would you shut up?!" I whispered harshly as he burst.

He let my legs go and slid out of me. Still breathing hard, he said, "You scared of that nigga, not me."

He zipped his pants up and sat down on the bed. I sat up, adjusting my panties, and scooted next to him. I was still breathing hard and pushing away the orgasm that never got to make its way out. I rested my head on his back, thinking that I needed to leave Shon alone. If I ever had a chance to keep my man, I needed to stop fucking his brother. How could I cry about him being downstairs with that bitch when I was upstairs with his brother?

Shon was fine. He was perfect. He had great dick. And he made everything better. But only for a moment.

I wanted Money, not him.

"What did you come over here to talk to Money about?"

"Business as usual, but I can wait since it sounds like he's busy. How you live like this?"

I shrugged. "It is what it is. I've made it through worse."

Shon just shook his head and dropped the subject. "I met with the connect a few days ago."

I lifted my head. "You did? You were serious, huh?"

I shook my head in disbelief of Shon's disloyalty. Yeah, he was fucking me, but this was on a whole new level of disloyalty. Shon, Money, and City had been getting money together for years. Even when City was taken away from them, they continued to build until he came back. None of this would be the same if Shon went through with going against them.

"Yeah, I told you. This ain't no fucking game," Shon answered.

"You need to really think about this. You're going to split the business up. That's crazy."

"I don't give a fuck. I want this paper. These niggas are happy with their lives, but—"

Shaking my head in disbelief, I asked, "What's wrong with that? Ain't none of us hungry."

"I'm doing this so that I can eat *better*."

"So just keep trying to talk them into it."

"I'm tired of talking to them niggas. They ain't listening."

"But this isn't going to work, Shon. So, what? You're going to be your brothers' competition?"

He shrugged nonchalantly. "If I gotta be."

263

Every Love Story Is Beautiful, But Ours Is Hood
by *Jessica N. Watkins*

When I gasped, his eyes bore into mine. "I keep telling you. You're scared of them niggas, not me."

CHAPTER FIFTEEN

BLISS DAVIS

"Money, I'm *tired*," I whined.

"Go to sleep then."

"I will if you leave!" Then I softly nudged him with my foot and he just chuckled. "C'mon now. Keandre been sleep for like two hours. Go back upstairs with your *girlfriend*."

He sucked his teeth and cursed, "Fuck that bitch."

"You don't live here, Money."

"I own this whole building. Fuck you mean?"

Money was laying across the foot of my bed like the king that he resembled, all majestic and what not with his fine ass. His chinky, bedroom eyes were staring into the television. He was watching highlights of the NFL playoff games on ESPN.

I wanted nothing more but to let him stay, but these games that he was playing were getting old. He was always down here with Keandre and me, reminding me of what could be and what perfection could be like. He was constantly reminding me of what we didn't have. He'd told me that he liked me being there, but I was starting to realize that he more so liked this set up. He was still Money; he liked me being there, but not enough to cuff me, not enough to leave his bitch, even though I made him feel better, took care of him better, and loved him better.

I was just happy that he hadn't tried to fuck me. With him having been around way more than before I moved in, I knew that I wouldn't be strong enough to fight him off if he did try.

"I start work soon."

Finally, his eyes left the television. "*Work?*"

"Yeah, *work.* Since you won't get me a place, I'll work for the money to get my own place."

I was lying. I hadn't found a job yet, but I was looking. I just wanted Money to take me seriously. But he didn't. This motherfucka laughed at me. He was loud as hell, cracking up. I just knew Zoe had heard him.

"Tuh! That's gone take you a minute, so you'll still be here for a while. Cool."

"I hate yo' ass!" This time I kicked him for real, and he just started cracking up laughing. "You're holding me hostage."

Every Love Story Is Beautiful, But Ours Is Hood
by *Jessica N. Watkins*

He looked at me, stared right at me with those bedroom eyes. It was so fucking hard for me to keep the stern look on my face

"You don't hate me. You like me holding you hostage."

I swallowed hard, getting rid of the lump of lust in my throat. "Fuck you."

ZOE MOORE

After Shon left, I snorted a few lines to keep my mind from obsessing over what Money could be doing downstairs. I sat on the toilet waiting for the intense high to spill over me. Soon, my heart began to race. The movement and voices downstairs suddenly became louder and echoed in the bathroom around me. My heart began to race more. The sudden rush fueled my anger and made me damn near mental as Money's laughs poured from beneath my feet.

In the same panties and bra, I stormed through our condo toward the front door and flew down those hardwood stairs in my bare feet.

Then I started kicking the door and began to scream his name, "*Money! Money!*"

I was kicking so hard that the walls were shaking around me. I was kicking and screaming his name until the door flew open and a pissed off Money appeared.

"Fuck is wrong with you?!" he barked.

He might have been mad, but I was madder and gave zero fucks! *Zero!*

"*You're* what's wrong with me! This is my

268

motherfucking house, and you're not going to keep disrespecting me in my own fucking house! You're my man! Not hers! She's a fucking side b—"

"Fuck this bitch! I'm whooping her ass!" Bliss' attempt to push past Money stopped my ranting. I squared up, getting ready to whoop her ass. But there was no need to. Money stopped her, holding her gently. "Move, Money! Let me go!" she spat.

She was attempting to claw her way out of his arms. Yet, every ounce of anger that he'd just had in his eyes for me had vanished as he laid his eyes on her. Looking at her, he was filled with compassion and *love*.

He held her tenderly and spoke to her soothingly. "Chill. I got this. Okay?"

She wasn't listening to him. Even though she had stopped fighting him, she couldn't answer because she was staring at me as I watched him love her and not me.

"I'm gonna take care of this," he told her intently. "Go check on the baby."

His words and the way that he held her hurt more than any physical blow that he could have given me. Watching them was killing me slowly. I couldn't take hearing or witnessing the way that he clearly loved her more than me anymore.

"No," left my throat in damn near a cry. "Stay here. This where you wanna be anyway."

I turned and ran up the stairs before my cries could escape. I did not want them to hear my tears. I barged through my front door that I had left halfway open. I ran into my bedroom with that fucked up, sickening vision of my man holding another woman more delicately than he had held me in a very long time. For as long as I had been with Money, he had never had that love in his eyes for me. He fucked me, he took care of me, but, God, he had never *loved* me like that. And it was devastating. It hurt so bad that I just wanted the pain to go away.

I went into my drawer and grabbed a bottle of pills. I didn't know what I was taking because they were a mixture of Percs, Xans, and Narcos. I took one and the other and then another. I lay there, waiting to pass out, waiting to see if Money would come. After ten minutes, neither had happened. The pain wouldn't disappear fast enough. So, I took more and more and more until *finally* everything went black.

by *Jessica N. Watkins*

KEANDRE 'MONEY' SAVAGE

"I'm outta here!" Bliss hissed as she stormed toward her bedroom. Even during this fucked up chaos, I still admired her big booty as it jiggled while she walked.

I tried to soothe her by saying, "Calm down—"

"No, fuck that! Don't tell me to calm down! Go tell that bitch to calm down. She is crazy as fuck, and I don't have to keep living like this! I'm leaving!" Bliss' arms flailed as she spat. She wasn't hearing me.

Finally in her bedroom, she snatched the closet door open. After pulling out a suitcase, she threw it on the bed.

"Where you gon' go?" I asked her.

"To go stay with my mama."

"You aren't taking my son all the way to Texas."

Her nose was still flaring as she said, "I have to do what I gotta do since you won't."

I gently grabbed her arm and let my guard down. "Bliss, please..."

I usually wasn't a weak dude, but fuck it. I knew I had to let go of that hard exterior when I realized that I was just as mad about seeing her potentially go as I was about my son leaving. I wanted her to be here with me just as much as I wanted my son here with me.

She saw the sincerity in my eyes so I kept begging. "I'll put you in a hotel tomorrow and get on top of finding y'all a house. You've been right all this time. This setup was selfish on my part. I'll have you outta here ASAP. Just please don't leave town."

With a deep breath, she let her guard down too. "Okay," she mumbled.

"Thank you. And I'll let you get some sleep."

She glared. "Bet you will now."

I ignored that slick comment and left out of the bedroom. I was about to go upstairs and beat the brakes off of Zoe. I wasn't one to put my hands on a woman, but she deserved this ass whooping that I was about to give her. She needed to realize that she didn't run shit. She needed to understand that she still had a roof over her head solely because my mother had raised me right. It had absolutely nothing to do with how I felt for her, because I felt absolutely nothing for this bitch anymore.

I flew up the stairs and pushed the door open. Without even closing it behind me, I quickly marched into the bedroom, ready to dead this bitch.

Every Love Story Is Beautiful, But Ours Is Hood
by *Jessica N. Watkins*

When I saw her lying across the bed, I sneered, "Hype-ass."

I figured she had to be doped up since she was passed out that fucking fast after straight spazzing just twenty minutes ago. I walked up to the bed and kicked it hard as hell in order to wake her ass up. Her body shook just a bit, but she didn't move much.

"Fuck," left my throat in a whisper as I noticed the white foam sliding out of her mouth, down her face and onto her neck. "Oh shit!"

Snatching my cell from my pocket, I dialed 9-1-1.

****

"She's stable. We pumped her stomach. We ran tests to assess any damage. There isn't any. We are going to keep her here for a few days for observation. She will also undergo a psychological evaluation. It's mandatory in this sort of case."

I nodded and replied, "She needs it."

The doctor was a bit shocked at how abrasive I was, but I didn't care. This move that Zoe had just made was a nail in her coffin. This bitch was fucking losing it.

What was weird at the moment was that I was more concerned about Bliss than Zoe. I couldn't make myself care about Zoe no matter what. She had done all of this to herself. Yes, I had cheated on her, but I had never in my life begged or even asked her to stay with me. But I had just begged Bliss to stay. That was the actions of a man who wanted a woman around. Zoe had never seen that from me. She was still with me because she was a glutton for punishment. I had never given her an ounce of hope that I would change.

"She's awake if you want to see her," the doctor told me.

"Thank you," was all that I said before I turned and walked toward the exit.

I had no interest in seeing that damn girl. She wanted some attention; now she would get more than enough attention when the doctors put her crazy ass on suicide watch.

ZYSHONNE 'SHON' SAVAGE

When I saw who was calling me, I sat back in the driver's seat and turned the Migos' album down.

"Juan, to what do I owe the honor?" I answered.

I wasn't expecting to hear from him this fast, but it was a good sign.

"Your reputation," he answered in his thick, Spanish accent. "I'm told that your family is highly respected in this business and that I would be a fool not to invest my product in the Savages."

I grinned and lightly punched the steering wheel with happiness. Then I coolly answered, "Damn right."

He chuckled at my cockiness. "I'm going to front you fifty bricks first. I want them moved and my money within two weeks. Can you handle that?"

"Of course I can. My buyers will be ready to move in a few weeks."

"No, no," he objected. "You get your buyers ready *now*. This deal will go down in the next few days or there will be no deal."

Every Love Story Is Beautiful, But Ours Is Hood
by *Jessica N. Watkins*

I mouthed, "Fuck," as my eyes rolled toward the ceiling. I had yet to confirm many of the buyers that I had contacted. I wouldn't be able to move that much weight that fast, but I told him, "I'll get it done. When can we meet?"

"I will send you the details soon. Have a nice night."

The call was disconnected before I could say anything else. I grimaced as I shoved my phone into my pocket and climbed out of the car. I walked through the hospital parking lot with the straight up bubble guts. This was my opportunity to be the man, as I had always dreamed. I had to get with my homies and confirm these buyers ASAP before my opportunity at billions fell through the cracks.

I shook that shit off, though, because I had more pressing matters to tend to. I had gotten a call from my brother a few hours ago. Zoe had overdosed. I was so disappointed in her that I damn near didn't want to visit her. But once Money let me know that she was awake, I knew I had to come check on her since he was so pissed at her that he didn't stay at the hospital with her. She was a fool for doing this to herself, but she didn't deserve to be alone.

It was damn near eight in the morning. I hadn't been sleep yet from trapping all day and night. And after that call

Every Love Story Is Beautiful, But Ours Is Hood
by *Jessica N. Watkins*

from Juan, I was hungry and ready to get this money. Fuck sleep.

Juan throwing these bricks at me this suddenly was a test. I knew it. And I was going to past this test with fucking flying colors.

Once I made it to Zoe's room, I knocked lightly before I walked in without waiting for a response. The room was dark despite the light from the television and the little sun that was able to enter through the drawn shades. Zoe was staring at the television, but she couldn't have been watching it because the sound was off.

After I sat in a chair next to her bed, she finally looked at me. She still didn't say a word, however. She just turned her eyes back toward the TV. I reached for her hand and held it. She wasn't my woman. She never could be. But she definitely was my homie. I had told her things that I had never even told my brothers. We had a bond on a different level. This was my friend, if not anything else.

Though she still wouldn't look at me, she had tears in her eyes. Beyond looking sad, she looked embarrassed and weak.

"You love that nigga this much?" I asked.

Every Love Story Is Beautiful, But Ours Is Hood
by *Jessica N. Watkins*

She looked at me as if my implication had hurt, but I knew why she had done this. Money had told me how it all went down. I didn't know whether Money's hurt had pushed her to this, whether she just wanted his attention, or both, but her overdose was definitely fueled by Money.

"You're beautiful. You're dope as fuck. Fuck that nigga. Leave him, especially if he's driving you to do some shit like this."

"Will you love me?" she asked dryly.

Zoe's question caught me off guard, but she kept badgering me. "If I leave him will you be with me and take care of me? Because I have nothing. I don't have shit. I don't have job experience or a fucking degree. Both of my parents are dead, and I can't go live with my auntie because her husband used to try to fuck me when I was ten. So, if I leave Money, I will have nowhere to go. So, will *you* take care of me?"

I was her friend, her *real* friend. In fact, I was too much of a friend to lie and tell her that after fucking her for a year, I would never choose her over my brother. So, I didn't. I didn't say anything.

She lay back on the pillow and gave her attention back to the television. Regretfully, she took her hand from mine as she said, "That's what I thought, so don't fucking tell me to leave him."

AKIRA WHITE

Hi, my name is Akira White, and I am addicted to City Savage. Completely and utterly fucking addicted to him.

"Uh! Mmmmm! Oh my gawd!"

"You're cummin'?"

"Yes, I'm cumminnnng!" I panted as my juices flowed and the orgasmic sensation washed over me.

He only spit my clit out long enough to smack my ass and say. "Good. That's number four." Then he sucked it back into his mouth.

Yes, he was counting every time I came all over his face, and, yes, it was indeed the fourth time. This man had waken me up eating my pussy thirty minutes ago and had yet to stop. I had cum so many times that I was weak and breathless. My hand was in his locs, trying to push him away from my sensitive clit, but he was relentless on my bud and would not let go.

Then, for the sixth time in twenty minutes, my phone started ringing. I had told Davion that I was going to my spin class. That usually bought me at least a couple of hours of uninterrupted free time, so I didn't understand why he was suddenly calling me back to back.

"Fuck," I groaned with irritation.

"Answer it," City commanded with a mouth full of pussy.

I ignored him because we both knew that it was Davion.

"Answer it," he fussed again and then smacked my ass.

"Ah!" I squealed, but I went ahead and reached toward the nightstand for my cell phone.

I was thinking that City would let me talk to Davion briefly, as I answered, "Hey." But nope! He kept slurping on this pussy, even more passionately and intently now.

My mouth fell open as I stared at the ceiling in disbelief of how superbly he was eating this kat.

"Hey babe. What took you so long to answer? You okay?"

"Y-yeah...I...I'm working out," I answered in pants as City slurped and sucked.

"Oh yeah? Sounds like you're getting it in too. Just call me back later."

"Okay," I hurried and said.

"Bye. Love yo—"

"Bye." I quickly hung up and this motherfucker started laughing. "That's not funny, City. Why did you do that?"

Staring up at me with my juices all over his beard, City never looked so beautiful. "Fuck that nigga. You're *mine*."

He always said that I was his. But I wondered what he meant by that since he had never asked me to be with him and never asked me to leave Davion. But, honestly, I really wasn't ready to make that decision yet. He had only been a single man for a few days, so Nova's epic return was still a fear in the back of my mind.

TARAJI GREEN

Shamar and I chilled in that hotel room all night. We fucked, ate, drank, and then fucked some more. The next morning, room service brought us breakfast and he ate syrupy strawberries off of this pussy. I couldn't believe how Shamar was acting with me all of a sudden. I mean, we had known each other for a long time and we were good friends. But he had never let his guard down physically or emotionally like he'd done the last few times I'd been with him. He was showing me a lover more than a friend. I had to admit that I was feeling the new man that he was revealing to me. Many men had shown me this kind of affection, but I didn't want it. Hell, Reggie had set my house on fire because I didn't want this from him. But I was cool with it when it came to Shamar. I had no fight in me when it came to him anymore. I had forfeited and was giving in.

We chilled all morning until I had a client. I had enjoyed the hell out of Shamar. Like, shit, that dude was really turning me into one of those love-sick chicks that couldn't eat or sleep without wanting to talk to bae.

Every Love Story Is Beautiful, But Ours Is Hood
by *Jessica N. Watkins*

I had been able to talk to him throughout the day between clients. But he never said that he was coming up to my shop, so I was surprised when I saw him walking through the door along with J Dante! As hairstylists and clients noticed the famous, award winning, hip hop artist, they started to gasp. Some even screamed as they took out their phones to take pics and videos. Despite his girlfriend being with him, these chicks were fighting for his attention.

I was star struck. J Dante's new single, "Dark" was off the chain and climbing the charts. He was touring all over the world and opening for rappers like Drake, Future, and Lil' Wayne. As a matter of fact, he was opening up that evening for the Migos.

"What's up, baby?" Shamar coolly greeted me as he walked up to me.

When he wrapped his arms around me and kissed my cheek, I felt like a bigger star than J Dante. All of the chicks in the shop were *haaaaating*!

"Hey, you," I purred. "What are you doing here?"

"My homie, J Dante, needs his girl's hair done for the concert tonight. Can you fit her in?"

I smiled at her. She was a beautiful girl with long natural hair that was perfect for a bomb-ass cut and color.

EVERY LOVE STORY IS BEAUTIFUL, BUT OURS IS HOOD
by *Jessica N. Watkins*

"Of course I'll fit her in," I answered as I smiled appreciatively into Shamar's eyes.

He leaned over and whispered into my ear, "Told you I got you."

I blushed and didn't hide it from these bitches that were soaking in jealously.

"And hurry up so we can hit up the concert tonight," he told me.

"You're taking me to the concert with you?" I was geeked!

"Hell yeah." Then Shamar reached back and grabbed my ass, and it was just what I'd needed. I needed that pinch so that I could know that I wasn't dreaming. When I let go and let myself like this man, it was breathtaking. I was so happy that it felt unreal.

CHAPTER SIXTEEN

SHAMAR SAVAGE

The J Dante and Migos concert was off the chain. Forget VIP seats; Me and Taraji were right on the stage while J Dante and the Migos were performing. I met J Dante through my brothers when they were serving him one day when he was in Chicago. He was in search of a good tattoo artist, and, of course, they sent him to me. We got cool over time because, after our first session, I was the only artist that he would let do his ink. So, even after the concert, he had let us backstage. That shit was epic.

Now, we were on our way to get something to eat to feed this liquor.

"Where you trying to eat at?" I asked Taraji.

She shrugged, looking pretty as hell with an intoxicated look over her chocolate face.

"I don't care. What's open?"

I shrugged as well as I started my ride. "Ain't no tellin'. It's damn near two in the morning."

"Maxwell's is cool."

EVERY LOVE STORY IS BEAUTIFUL, BUT OURS IS HOOD
by *Jessica N. Watkins*

I had to break out in a grin.

She giggled and asked, "What are you smiling so hard at?"

"You are the only bougie chick that I know that will still do hood shit like eat Maxwell Polishes at two in the morning."

"I am *not* bougie."

"Shiiiiid!" I teased.

"How am I bougie?"

"'How am I bougie?'" I mocked her. "First of all, you *sound* bougie."

"Asshole—"

My phone started ringing. Since it was so late at night, I got nervous. I was hoping that it wasn't one of my hoes because Taraji was so close to me that she could see the name on the screen. We had had such a good night. I was more than ready to get in that pussy. I had earned some brownie points by getting Taraji that celeb client earlier that day, so I knew that she was going to suck the skin off my dick. The last thing I needed was for some random bitch's call to piss her off.

I discreetly exhaled with relief when I saw that it was my brother, City.

"What up, big bro?" I answered.

EVERY LOVE STORY IS BEAUTIFUL, BUT OURS IS HOOD
by *Jessica N. Watkins*

"What up, man? You busy?"

"Kinda sort." Then I chuckled devilishly so that he could get the hint.

"I get it, I get it. I won't keep you long. You heard what happened?"

"No." Then I noticed his line of questioning and became curious. "Why? Something going on?"

The first people that I thought of was Kaos and Mayhem's bad asses. I just knew that he was about to tell me that them lil' niggas had fucked up my shop or something.

City took a deep breath and told me, "Zoe tried to kill herself last night."

My eyes bucked. I sat back in the driver's seat. Taraji noticed the blank look on my face and sat up in concern.

"*Tried*? So, she's still alive?" I asked.

"Yeah. She took a bunch of pills, but, luckily, Money found her quick. They pumped her stomach. They are going to keep her for a few days for observation."

"Damn, man. That shit is crazy. Money cool?"

"He's cool as he can be. He's a'ight, just pissed that she would pull a stunt like this."

"I can understand that."

Every Love Story Is Beautiful, But Ours Is Hood
by *Jessica N. Watkins*

"I was just letting you know what the word was, though. Go ahead and finish your night."

"Cool. I'll go visit Zoe tomorrow."

"Bet. Call me. We can ride together."

"Cool."

As I hung up, Taraji quickly pressed, "What happened?"

"Zoe tried to kill herself last night."

Taraji gasped and threw her hand over her mouth. Even though my brother had just told me, it felt so unreal to say it. I shook my head in shame as I put the car in drive and finally left the parking lot of the Pavilion.

"That's crazy," she said with a sigh.

"Shol' is. Speaking of crazy, they still haven't arrested Reggie?"

"Nope."

I shook my head, still in shock of how crazy things were getting. "What's up with these crazy motherfuckers? Zoe trying to kill herself, and Reggie is setting houses on fire. Love drives people insane. I don't want nobody to love me that much."

"What do you mean?" Taraji asked.

EVERY LOVE STORY IS BEAUTIFUL, BUT OURS IS HOOD
by Jessica N. Watkins

"Zoe's been tripping for a minute. Money done drove her ass crazy by cheating on her and shit. Then the nigga moved his side bitch downstairs in his—"

"What?! He moved Bliss in?!"

I had to laugh at the way Taraji's eyes were bucked. They were damn near spilling out of the sockets. "Yep. Bliss needed a place to stay because her crib caught on fire around the holidays. It was taking him a minute to find the right spot for his son, and she was threatening to leave town to go live with her family. Money lives in a two-flat, so he moved her in the vacant apartment downstairs until he found her a place."

"That's fucked up. See? That's why I was avoiding getting my feelings involved with a nigga. I'd fucking kill you if you did something like that to me."

Whaaat? I had to stop the car. We were at a stop sign, but since the streets were vacant, I just sat there looking at her with this teasing grin on my face.

"What are you looking at?" she asked.

"You said *was?*"

"Was what?"

"You said that's why you *was* avoiding getting your feelings involved with a nigga. I passed English class. That

Every Love Story Is Beautiful, But Ours Is Hood
by *Jessica N. Watkins*

means past tense, motherfucka..." Taraji started giggling. "Which means *presently* you do have feelings for a nigga."

She was blushing, and she couldn't hide it. She looked out the window to avoid my eyes, but nah, fuck that, I wasn't letting her slide with that. This girl had been acting like *she* was the man in this fuckship. She thought just like a man; that's why I thought she was so cool. She had no feelings and no filter about not wanting to be in a relationship or getting in her feelings.

"Who you got feelings for, Taraji?" I was teasing with her, smiling from ear to ear.

"I ain't got feelings for nobody, nigga!" But her smile said different.

"So you gon' lie to me?"

"Will you drive?! We been sitting at this stop sign forever. We both been drinking, and I ain't trying to go to jail tonight. I want some dick."

She was still giggling, but as soon as I slid my hand on her exposed thigh, the humor left her face and anxiousness slipped into her expression. She bit her lip as she stared into my eyes.

"It's okay if you got feelings for me—"

"I do not have feelings for y—"

Every Love Story Is Beautiful, But Ours Is Hood
by *Jessica N. Watkins*

"So you're still going to lie to me?" My hand slid up her thigh, and I allowed my fingers to tickle that pussy, which was covered by black lace. Her head slightly fell back as her eyes rolled to the ceiling.

"Stop lying to me," I pressed. "Answer the question."

"Yesss..." She exhaled as if she didn't want to admit it. "Yes, I fucking have feelings for you. Okay?" Then she reluctantly looked at me.

That, her admission, made my dick hard. I gently grabbed her face and kissed her as I continued to play with her pussy.

"Mmmm," she moaned into my mouth with a, sort of, whimper attached to it.

I reluctantly let her go. Had I kept kissing her, I would have had my dick out in the middle of the street. I put the car in drive and drove off. There was some awkward silence until I heard a cynical chuckle leave Taraji.

"What are you laughing at?" I asked.

"Oh, you feeling me too, nigga," she answered, still laughing.

"What made you say that?" I asked, playing it off. "How you figure?"

EVERY LOVE STORY IS BEAUTIFUL, BUT OURS IS HOOD
by *Jessica N. Watkins*

"You put our picture on Instagram!" she said with a teasing laugh.

Then she quickly flashed her phone in front of my face and moved it so that I could see the road. I hadn't seen what she was showing me, but I didn't have to. I knew what it was. I had taken a couple of selfies of us while at the concert on stage. And, yeah, I had posted one on my Instagram. Fuck it. If all my bitches stopped talking to me because of it, I really didn't give a fuck. I was cool with who I was riding with.

"That's a cuff move, nigga," she continued to tease.

That was true, but she didn't need to know that. "Whatever."

BLISS DAVIS

I never thought that I would be this sad when I finally moved out of Money's building. I thought I would be ecstatic and relieved. But I wasn't. I was hurt like hell. I missed Money's presence already, and I hadn't even left yet.

He wasn't my man and he hadn't even touched me lustfully or fucked me. Yet, I still didn't want to leave. That let me know that I had to get the hell up out of there. He had a bitch try to kill herself over him. I wouldn't be the next girl to go crazy over that man.

"You ready?"

You know who else looked sad? Money. I looked at him as he leaned on the doorframe of the bedroom. I had never seen him look so weak and uncomfortable. Money was a fearless goon, a gangsta. But standing in that doorway, he had fear.

"Yes, I'm ready," I told him. "I have mostly everything. I can come back later for the rest or you can bring it to me."

I picked Keandre up from the bed while Money went to grab the last suitcase. I was on my way to yet another hotel until Money got me a place, which he swore would be soon. I

Every Love Story Is Beautiful, But Ours Is Hood
by *Jessica N. Watkins*

was tired of my baby being in hotel rooms that weren't conducive for him. But this building wasn't safe for him either, not with bitches overdosing over his daddy living above our heads. If she was willing to kill her motherfucking self, she would definitely be willing to kill me or somebody else. I was sure of that, so I was out.

"Bliss..."

I didn't like the sound of his voice, so I didn't even want to turn around. I kept walking, so he urged a little louder, "Bliss!"

I reluctantly turned on my heels and saw him still leaning in the doorway. He hadn't even attempted to grab my bags.

"What?" I asked.

"I don't want you to go."

Why is he doing this?

"I'm only going to a hotel. You can come see Keandre anytime you want. You know that."

"That ain't enough. I want y'all here. Both of y'all. I love being with my son, and I love you being here with me. I *want* you to be here with me."

"I can't live here with that girl acting crazy like that. It ain't safe for me, and it ain't safe for my son."

Every Love Story Is Beautiful, But Ours Is Hood
by *Jessica N. Watkins*

"Fuck her. I ain't talking about her. I want to be with *you*."

I turned my head. How did he want to be with me? I didn't know what that meant. Did he want to be with me or just want me in his presence so that he could reap the benefits while staying with Zoe? I didn't know if I wanted to know the answer to that. I went to walk towards the front door, but I felt a tug on my arm that stopped me. I turned back to see Money staring deeply into my eyes.

If I didn't know what he meant before, if I didn't want to know, he was going to clarify anyway. "You hear me? I want you. I want *you*, not Zoe. I want you. I want to be with my family."

I had waited to hear this from Money for so long. After a year and a half of wanting him and praying for God to give him to me, I felt relief. I felt closure. I felt like I wasn't crazy; that I was in fact good enough, and I could in fact make him happy.

"You haven't even given me any pussy, and I still want you. This is not about just wanting to fuck you. I want you to be mine. I want us to be a family. I know I'm a fucked up man with doggish ways, but I know you can change all that. You *have* changed all that. I haven't been with nobody or even thought about pussy since you got here. That's because I've been content with you. I want *you*, baby."

My heart fluttered. I was fighting tears. Finally, what I had always wanted was being offered to me.

However, it still wasn't right. "Then leave Zoe."

KEANDRE 'MONEY' SAVAGE

"A'ight."

Bliss didn't believe that, though. She just stood there staring at me with doubt in those pretty eyes. I understood why she wouldn't believe me. I had been playing with this woman's heart since the day that I met her, so I wasn't surprised that she didn't believe a word that I was saying.

"All I can do is show you. Will you agree to at least let me show you?"

Finally, she sighed. It was as if she was letting her guard down against her better judgment. "Okay, Money."

She probably was just saying that to shut me up, but I had finally matured enough to realize that with Bliss was where I wanted to be. I wasn't no pussy nigga, and I never had been. Whatever I wanted, I made sure that I got. Only this time, I couldn't take it or buy it. I had to man up and earn that shit.

****

EVERY LOVE STORY IS BEAUTIFUL, BUT OURS IS HOOD
by *Jessica N. Watkins*

Bliss and I really didn't say much more to each other after that. There was nothing more to say. I needed to prove to her that I wanted her by leaving Zoe. Nothing more. Nothing less. I was in my own head as I trailed behind her to the hotel that was five minutes away from my crib. I knew that I had to and wanted to leave Zoe's crazy ass for more reasons than wanting to be with Bliss. Zoe and I had been over for a long time. We were emotionally separated, but physically living together, only fucking when we wanted to get off. Our relationship had been over for a long time. I had never loved her. She had loved me, but it was for all the wrong reasons. And, now, she was only still with me out of competition, instead of love.

However, regardless of the absence of love between us, we had history. So, as I left my family at the hotel and made my way to the hospital, I knew that leaving Zoe wasn't going to be easy. I definitely had to wait until she was released from the hospital. I feared what she would do to herself next when I finally left her, but I could no longer stay with her and be miserable because this bitch wanted to ruin or end her life because of me. I had enough bullshit to deal with in the streets. I battled with niggas all day, every day, so

Every Love Story Is Beautiful, But Ours Is Hood
by *Jessica N. Watkins*

the last thing I wanted to do was continue to come home to a warzone.

Fuck that.

After leaving the hotel, I went to the hospital to check on Zoe. She called herself mad at me, so she wasn't answering my text messages. Since the damn girl didn't have any family, I was trying to be there for her. Despite our relationship being over, we were family. Zoe was that to me, as well as my brothers and sisters. We cared about her, but all she cared about was winning me.

"What up?" was all that I said as I entered her hospital room.

She continued to stare at the television without responding.

"Did they say when you could be released?"

"After I have a psych eval," she mumbled.

"Good."

Her neck snapped and her head swung around toward me.

"I didn't mean it like that," I corrected. "I just think it'll be good if you talk to somebody."

"I don't need no fucking therapist," she sneered. "What I need is for you to love me like you're supposed to."

EVERY LOVE STORY IS BEAUTIFUL, BUT OURS IS HOOD
by *Jessica N. Watkins*

TAYE 'CITY' SAVAGE

"What, man?" I spoke into the phone.

"Excuse me?" Nova shrieked. "That's how you're going to answer the phone for me?"

I grimaced. Cuffing my forehead in irritation, I lay back on the bed in the suite. I should have kept ignoring this girl's calls. I knew that nothing good was going to come out of answering it. The only reason that I had decided to go ahead and answer was because Akira was due to arrive soon, and I didn't want Nova's calls interrupting any of my time with her.

"You've been gone long enough. It's time for you to come home now."

This bitch was really talking to me like she was my mother. "See? This is your problem, you think you run shit. You don't run me," I fussed.

She sucked her teeth. "So, you left me for real?"

I shook my head in disbelief in how self-absorbed she was. Every day that she had called asking me where I was and why I hadn't been home, I told her very clearly that it was never my home and she was no longer my girl. Apparently, she thought it was a game. But I was willing to do or say whatever I had to make her realize that this shit was far from jokes and riddles.

I for sure was done with Nova. "Hell yeah. Why the fuck don't you get that?"

"Because it will *never* be over between us, City. It's you and me."

"No, it's been you and my money, but that shit's dead."

She sucked her teeth and simply said, "I'll give you a few more days to come to your senses."

A mocking laugh left my throat. "Give me all the days you need. Let me know when you realize that yo' ass is single."

I could hear her yapping, cursing, and threatening me. I also heard knocks on the suite's door, so I hung up on her ass.

Walking to the door, I could only shake my head in shame for myself. This was all my fault. I should have been man enough back then to realize what was important. I was just being money hungry and wanted a chick in the streets looking out for me while I was on the inside. I didn't realize that while having a woman to hustle with you, you needed her to want you for you.

That realization only came with maturity, however.

****

I felt bad that the most time that I spent with Akira was inside of her. I couldn't help myself, though. A nigga had been deprived for so long. I couldn't help but want to be inside of some good pussy now that it was finally at hand.

After cumming twice, I was done...*for now*. So, Akira lay in my arms as we attempted to catch our breaths.

"I'm leaving town tomorrow morning," I heard her say as her head was buried in my chest. I could feel her fingertips lightly tracing my chest.

I laced my fingers inside of her hair and started to massage her scalp. "Where are you going?"

"I have to go to the Super Bowl."

"Damn, I was hoping to watch it with you."

"Really?" She sighed. "I wish we could, but I have to go."

"I understand. Have fun."

She chuckled. "Have fun, huh? Why is this so easy for you? Why are you so okay with me being with Davion?"

Every Love Story Is Beautiful, But Ours Is Hood
by *Jessica N. Watkins*

"I can't hate on that man if that's who you choose to be with. If he makes you happy, who am I to talk shit? I want you to be happy."

That was some bullshit. I wanted that pussy to be all mine. The only reason I hadn't snatched her away from that lame nigga is because I was getting out of my own shit first.

"Why do you always say that? That you just want me to be happy? What about what *you* want?"

"Because it's simple; be with who makes you happy. I love you enough to want you to be happy, whether it's with me or not."

She lifted her head and looked into my eyes. "You *love* me?"

"How could I not love you? I care about you enough not to hurt you by forcing you to do anything. But I *will* make you if you take too long. I'm only willing to share you for so long."

"*You* make me happy, but you scare the shit out of me as well."

I figured I did. Davion was safe while I was a huge risk. I had hurt her before, and a few weeks of fucking wasn't going to take away that pain or the hesitation to trust me again.

CHAPTER SEVENTEEN

TAYE 'CITY' SAVAGE

"Deuce, what's up with that jogging suit, man?" Kaos teased our father. "What the fuck is that? *Pleather*? You falling off? Pimping must be dead like a motherfucker."

The room erupted with deep laughs. The living room was filled with the Savage men—all of my brothers, my father, and me. Bliss, Taraji, Yummy, Tanisha, and Nova were in another room with Keandre, the only Savage grandchild so far. One of my father's girlfriends was with them too. They were preparing the Sunday dinner as we watched the game. Since we were kids, we had watched the Super Bowl as a family because football was my father's favorite pastime.

"Pimpin' ain't dead. Hoes just scared," my father barked.

The room went up again in boisterous hollers and laughter.

"This nigga..." I chuckled with a shake of the head.

"I know you ain't laughing, Money," Deuce barked. "You are the biggest pimp in here. Got your side bitch in here while your main bitch is in the hospital. You's a cold motherfucker, boy."

"Oooooouuuuu!" Mayhem taunted.

Suddenly, Money didn't find shit funny at all.

"That *was* a bold move, bro," I told Money, who was sitting beside me on a barstool at the bar at the back of the room.

Money sucked his teeth. "Fuck that bitch. Zoe is crazy as fuck."

"She's been crazy. You just feeling Bliss now, nigga. You ain't slick," Shon chuckled.

Money ignored Shon, and I knew why. He didn't trust that Shon wouldn't tell Zoe everything. But when the conversation in the room silenced as the game came back on, Money leaned toward me.

"I *am* feeling Bliss, bro," Money confessed.

"You already told me that. I know."

He shook his head. "It's deeper than what I thought, though."

"Deep like how?"

"Like I wanna leave Zoe." My eyes bucked as he continued. "Not for Bliss, for *me*. Being around Bliss just showed me what a happy household could be like and how it's supposed to be. Zoe ain't been happy in a long time and neither have I. This shit is becoming unhealthy—*literally*."

I nodded. "I feel you. I'm kinda going through something like that myself."

"Is Akira why you left Nova?"

"Like you said, Akira showed me why I should leave Nova. But I didn't leave Nova for Akira because Akira is engaged."

Money sucked his teeth and waved his hand dismissively. "Fuck that lame-ass nigga."

Those were my sentiments exactly, but I cared about Akira enough not to put her in a fucked up position. I knew that if she was with me, I would take care of her better than that lame nigga ever could. But I was giving her a chance to make that decision herself before I made it for her.

As I laid eyes on Nova leaning in the doorway of the living room, even if there was no love in the relationship, it was hard to get rid of your girl when she was like family, even though she had stopped being your woman a long time ago.

I grimaced as she motioned for me to meet her in the hall.

"I'll be back, man."

Every Love Story Is Beautiful, But Ours Is Hood
by Jessica N. Watkins

Since Money saw the exchange, he just nodded with a chuckle. I think he was enjoying somebody being in the same fucked up predicament that he was in.

I had figured that Nova would want to have some kind of conversation when she saw me today. I had been gone for over a week now with very little communication with her. My mind wasn't on her at all. Much of that had to do with me having my dick in a better woman than her most of the time.

"What up?" I spat once in the hall.

"What's up with Money bringing that bitch in here?'

"Don't call her that. Watch your fucking mouth."

She folded her arms tightly across her fake breasts, shifting all of her weight to one foot. It got under her skin that no matter what she had done for me while I was inside, I still treated her like the next bitch. She wanted to be put on a pedestal so bad that she put herself on that motherfucker. I was happy to snatch her back down off of it, though.

"That's just disrespectful as hell for him to have her in here," Nova snarled.

The nerve of this bitch. This was Nova's problem. She thought she ran everything and everybody. I could smell the tequila on her breath, so clearly she was so drunk that she thought she called shots around here.

EVERY LOVE STORY IS BEAUTIFUL, BUT OURS IS HOOD
by *Jessica N. Watkins*

"That's not your motherfucking business."

"You may think you've left me, but—"

My deep chuckle cut her off. "*Think*? I did."

"Whatever. Like I said, you may *think* you've left me, but this is still my family, so it *is* my business."

"Bitch, is you crazy?" I threatened. "This is not your family."

She looked me up and down and snarled.

I ignored that and went back to watch the game. That bitch didn't know how close she was to being disrespected in the same way that Zoe was being disrespected. Only difference would be that if Akira acted like she wanted to leave that lame-ass nigga, I would be parading her back and forth through this motherfucker right in Nova's face.

As I sat down and got back into the game, I wished that I had been a dirty enough nigga to make that move just to bring Nova down on her level even more. Nothing would humble her more than seeing Akira here with me. But I respected Akira too much to make her leave Davion. Besides, I didn't want to force her to leave him, I wanted her to do it on her own so that I would know that she was confident in where she wanted to be. To me, that nigga didn't exist. Akira was mine; always had been and always would be.

BLISS DAVIS

"I can't believe that I let this nigga trick me into coming here."

"Tricked you?" Taraji asked me.

"Yes, he tricked me. Money only told me that he wanted me to bring Keandre over here so that Deuce could spend some time with his grandson. He never told me that it was a damn family dinner."

Taraji, Yummy and Tanisha giggled as I took another sip of the margaritas that Deuce's girlfriend had made. They were so strong and had all of the girls buzzed.

"It's not funny," I whined. "He got me in here looking like the good mistress. I don't want to be here. Zoe is his woman, not me."

"Have you all heard anything about how she's doing?" Taraji asked us.

"Me and Yummy saw her this morning. She should be released tomorrow. She looks horrible, though."

Yummy nodded. "Yeah, she does. She's emotionally sick."

EVERY LOVE STORY IS BEAUTIFUL, BUT OURS IS HOOD
by *Jessica N. Watkins*

"That's why I don't feel right being here," I told them. "I just don't feel right, especially after what Zoe did."

Yummy sucked her teeth and waved off my guilt. "You're here because Money asked you to come. You're Keandre's mother. At some point, Zoe is going to have to get used to that. Although it's obvious that Money is feeling you way more than he has ever felt Zoe."

"Is it that obvious?" I asked.

I didn't even bother to hide the grin on my face. I didn't have to. I knew these girls well. I had met Taraji when Shamar came to visit his only nephew. She was with him a few times after that. Yummy and Tanisha used to come over often to play with Keandre before my house caught on fire. Even afterwards, they'd visited the hotel and had been to the apartment that Money gave me to spend time with him. They had babysat Keandre a few times as well. I knew them all just as well as Zoe did. So, if I hadn't told them that I still loved Money, I was sure that they could already tell.

Just as Yummy was about to answer, her eyes locked on something and she stopped. It was Nova walking past the doorway of the den where we were chilling as Keandre played with his toys in the middle of the floor.

Once Nova was gone, Yummy rolled her eyes and said, "That bitch is being extra stank today."

"Ain't she?" Tanisha agreed as she snacked on Flaming Hots.

She was so young. She was only sixteen years old, but she was already so beautiful. She had mature features that were very similar to the rest of the Savages. Though she and Yummy had different mothers, they looked more like twins than Kaos and Mayhem did.

"She didn't even speak," Taraji fussed with her nose turned up. "She acts like I don't do her hair. You don't piss off your hair stylist."

We all laughed as I added, "Exactly. She's always been stank. She thinks she's better than every fucking body."

Yummy sucked her teeth. "She isn't better than me, with all that bad work she got done. Why the fuck didn't nobody tell her to stop getting all those injections? Her booty looks like a big-ass, fucked up shaped watermelon sitting up on two sticks."

I giggled uncontrollably.

"Anyway," Taraji said through laughs. "Yes, it's obvious that Money is feeling you, Bliss. You don't see how he looks at you?"

EVERY LOVE STORY IS BEAUTIFUL, BUT OURS IS HOOD
by *Jessica N. Watkins*

"I see it, but, girl, I got post-traumatic stress. I told him that if he really wanted me, he needs to leave Zoe. But I gave him that same ultimatum a year and a half ago, and he played me. He chose her."

Yummy shook her head. "I don't think he will now."

"How do you know?" I asked.

"Do you not see that crack-head bitch?!" Tanisha snapped with a chuckle.

I laughed and told her, "Shut up."

"Seriously," Tanisha went on. "I be seeing her all on Instagram looking whack as hell. She do all the drugs. It's so obvious. I'm from the hood. I know how a crack head looks."

"He chooses to sleep in the same house with that crack head every night," I reminded them.

"Just be patient. It's coming," Taraji told me.

"I've been patient for a year and a half, Taraji."

"And even after all of that time, you still love him, so keep holding on," she insisted.

"Are *you* holding on, though?" Yummy asked Taraji with a smile.

Taraji tried to play stupid. "To who?"

"To Shamar, heffa. Don't play dumb," I answered for Yummy. "I see you done made it to the family dinner too."

EVERY LOVE STORY IS BEAUTIFUL, BUT OURS IS HOOD
by *Jessica N. Watkins*

"And I got tricked too," Taraji said. "He told me that we were watching the game with his father. He didn't tell me that the whole damn Savage family would be here."

"Well, he already outed y'all on social media, so meeting the family officially was next," Tanisha told her.

"I don't see why, though. We aren't even in a committed relationship. That's the last thing that Shamar wants."

"Well, you are the only girl that he has ever brought around the family," Yummy told her. "The other hoes I have only seen in passing, and I haven't seen them since he started hanging around you more."

All Taraji said was, "Humph," but I could see the smile bursting through those big, juicy lips. Damn, I don't even see how she and Shamar ever kissed. They probably swallowed each other's heads every time.

"So, see? A committed relationship may be in your near future, girlie," I told her with a slight nudge in the side.

Taraji replied, "But I'm not even sure if that's what I want."

"Why not?" I asked.

"I'm scared," she confessed.

"Of what?"

Every Love Story Is Beautiful, But Ours Is Hood
by *Jessica N. Watkins*

"Being hurt. Hell, I got post-traumatic stress too."

I couldn't argue with that. I was sitting there like a scared little girl. I had once again tried to give Money a chance, not knowing if he would do right by it. But I guess if he were to choose Zoe this time, I could finally walk completely away, knowing that I gave it my all.

KEANDRE 'MONEY' SAVAGE

Tonight just further proved that Bliss belonged with this family. She just looked better in the picture. I wasn't swapping out the old model for a new one. I was replacing one with who was supposed to be there in the first place.

I should have chosen right the first time. Bliss had always loved me better, but I was trying to be some kind of typical hood nigga that had his main bitch stunting while he had the good woman on the side. I was whack as fuck for that.

As I watched her undress in the bedroom of the suite that I had put her up in, I wondered how I could've been so stupid to play with this girl's heart for two whole years.

"Thank you for carrying Keandre up here. That boy is getting heavy."

"You don't have to thank me for that," I told her.

Bliss wasn't even looking at me. That was a good thing because she didn't see me slobbing as she took off her jeggings. Her ass was so fucking phat. My dick hardened in my jeans.

Every Love Story Is Beautiful, But Ours Is Hood
by *Jessica N. Watkins*

Bliss had me fucked up. If she thought that she was going to keep walking around me with that ass out, and I wasn't going to stick my dick in her, I was about to show her that she was dead-ass wrong.

Fuck this. I had been respecting her pain for long enough. Yes, I had all plans of being more careful with her heart this time around, but baby girl was about to give me that pussy. I stood from the bed and walked up on her with a dick hard as concrete running toward her thick ass. Before she even knew what was coming for her, I spun her around, locked my fingers in her red waves and kissed her.

"Money, what—" she mumbled into my mouth, but I kept kissing her in order to bury any of the rejections that were about to come out of her mouth.

I used my massive weight to force her toward the bed. She held on to my waist, squeezing my T-shirt. She had finally stopped trying to fight me with her words, although her body had never tried to fight it.

I laid her on the bed, standing between her bare, chocolate milky legs. I stared down on her as I removed my shirt. I saw her doe-shaped eyes squint as she admired my chest decorated with a mural of tattoos. After I dropped my jeans and boxers, and my hard dick was pulsating toward her,

Every Love Story Is Beautiful, But Ours Is Hood
by *Jessica N. Watkins*

I slipped her out of her panties, parted her thick thighs and revealed the pale pinkness of her creamy pussy. I glided my fingertips over her inner thighs, and she shivered under my light touch. My fingers traveled higher, into her wetness. She thrust her pelvis up, so that her pussy met my fingers. I felt how drippy wet it was, and my dick jumped with impatience.

Gawd damn, I had to be inside of her. I couldn't wait any longer.

I climbed onto the bed, hoisted her legs onto my shoulders and dove in.

Her gasp was so loud that it filled the quiet air around us. Mine was so loud that it overshadowed hers. This pussy was tight. It hugged me. It grabbed my dick and snatched me in deeper and deeper.

****

Bliss and I hadn't fucked in a year and a half, and I had taken my time to get back all of the time I had lost. After the umpteenth nut, I looked over at the clock and saw that it was damn near two in the morning. I looked over at Bliss, still trying to catch my breath. Sweat was pouring from her beautiful nakedness as she stared at the ceiling.

I wondered what she was thinking. But she was a woman, so I didn't have to wonder for long.

"So what does this mean?" she asked, finally breaking her silence.

"What do you mean?"

She turned on her stomach, rested on her elbows and said, "I mean, are you going back to her? Have you left Zoe? Is it me and you?"

I turned on my side in order to be closer to her, hoping that she saw the sincerity in my eyes. "Yeah, I'm with you. My heart is with you, but I need some time to leave officially. It's going to be hard."

Her eyes rolled. "What's so hard about it? Just leave her."

"It's not that easy."

Her voice got louder as she spat, "Why the fuck not?!"

I wanted to tell Bliss that even though I didn't want to be with Zoe anymore and that I had never loved her, she was family. And she was sick right now, so I needed to deal with leaving her carefully. It was only fair. I was tired of hurting her just as much as I was tired of hurting Bliss. It was time for

319

Every Love Story Is Beautiful, But Ours Is Hood
by *Jessica N. Watkins*

me to be a better man to everyone in my life. But I knew that none of that would be a good enough answer for Bliss. All she wanted to hear was that I had left Zoe.

"Why do you even care if it's not going to be easy?"

I saw the tears in her eyes and felt like shit. I didn't know the words to tell her that would make her feel better about this. This was new to me. I was trying to be caring, wanting, and loving. Shit, a nigga was still learning, so how could I make her understand this if I didn't?

"Huh?!" she pressed. "You didn't give a fuck if it was

easy to break my heart, so why

are you so fucking timid to break hers?!"

"Bliss, be quiet before you wake up the ba—"

"Fuck that!" she shouted as she sat straight up.

I reached for her, trying to calm her down and she spat, "Don't touch me! I'm sick of this shit! I'm sick of you constantly choosing that bitch over me! Get out!"

"Bliss, wait I—"

"*Get out!*" she screamed at the top of her lungs.

Shit, I had guns and drugs on me, and we were in a five-star hotel. If she was about to spazz out, then I was most definitely going to get the fuck out of there. She burst out in tears as I got out of bed and dressed.

EVERY LOVE STORY IS BEAUTIFUL, BUT OURS IS HOOD
by *Jessica N. Watkins*

"I hate you," she cried softly. "I fucking hate you for constantly doing this to me."

I wanted to soothe her, but there was nothing to say. I walked out, knowing that nothing would make this better until I left Zoe.

CHAPTER EIGHTEEN

AKIRA WHITE

"Damn, City," I moaned. I tried to use my hands to control his strokes. I put them on his hips, trying to slow him down, but he lightly swatted my hands away.

"Unt uh. Don't stop me. I'm getting all this pussy. I missed you."

"Fuck!" I winced sharply.

City was showing my body no mercy. He was on top of me, forcing my legs on his shoulders as he hovered over me, bringing my knees to my chest. He was so deep inside of me. My French manicured toes curled next to each of his ears as they braced on his shoulders. Every now and then, he would turn his head and kiss them as sweat poured from his brow.

I had only been gone for two days, but he was fucking me like he hadn't had this pussy in two years. I allowed myself to release the pressure through my throat in loud moans so that I could take every inch of him. I wanted all of it; the pain, the pressure, and the immense pleasure. I never

EVERY LOVE STORY IS BEAUTIFUL, BUT OURS IS HOOD
by *Jessica N. Watkins*

wanted him to stop, no matter how severe the beating, because I'd missed him too.

The Super Bowl was off the chain. Houston was lit the whole weekend. Yet, the entire time, I just wanted to rush back home to City. I couldn't wait to get back to this hotel suite and in his arms. As soon as I landed this morning, I told Davion that I was heading to a yoga class and afterwards a day full of errands. Then I ran to where I wanted to be. Davion was where I was, but City was slowly but surely turning into where my heart wanted to be.

Finally, after fifteen more intense, euphoric minutes, he suddenly pulled out of me and came all over my stomach. He grunted, "Urrrrrrrrrgh! Fuck!" as his seed spilled out all over me.

There was nothing sexier than seeing a 6'4", massive man buckle because of the way your pussy made him cum so hard. I smiled up at him with admiration all over my face as he wiped off my stomach.

"What are you looking at?" he asked as he started to clean himself.

"You. You're so beautiful."

"*Beautiful?*" he asked curiously. "I'm a grown-ass man."

Every Love Story Is Beautiful, But Ours Is Hood
by *Jessica N. Watkins*

"Grown-ass men can be beautiful in a masculine way."

He threw the towel that he'd used to wipe us both clean on the floor. Then he pulled the covers over us and spooned with me. I closed my eyes as he secured me under him. With my eyes closed, I enjoyed his scent, his touch, and just being in his presence. These were the moments that let me know that our connection wasn't just physical. Our connection wasn't birthed from the orgasmic hours that we'd spent with each other. Our connection started to develop years ago, during times like this, before the physical had ever occurred.

"I wish you'd never gone to jail."

He chuckled sarcastically. "Shit, me too."

"I mean, of course, I wish you'd never lost ten years of your freedom. But, for me, I wish you'd never left so that I could have just been with you from the start."

"We still have a chance."

I smiled into the sheets, so happy to hear him say that. I hadn't physically left Davion, but I had emotionally left him already. As a matter of fact, he had never had me emotionally, only content. However, City was showing me that there was way more to life than just being content.

"I don't want to hurt anybody," I admitted.

EVERY LOVE STORY IS BEAUTIFUL, BUT OURS IS HOOD
by *Jessica N. Watkins*

"Do you feel like you're about to hurt somebody?"

City had never asked me to leave Davion. He had never pressured me to decide. But I wanted to be his nonetheless. I was willing to risk a forever with Davion for an attempt at happiness with City.

"I think so."

EVERY LOVE STORY IS BEAUTIFUL, BUT OURS IS HOOD
by *Jessica N. Watkins*

TARAJI GREEN

I don't know what it is that you've done to me
But it's caused me to act in such a crazy way.
Whatever it is that you do when you do what you're doing
It's a feeling that I don't understand.
'Cause my heart starts beating triple time,
With thoughts of loving you on my mind.
I can't figure out just what to do,
When the cause and cure is you.

"*I geeeeet sooooo weak in the knees, I can hardly speak.*
I loooose all control and something takes over me!!"

I was singing at the top of my lungs in the mirror in my bathroom. My brush was my microphone. I was feeling every word of this song because I was weak as hell for Shamar.

Ever since the dinner at his house, he had barely left my side. I was either at his house or he was at mine. I hadn't spoken to any of those other dudes on my roster. I was happy with Shamar...genuinely and truly.

Although it was thirty degrees that day, I felt warm on the inside. I felt that fire inside of my heart and had been

EVERY LOVE STORY IS BEAUTIFUL, BUT OURS IS HOOD
by *Jessica N. Watkins*

trying to put it out for weeks, but fuck it. I gave up. I was letting that fire burn. Just a few weeks ago, I was a heartless bitch that was fucking them and leaving them. I was cool not being attached to a man. But the feelings I had for Shamar were knocking the cool right out of me.

He hadn't said anything about us being in a committed relationship. That was okay with me, however. I was having a hard-enough time dealing with these feelings for him. I couldn't take being in a committed relationship on top of it. I was good with taking things slow, if it meant things working out for the both of us in the end.

Finally dressed and ready to go, I left the bathroom with a smile on my face. I cut off the Old Skool R&B station that was playing through the Pandora app on my phone. Then after turning off lights around my place, I collected my keys and purse and headed toward the front door. I was on my way to the salon. I had a shitload of clients that day.

Once I was outside, I slipped on my shades. Though it was still winter, the sun was shining bright. I couldn't help but notice the smile on my face and the pep in my step.

Yet, just as I was marinating in the memories of the sex Shamar and I had the night before, that smile melted off of my face when I saw Reggie running toward me. I should

EVERY LOVE STORY IS BEAUTIFUL, BUT OURS IS HOOD
by *Jessica N. Watkins*

have run the other way, but I couldn't move. I was stuck, standing on the sidewalk watching Reggie running toward. My feet were implanted in fear. I should have screamed, but confusion had left me speechless.

However, others did scream just as he ran up on me. As soon as he grabbed me, I started to fight him off as it felt like he was pulling me into a specific direction. I heard bystanders' screams and pleas for help as he was he able to drag me across the grass.

"*Help*! *Heeeelp*!" I had finally found my voice, but it was too late. Reggie was throwing me into the back seat of his car. I tried to kick and scream. I was shouting at the top of my lungs. "*Noooooo*! Help!"

Then, suddenly, a hard blow to the head rendered me unconscious.

SHAMAR SAVAGE

As I hung up my cell with an odd look on my face, my client, Brandon asked, "What's wrong?"

"Nothing. My girl isn't answering the phone. Just wondering what's going on," I told him as I returned my phone to my pocket. "It's not like her."

This was my third time trying to call Taraji. She hadn't answered any of my calls or replied to any text messages all morning. I wondered had I done something to piss her off. I ran down in my head what I had said before I left her that morning, wondering if I had put something fucked up on social media. You know, little shit that women get mad at— but I hadn't.

"You need a minute?" Brandon asked.

"Nah. She's probably just busy at the salon."

"Your girl, huh? When did you settle down?'

Brandon was a homie from the hood that I had grown up with. Our life had gone into two totally different directions, however. He had gone from a project dude to a minister at a mega church. That's how he became a client of mine. I specialized in cover ups, and he had been coming in over the last couple of months getting some of the gang and street affiliated tattoos that he had gotten when he was younger covered up.

"Well, she isn't technically my girl," I explained as I started back drawing his cover up on his right forearm.

"Do you like her?"

I cringed. I knew he was about to start preaching as he always did whenever he came to the shop. I didn't mind, though, because he always spit the truth and dropped some much needed knowledge on me every time.

"Then why isn't she your woman?"

I shrugged. "I'm scared, I guess."

"Scared of what?"

"Settling down, responsibilities, taking care of somebody other than myself, and having babies."

He chuckled. "I get it, I get it."

"I've never even had a woman before. I just mess around."

"Well, the Bible says: 'He who finds a wife finds a good thing and obtains favor from the Lord'."

"Wife? Whoa. See? That's what I'm talking about. We're talking about me committing to a woman and you're

EVERY LOVE STORY IS BEAUTIFUL, BUT OURS IS HOOD
by *Jessica N. Watkins*

bringing up a marriage already. That's exactly what I'm scared of."

"Well, that's how God intended it. You find a good woman, your good thing, and then you marry her. That's the point. It's too many men just sleeping around with good women when they should be making honest women out of them and giving them rings. The Bible also says that a man should not be alone. It's meant for us to court and marry when we find that good thing, and she's your good thing."

Quickly, I looked at him questionably before I focused back on sketching. "How do you know?"

He chuckled. "The way your face looks like you want to kill something or somebody because you haven't talked to her all day."

I laughed, but I was too ornery to verbally agree with him. But in my heart, I knew that he was right. I had been feeling everything that he was saying. I had never been scared of nothing in my life, but Taraji scared the fuck outta of a nigga *for real*. She was everything that any man could ever want, and it was time that I cuffed her before it was too late.

ZYSHONNE 'SHON' SHAVAGE

That morning, I received a text with a time and location from an unknown number. I knew that it was Juan with the time and location of the drop. He'd been right; he wanted this deal to go down right away.

That afternoon, I was meeting Juan's workers on the lakefront. In early February, the lakefront was abandoned. As instructed, I parked next to the white Suburban, popped the trunk, and sat back as two Columbians transferred four laundry bags into my trunk. I knew that inside of the laundry bags, amongst the dirty clothes, was my future, the beginning of my very own empire.

After I heard the tap on the trunk, indicating that they were done, I put my trap car in reverse and headed back to Lake Shore Drive feeling like "that nigga." With the wholesale price that Juan was giving me for these bricks, I had positioned myself to make a six-hundred-thousand-dollar profit. Then I would explain to Juan that my brothers had nothing to do with this deal, that it was all me. I was sure that he would be pissed at first because I had lied to him, but after a nigga brings you over a million dollars in less than a week,

EVERY LOVE STORY IS BEAUTIFUL, BUT OURS IS HOOD
by *Jessica N. Watkins*

you can't be mad at him for too long. Then I would have the relationship that I needed with a connect to turn my own name into an empire. Fuck an empire, my shit was going to be a kingdom, and I would be the king.

I deserved this shit. Money and City were being some pussies. It was money to be made out here, and I was about to get that shit.

"Oh fuck!" I shouted when I saw the Chevy speeding up behind me. I watched, waiting for it slow down, but it never did. I knew that it was about to smack into the back of me, but I had nowhere to go. I had just exited off of Lakeshore Drive and was at a red light. I was surrounded at all sides. There was nowhere for me go to before the Chevy smacked into me.

The collision was loud as my head hit the steering wheel, but the ringing in my ears made me deaf. As I tried to gain my composure, I saw three niggas jumping out of the Chevy. One was going inside of the trunk that had popped open during the collision. When I saw the guns in the hands of the other two, I realized that I was being robbed.

"Oh shit!" Adrenaline rushed through my body. Suddenly, I didn't feel the pain of the impact anymore. I reached under the seat for my gun and rushed out of the car, shooting wildly in their direction. But them niggas were ready. The two other dudes started shooting at me, protecting the nigga that was emptying out the trunk. Their bullets were flying back. I hit the ground and climbed back into the car. Along the way, glass shattered around me. I could hear people screaming and tires screeching. I had to get the fuck outta there. I threw my car in drive and hit the gas, not giving a fuck if I hit somebody. Luckily, I didn't as I sped down the road going ninety. The bullets had stopped, but I didn't for ten blocks until I found a self-car wash to pull into and hopped out.

My heart was beating out of my fucking chest. "*Fuck, fuck, fuck, fuck, fuck!*"

I had never been a praying man, but as I ran to the back of my ride, I prayed. But my prayers went unanswered. The trunk was empty.

"*Fuck!*"

****

"What the hell is wrong with you?"

EVERY LOVE STORY IS BEAUTIFUL, BUT OURS IS HOOD
by *Jessica N. Watkins*

Zoe looked at me with fear in her eyes as I burst into her hospital room. I knew that the events of the day were all over my face. I could feel the anxiety in my chest. Fuck! My life was over.

"I got set up," I blurted out as I started to pace the floor.

Her eyes bucked. "By who? What do you mean? What happened?"

"I don't know by who! Juan? The niggas I had set up to buy the work? I don't know."

"Wait, wait, wait," Zoe chanted. "Who is Juan? What the fuck is going on? What happened?"

I tried to slow down my breathing, but, fuck, I couldn't. This was fucked up - real fucked up. I didn't even know how this had happened. Besides the few people that I had arranged to sell the bricks to, nobody knew about this but Zoe, and she hadn't even known that the deal was going down today.

I was still pacing as I told her, "I got a connect to front me fifty bricks. He thought that this deal was with me, City, and Money; though. I told you that I wanted to do my own thing. I didn't tell Money or City."

"Why the fuck not?!"

Every Love Story Is Beautiful, But Ours Is Hood
by *Jessica N. Watkins*

"They kept shutting me down, and I was tired of living like this."

"Like what? Good? You ain't hurtin'!"

"Just listen!"

Zoe folded her arms, glaring at me, but she shut up and let me finish.

"I got in some shit and have nobody else to talk to, so please just listen to me. I lied and told the connect that City and Money were behind me on this because he wouldn't have believed that I had trusted clientele to move that much weight. So, he agreed to front the work and arranged for the drop today. I got there and everything went downhill. After the exchange was made, I got a few blocks away and some niggas rammed into my car and straight ambushed me. They went straight for the trunk. I jumped out shooting, but it was two of them with guns and one of me, so I climbed back in the car and sped off. But it was too late. Them niggas got me for *everything*."

The color left Zoe's face. She had already looked upset from being in the hospital for three days, but now she looked sick for real. And I couldn't blame her. This shit was fucked up. My life was over. I was sick too.

Every Love Story Is Beautiful, But Ours Is Hood
by *Jessica N. Watkins*

"I got set up," I said again in disbelief. I couldn't believe this shit. I had been hustling for years and a nigga had never gotten me.

"By who?"

"I don't know." This was the first time that I had ever felt weak and helpless in my life. This was the first time that I didn't know what to do.

"*This* was why you shouldn't have lied in the first place. You don't have a history with those motherfuckers. For all you know, whoever these niggas are they were about to work with could have been following you for days because they knew this drop was about to happen." Her eyes were still falling out of her face as she looked at me. "You have to tell Money and City."

I immediately shook my head. "Fuck no. Hell no."

I couldn't tell my brothers anything. This would only prove to them that they were right, that the whole hood had been right. It would only prove that I was a mistake that would never be shit but City and Money's little brother.

"Why not?" Zoe pressed.

"I'm not telling them shit!"

"You need them."

"Fuck! Just let me think!" I spat.

EVERY LOVE STORY IS BEAUTIFUL, BUT OURS IS HOOD
by *Jessica N. Watkins*

For the first time since I'd hit the streets, I didn't know what the fuck to do. All I did know was that no matter what, I was in debt with the Columbians for over a million dollars.

Chapter Nineteen

TAYE 'CITY' SAVAGE

"Let me run in here real quick," I told Akira just as I unlocked the door to my old crib.

Akira giggled. "Don't sound so excited."

"I hope this bitch ain't here." But just as I said that shit and looked up, Nova was glaring at me from the stairwell.

"Let me call you back," I told Akira quickly.

"No bother. I'm on my way to the hotel. I'll see you soon."

"Okay."

I closed the front door and hung up, but something told me that I needed to go right back out the door. I was having a good-ass day. I had been in some good, tight pussy all morning. Then Akira was gon' meet me back at the hotel. I wasn't going to fuck her all night, though. My father had taught me right. I needed to romance her inside and outside of the bedroom, so I planned on taking her out that night. I had great plans, so the last thing that I wanted to do was have this confrontation that Nova looked like she was intent on having.

"Hello," she spat. "Finally deciding to come back home, huh?"

"This ain't my home, which is why I am coming to get the rest of my shit."

Whether I was fucking Akira or not, I was done with this self-righteous bitch. I had been in prison too long to come home and deal with this bullshit. I was Taye *Motherfucking* Savage. The last thing I *had* to do was deal with a bitch that didn't want to love, fuck or suck me right.

Nova's sarcastic laugh made my fucking skin crawl. As I walked up the stairs by her, I wanted to slap that silly-ass smile off her face. I didn't, though. I kept my composure because this bitch wasn't going to be the reason why I ended up back in prison.

"You can't leave me!" she shrieked as she followed me up the stairs.

"The fuck I can't. I already have."

"You wouldn't have shit if it wasn't for me!"

I could only laugh, and that pissed her off.

Every Love Story Is Beautiful, But Ours Is Hood
by *Jessica N. Watkins*

"You got that lil' girl sucking your dick, so now you think you can do better than me? That bitch ain't got shit on me, motherfucker!"

"Whatever bitch you're referring to has more than some shit on your shallow ass, I'm sure."

She gasped. "So you *are* fucking that bitch!"

"What bitch?!" I barked as I stormed in the bedroom. I raced toward the closet in a hurry to get my shit so that I could get the fuck out of there before shit went further south.

"*Akira!*"

Akira, Akira, Akira... Nova kept Akira's name in her mouth. She was right, but there was no way that she could have known that for sure. Everything in me wanted to tell her yes, Akira's young ass had taken "her" man. However, since Akira hadn't left Davion yet, I didn't want to jeopardize her safety while at home by putting our relationship out in the streets.

"If I am, so the fuck what? You ain't fucking me, so why do you give a shit who's fucking me?"

"You are *my* man! This is *my* family! I built this shit!"

"Wow!" I laughed again.

"Fuck you!" she screamed just as I felt her attacking my back with punches that felt like mosquito bites.

EVERY LOVE STORY IS BEAUTIFUL, BUT OURS IS HOOD
by *Jessica N. Watkins*

My jaw tightened as I tried to collect my things while she called herself fighting me. She was trying to hurt me, but all she was doing was annoying the fuck outta me.

I reached back and pushed her. "Get the fuck off me!"

She stumbled and fell back, her butt hitting the carpet. She started to seethe as she stood up from the carpet.

At that point, anything that I didn't have, I didn't need. I had to get the fuck out of there before I killed this girl. With whatever I had been able to stuff in a duffle bag, I started walking toward the bedroom door.

Just as I stepped foot into the hallway, a gunshot pierced the air.

"Shit!" I yelled as I ducked. Then I darted down the stairs as I heard Nova screaming behind me.

"*Fuck you, motherfucker*! I'm that bitch!" *Pow!* "You don't fucking leave me after all I've done for you!" *Pow! Pow! Pow!*

****

Akira was trying to hold in her laugh as she sat across from me at V 75. I'd had all plans to wine and dine her tonight,

Every Love Story Is Beautiful, But Ours Is Hood
by *Jessica N. Watkins*

but after that move Nova had made, I told Akira to throw on some jeans and meet me on the Southside because we were going to get some drinks where the bartender poured heavy. I needed it.

"You are lying," she said as she unsuccessfully held in her laugh.

"I ain't lyin'. That bitch tried to kill me," I told her.

I shook my head as I relived the moments that I thought my life was going to end. Bullets had flown by my ears. With each step that I took, I swore it would be my last one. I thought I was a dead man until I made it out of the front door.

"I'm sorry that happened to you for real," Akira insisted as she finally stopped laughing. "I know that I'm your side bitch—"

"You are *not* my side bitch."

"I kinda am. But, anyway, regardless of our situation, I am very sorry that your relationship ended like that. I hate that woman, but I hate that you had to go through all of that as soon as you got out of prison."

I shrugged as I took a sip of the double shot of 1738. "It is what it is. I was already done with her ass. She was already dead to me. Today only put the nails in her coffin."

Every Love Story Is Beautiful, But Ours Is Hood
by *Jessica N. Watkins*

"Really?" Akira asked me with disbelief. "After all this time and everything that you all have been through, how can you be so sure that you're done?"

"You mean besides the fact that she just tried to kill me?" I spat.

Akira chuckled, but answered, "Yeah. Women try to kill their men every day and many of those men stay. Men seem to like crazy women for some reason."

"I was already gone, though. You know me. I'm not a soft-ass nigga. The streets raised me, so ain't a soft bone in my body. But when it comes to a woman... *my* woman ... Nova never fit the bill. The hardest nigga needs to be loved right by the woman he's taking care of, and Nova wasn't doing that. After all that I have given that girl, I deserved for her to love me right. Everybody does."

Akira's soft, delicate hand slipped on my thigh as she scooted closer to me. "Then let me love you right."

Ignoring the way that my manhood was jumping, my eyebrow rose. I asked, "You want to? You want that responsibility?"

"I always have."

"*Word?*"

She smiled pretty and nodded. "Word."

EVERY LOVE STORY IS BEAUTIFUL, BUT OURS IS HOOD
by *Jessica N. Watkins*

"You ready for that?"

"I'm more than ready."

BLISS DAVIS

"Fuck you," I groaned as I hit ignore on my cell and threw it in my purse.

I was ignoring yet another one of Money's calls. He had been calling me all day, but I didn't have shit to say to him. He had done it to me again. He had tricked me again.

When he had sex with me last night, I thought that he was choosing me. I thought surely he wouldn't sleep with me after all that we'd been through and still go back to Zoe. It didn't even break my heart when he told me that he needed time. No, it didn't hurt because at this point, my heart was numb to the hurt that Money could inflict on it. But I did feel stupid as fuck and used.

So, yeah, fuck Money. That morning, I woke up with the plan to get all of my shit, pack it in my car, and drive down to Texas without telling his ass. My mother had wired the gas money that I needed through Western Union and I had already picked it up. All I had to do was get the rest of my things out of the apartment in Money's building. I had to get the hell out of Chicago. I needed a new start so that I could finally get Money out of my system for good.

EVERY LOVE STORY IS BEAUTIFUL, BUT OURS IS HOOD
by *Jessica N. Watkins*

I got out of the car, hoping that no one was home. I didn't know if Zoe had been released from the hospital yet, but I didn't give a shit. Since Money couldn't leave that bitch, she could have him. I was done hoping and wishing that he would leave her crazy ass and choose me. So, if she was home and wanted to pick a fight, she was going to fight with herself because I was done fighting over this man.

Luckily, the building seemed quiet. So, I creeped into my old apartment as quietly as I could. There was only a few of me and Keandre's things still left inside, so I didn't plan on taking long. I darted into Keandre's bedroom and threw the diapers, wipes, and toys into a garbage bag that I had brought with me. Then I ran into the hall closet to get my laptop, a few purses, and other things that I'd left.

With a sigh of relief, I walked toward the front door, happy that I was seemingly about to make it out of the building without running into Money or his crazy-ass girlfriend. But as I closed the door quietly, I heard noises coming from upstairs that sounded so familiar. They were familiar because it sounded like the same feminine moans that Money had made leave my throat lustfully the night before.

I gasped and held my chest. "This motherfucker."

I was not hurt, however. He had just pulled out of me, and he was fucking his bitch already? No, I wasn't hurt; I was enraged!

I dropped the garbage bag in the hall and ran up the staircase that seemed endless. I was still done fighting over Money, but this fight wasn't about to be with Zoe, it was going to be *with* Money! This nigga was not about to keep getting away with playing me!

Once up the stairs, I stopped at the front door. I twisted the knob to see if it was open, and, just my luck, it was.

"Ahhh! Yes! Right there!"

At first, I wasn't hurt. On my way up those stairs, I didn't feel pain, only rage. However, as I listened to their heavy breathing and moans, my heart crushed all over again. Money had really convinced me that he wanted me and his family, but that was a lie. It was all more fucking lies. However, as I walked into the bedroom, I knew that this was the last time that Money would get to lie to me. I was so done. Money would never get the chance to hurt me again.

I could feel the tears stinging my eyes as I tiptoed into the bedroom. I looked toward their moans and was never expecting what I saw.

EVERY LOVE STORY IS BEAUTIFUL, BUT OURS IS HOOD
by *Jessica N. Watkins*

To my dismay, I gasped out loud. "Uh! Oh my God!"

EVERY LOVE STORY IS BEAUTIFUL, BUT OURS IS HOOD
by *Jessica N. Watkins*

ZOE DAVIS

"Zoe," I heard Shon say my name in a warning tone.

I ignored him as I bent down over the dining room table and took the three lines of coke so quickly that he didn't have time to stop me. Fuck whatever Shon had to say. This would be my last time getting high, my last hurrah, so I was about to get higher than the Empire State Building.

I heard Shon suck his teeth and blow his breath like he was frustrated.

I turned on my bare heels and told him, "Don't start. I didn't overdose off of cocaine, Shon."

"Does that fucking matter?" he sneered.

"Look, I didn't invite you over here for a lecture. I invited you so that you could give me some of that dick. I missed it."

"Where is Money?"

I chuckled. "You care?" When he just looked at me with this serious, solemn expression, I rolled my eyes. "He had some business to take care of."

"And Bliss?"

Every Love Story Is Beautiful, But Ours Is Hood
by *Jessica N. Watkins*

"She moved out. So..." I smiled and licked my lips. "We got some time."

I wasn't let down when he didn't look like he was game. He did have a lot on his mind, like one million dollars. I felt bad for him. I was in love with his brother, but I cared about Shon. I hated the stressed look on his face and wanted to suck it out.

I was back home after a few days of being in the hospital. I was so tired of thinking, stressing, and crying in that hospital bed. I had thought that my life was fucked up until the nurse gave me that news at the hospital and revealed that my troubles were only starting.

Just as the adrenaline rush started to hit me, I was ready to get some dick to take with me to cloud nine. But I still didn't see any lust in Shon's eyes as I took his hands, stood him up from the dining room table, and led him into the bedroom. But since all that I had on was a thong, I knew that his dick would get him ready just by watching me walk.

Once inside of the bedroom, I sat him down on the bed. I unzipped his jeans and pulled them down. He may not have been in the mood, but his dick sure was. It bounced out and hit his belly button with a thump. My mouth started to salivate as I knelt down before him. Once on my knees, I used both hands to bring his dick to my mouth. Then I spit on it, lubricating it. Using no hands, I slurped his dick down my throat just how I knew he liked it.

"Mummph."

The only time that a goon like Shon lets his guard down is when his dick is in a wet mouth or pussy. Hearing his rare vulnerability was such a fucking turn on. So, I used one hand to play with my pussy as I continued to allow his huge manhood to bang violently against the back of my throat.

"Gawd damn, girl."

"Mmmm," I managed to moan as I sucked.

"Fuck this. Come sit on it."

I looked up at him. He lusted after the sight of my wet mouth. I felt his dick harden in my hand.

I smiled as I told him, "I'll be happy to."

With each second, I was becoming higher and higher. Sex off of drugs made the dick feel like pure magic. So, as I sat on it, I felt the room spin. He braced himself on the edge of the bed. I rested on my tiptoes and started to bounce hard and fast. I was in control, but only for so long. He soon gripped both of my ass cheeks and started to fuck me back.

"Ahhh! Yes! Right there!"

EVERY LOVE STORY IS BEAUTIFUL, BUT OURS IS HOOD
by *Jessica N. Watkins*

I felt such intense pleasure. It didn't matter whether it was the dick, the coke, or both. I was riding this dick until I forced my first orgasm down.

"Uh! Oh my God!"

I jumped out of my skin when I heard a female voice shout. Then my world began to crumble as I saw Bliss standing in the middle of the bedroom floor with her eyes falling out of their sockets. Her mouth was just stuck open at first as if she didn't know what to say as Shon and I scrambled to put our clothes on.

Then a sarcastic, somewhat psychotic laugh rumbled from her mouth. "Ah hell nah! I can't wait to tell Money this shit!"

She turned to walk toward the door, but in a bra and thong, I charged toward her and tackled her.

"Bitch, you ain't telling Money shit!"

I was on top of her drilling her ass! I felt her hitting me, but my adrenaline was so high that I didn't feel shit. The only thing I felt was Shon's hands on me, trying to pull me off of her.

"Let me go! Fuck this bitch!" I screamed at him.

"Fuck *you*, bitch!" she shouted back.

Every Love Story Is Beautiful, But Ours Is Hood
by *Jessica N. Watkins*

I was fighting both her and Shon, who was trying to stop this fight. Then I could see his gun shining on his waist. I reached for it and cocked it. That's when the two of them froze. Still breathing hard, I stood to my feet, standing over this bitch that had already ruined my life enough. I couldn't let her take Money from me like this.

"You ain't tellin' Money shit!" I spit as I gripped the gun tightly. "Bitch, I'll kill you first!"

I would. I was already high as fuck. I wasn't thinking rationally. I was sweating. The anxiety of Money finding this out was making me crazy. I thought about him knowing about me and Shon and got sick to my stomach. I would kill this bitch first before I let her ruin me again.

"Are you fucking serious, Zoe?" I heard Shon sneer. "Put the fucking gun down."

"No! She's gonna tell Money!"

"So!"

"What do you mean *so*? I need Money and so do you!"

"Fuck that sh—"

In the seconds that it took for me and Shon to go back and forth, my attention was off of Bliss long enough for her to crawl from under me and toward the door.

EVERY LOVE STORY IS BEAUTIFUL, BUT OURS IS HOOD
by *Jessica N. Watkins*

"Bitch!" I shouted as I pointed the gun at her again. But just as I tried to pull the trigger, Shon snatched it from my grasp. I watched in horror as Bliss stood to her feet and took off for the front door. I took off after her. I couldn't let her leave. I couldn't let her tell Money. If she did, my life would be over.

I caught up with her just as she'd ran through the front door and reached the stairs. In her rush to take flight, I watched her trip and take a hard fall. I could literally hear her body hit each the stairs violently as it bounced off of one and then the next. Her head and body made a loud thud, as she rolled down the flight of twenty hard stairs. Once at the bottom, her head hit the concrete in front of the security door with such a loud crash that I even flinched.

I stood at the stop of the stairs with my hands horrifyingly cuffing my mouth. I watched unbelievably as blood started to run from Bliss' nose.

"Oh my God!" Shon screamed in horror behind me.

I hadn't even noticed that he was there witnessing this as well. He ran by me, flew down the stairs, fell to his knees and hovered over Bliss' body as if he was checking to see if she was okay.

"Call the ambulance!" Shon shouted.

Every Love Story Is Beautiful, But Ours Is Hood
by *Jessica N. Watkins*

"Is she breathing?"

His face contorted, as if he were wondering why the hell I'd asked. "I don't know. Call the fucking police!"

I'd heard him, but I couldn't say anything. I just stared.

"Zoe!" I couldn't move. I was stuck, wondering what to do. "Call the fucking ambulance, Zoe!"

"No," I finally said.

"What?! Why not?"

"No!" I pressed. "She is going to tell Money."

"After everything that nigga has done to you, you give a fuck if she tells him?! Are you serious?! Call the fucking ambulance!"

"Shon, if she tells Money, my life is over. Your life will be over too because your family is going to disown you, and you need them to pay off the Columbians!"

He stared at Bliss' lifeless body for seconds that felt like deafeningly quiet hours. Then, it was as if he finally realized that I was right because he stopped pressing that I call the police.

"Is she breathing?" I asked again.

He bent down, putting his ear to her mouth. Then, he sadly said, "No."

I sighed with relief.

EVERY LOVE STORY IS BEAUTIFUL, BUT OURS IS HOOD
by *Jessica N. Watkins*

"Go get dressed and get the hell out of here." His voice was so low. I knew that he didn't want to do this, but he was doing what he had to do. "I'll get rid of her body."

Chapter Twenty

SHAMAR SAVAGE

"What the fuck?" I asked myself. I was standing in front of the security door at Taraji's apartment building. I had been ringing her bell for five minutes, but I didn't get an answer.

After my last client at the shop, I headed over to her place. It was pissing me off that she hadn't answered my calls all day. I had even sent her text messages asking her to at least let me know that she was okay, but I still got no reply.

I had seen her car parked on the street, so it was pissing me off that she was shutting me out.

She was running from me; I knew it. For a year, she had been telling me that she didn't love *love*, that she loved sex. And even though she had admitted that she had feelings for me, her suddenly distancing herself from me was evidence that she was running from those feelings while I was running toward them. Brandon had put something on my mind that had been marinating all day, and it was only boiling over, the more it was becoming evident that Taraji was

358

Every Love Story Is Beautiful, But Ours Is Hood
by *Jessica N. Watkins*

pushing me away. I wanted to give Taraji everything that a man was supposed to. She was my good thing. She was mine. I was ready to make her *all mine*.

To be in love was to be old and young, smart and dumb, a virgin and a hoe, every day, and in every way for a complete stranger. That shit is scary as fuck, but I was ready to be scared with Taraji. I was finally ready to admit that and cuff her like a real man should.

But it looked like it was really too late.

AKIRA WHITE

"So, you finally decided to come home?"

I took a long, deep breath. I knew that Davion would eventually say something about me constantly being gone. I figured today would be the night that he would because I'd left him that morning after we landed and hadn't seen him since. It was now well into the afternoon, and the last thing that I wanted to do was argue. As a matter of fact, the last thing that I wanted to do was get in the bed with him. I wanted to be with *City*.

I didn't avoid Davion's eyes as he stared at me from the couch. I closed the front door, but I didn't take off my coat or remove my purse from my shoulders. I just stared at him, wondering if he had any potential to make me feel at least one half of the way that City did. But I knew that the answer to that was no.

"What's going on with you, Akira?" he fussed with concern all over his face. "You've been showing your ass the last few weeks. You've been gone all day, coming home in the middle of the night, and not answering my calls. What's up?"

Every Love Story Is Beautiful, But Ours Is Hood
by *Jessica N. Watkins*

I continued to just stare at Davion, and I saw the fear in his eyes. I saw the fear in him for what answers I would give him.

"Are you cheating on me?"

I only sighed. I knew the answer was in my eyes, so I decided to just admit it, "Yes, I am."

It's crazy how it left my mouth so easily. Admitting to him that I was sleeping with City was easy because I felt like City was right, being with him was right. Davion was what was wrong. Yet, my admission was only the easy part. Looking at the hurt in Davion's eyes was hard. I didn't love him, but I damn sure didn't want to hurt him.

"I'm not happy," I admitted with a sigh. "You're a good man, and that's why I have been content. But contentment is not enough. We are just dealing, and I am too young to deal."

Davion's nostrils flared as he glared at me. "Who is he?"

I shook my head. I was disappointed. Even after all of this, Davion didn't care about my unhappiness, that wasn't his focus. He just wanted to know who "he" was.

Reaching for my ring, I answered, "That's not important."

EVERY LOVE STORY IS BEAUTIFUL, BUT OURS IS HOOD
by *Jessica N. Watkins*

As he watched me remove my engagement ring, I saw his breathing become sporadic. "So, you're leaving me for this nigga?"

"I'm leaving you for *me*, Davion." I placed the ring down on the coffee table nearest me. "I'm sorry," was all I could say. I hated that I was hurting him, but as I walked toward the front door, I had never felt so free.

When Davion didn't stop me, I figured that this was all meant to be. I figured that it was fate. And despite how bad I felt for hurting Davion, I was so happy as I drove back to the hotel. I didn't know what the future held, but I knew that as long as my future was somewhere under and next to City, I would be happy.

However, when I got back to the hotel, I realized that I was sadly mistaken.

He had told me that he was staying in for the night when he left, so when he didn't answer my calls when I was on my way back to the hotel, I figured he was asleep. So, I used the key that he had given me before I left to let myself back in. I was surprised when I walked in and saw City standing in the middle of the living room of the suite with the weirdest look on his face.

EVERY LOVE STORY IS BEAUTIFUL, BUT OURS IS HOOD
by *Jessica N. Watkins*

"Hey, you didn't see my calls?" Then I noticed that he was fully dressed. "Where are you going?"

"I'm going home," he said as if those words would mean nothing to me.

My heart filled with so much dread as I stuttered, "W-why?"

"I'm going back to Nova."

My breath escaped me. I forced out, "*What? Why?*"

"I have to rock with my girl. She was down for me. I can't hurt her like this."

I couldn't wrap my head around this sudden change or the mysterious way that he was so cold and distant with me. But what I could wrap my head around was the familiarity of this. He had done this to me before. He had switched up on me in the past. He had chosen Nova over me before.

I didn't want him to see me cry. He didn't deserve to see my hurt or my tears. So, I simply said, "Okay." But it came out in croaks and cracks just as the tears started to flow. I turned quickly on my heels and hurried for the door.

"I'm sorry, Akira," I heard him say behind me.

I replied by simply shutting the door.

EVERY LOVE STORY IS BEAUTIFUL, BUT OURS IS HOOD
by *Jessica N. Watkins*

So much of my heart wanted him to come after me, to chase me, and profess his love for me. But the longer that I waited for the elevator, and the door of that suite never opened, I understood that he wouldn't and that he had played me once again. Only this time, I was old enough to know better. So, I felt so stupid for allowing the dick to trick me again.

City Savage had struck again.

TAYE 'CITY' SAVAGE

I felt like I had returned to the past, like it was ten years ago. I felt like once again, I would never see Akira again.

That fucked with my soul. It hurt more than it did when they gave me that ten-year sentence. I would have preferred to do ten more years than inflict anymore pain on her, but my hands were tied.

"You made the right choice."

I hated the sound of this motherfucker's voice as he crept out of the bedroom. If I could have gotten away with shooting his ass, I would have. I was quietly contemplating how I could. I couldn't kill him in this hotel and get away with it, but this son of a bitch was making the pure savage in me emerge. I was ready to dead this nigga the first chance that I could.

Detective White saw me calculating in my head. He knew that I was contemplating what I could do to him and when. "Don't underestimate where my influence reaches, son. I got eyes in the back of my head, and I'm two steps ahead of you, which is how I ended up here in the first place."

Every Love Story Is Beautiful, But Ours Is Hood
by *Jessica N. Watkins*

It was clear that he was two steps ahead of me. I realized that when I opened my eyes to a gun pointed to my head after falling asleep. He had cocked his pistol before I could even reach for my gun. That was the second time in twenty-four hours that someone had tried to kill me. So, I just lay there, figuring that if God had planned this to be my time, then so be it.

However, Detective White quickly explained to me that my life and freedom would remain as long as I left his daughter alone, and, if I did, I would not be the only person that would pay.

"Fuck you," I spat. I wasn't even looking at Detective White as I cursed him. My eyes were on the door, hoping at any moment Akira would return. But I knew that she couldn't.

Not this time.

It was over.

"You can *fuck* anything you want, as long as it's not my daughter," Detective White taunted. "Like I said before Akira came and interrupted us, if I find out that you are anywhere near her again, I will send the police, the district attorney, the Feds and everybody else to raid every address that I have on you until I find enough evidence to put your *entire* family away for a very long time, including your punk ass father." My

EVERY LOVE STORY IS BEAUTIFUL, BUT OURS IS HOOD
by *Jessica N. Watkins*

teeth fiercely gripped my bottom lip in rage as my nostrils flared. Yet, he continued to taunt me. "Yea, motherfucker. I know Deuce. Imagine my surprise when I was running your background and learned that your father was the pimp that turned Akira's mother out. He is the reason why my baby girl suffered for fourteen years. You all have managed to stay under the radar all of this time because no one knew about your organization. But, now, I do. You Savages are eating off of illegal money that involves every single member of your family, and I would love to make sure that all of you are indicted. Just try me."

I heard him walking toward me. Then I felt his hand on my shoulder. I glared at him, and he simply smiled cynically.

"Stay away from my daughter, and, in exchange, I will stay away from your family."

As I had been the entire time that he was there, I said nothing. This motherfucker didn't deserve a word from me. But he didn't need me to say anything. He'd witnessed my agreement when I sent his heartbroken daughter out of here.

I was fucking fuming as he strolled toward the door as if he hadn't just made me break his daughter's heart. That was something that I swore to myself and her that I would *never* do again. But he had forced my hand. The only thing in this world that I cared for more than myself and Akira was my family. I had done ten years to keep them free, and I would continue to do whatever it would take to ensure that they all remained that way.

Yet, nobody *made* City Savage do a motherfucking thing. This nigga had backed me into a tight corner, but I was plotting on coming out swinging.

NOVA JEFFERSON

"Arrrgh!"

"Yes, baby," I encouraged him. "Oh, *God*, yes!"

On all fours, bracing myself on my knees and elbows, I was getting the best dick of my life.

"*Fuck*, that ass is so pretty," Ice grunted as he smacked my ass. The sound of the contact of his hand and my ass echoed against the walls of his bedroom. When I started to through this ass back, he encouraged me with another smack on the ass. "That's it. Throw that big motherfucker back on me."

Then, he grabbed my tiny waist and started to hammer that big dick into my drizzling center over and over again until that wet smacking sound started to overshadow our moans and I could feel his sweat raining down on me.

I panted heavily, "Right there! Right fucking there! That fucking dick feels so gawd damn good! *Shit!*"

"Urrrgh, I'm cumming, baby," he growled just he pounded a few more times and then... "Arrrrrrgh!" I could feel his nails digging into my waist as he released into the rubber.

Every Love Story Is Beautiful, But Ours Is Hood
by Jessica N. Watkins

I felt so much relief as he pulled out of me. I was a tall, thick woman, so I liked my men the same, and Ice was definitely that in physical size, and so was that dick. I collapsed on my stomach, breathing heavily, trying to recover from the hour of pure, rough, freaky, just nasty fucking that Ice and I had been doing.

After taking off the condom and dropping it on the floor next to the bed, Ice lay down, breath still choppy as hell as he spooned with me with his face in my neck.

"You ready to get this money?"

A pleasant smile crossed my lips. "Hell yea. You know I am."

"We gotta get rid of those bricks ...and fast."

"You know me; I'm ready to work whenever you are."

I felt his lips touch my shoulder. "I know, baby. That's why daddy loves you."

A satisfied smile spread further across my cheeks in the darkness of the bedroom. I was so ready to get this money that I could taste it.

I was a woman that was used to being kept. Although City ensured that I was well taken care of while he was locked up, I still got lonely over the past ten years. I had secretly dated many men, but I liked a certain type of man. I liked my

Every Love Story Is Beautiful, But Ours Is Hood
by *Jessica N. Watkins*

niggas hood. I liked a hustler. Even though I had a man taking care of me, there was no way that I would give this pussy to a man that wasn't paid and willing to spoil me with his money. But most hustlers on that level in the Chi was too scared to fuck with City's old lady...until I met Ice. He was a made boss that was a gorilla in these streets. He feared no man, so he was game to fuck with me when we met two years ago.

Over those two years, Ice and I blossomed from casual dates and sex to a passionate union that I was obsessed with being immersed in. My loyalty was with City, but my heart and body were committed to Don. He had been able to give me the love and attention that City never did before he got locked up and couldn't because he was away.

When City got out, I still fucked with Ice for a few days, but Ice wasn't willing to share. He'd been under the impression that I was going to leave City because he had more than proved that he could take care of me. I loved Ice, but I owed City my allegiance. So, Ice stopped fucking with me. Yet, when City left me, I came crawling back to Ice on bended knee. He wasn't going at first. This cocky motherfucker made me work my way back in. But I had the perfect way to win his heart; a come up. A hustler like Ice

EVERY LOVE STORY IS BEAUTIFUL, BUT OURS IS HOOD
by *Jessica N. Watkins*

never slept on a come up, so when I told him about Shon's shipment from the Columbians, he got all over that shit.

I had learned about Shon's deal with Juan when one of Don's homeboys, Country, put a bug in my ear. He told me that one of his boys had been talking to Shon about buying some work. Since I was so heavily involved with the Savage organization, I knew who they sold their work to and when they had shipments of work coming in. Since none of that matched up with what I was being told, I knew that Shon was setting up some business on the side. So, I told Country to play Shon very close so that I could know more. He was happy to oblige once Ice got on board and paid for his participation.

Don ensured that Country would never tell of our involvement in setting Shon up by silencing Country forever with three bullets to the head. I had also silenced the Savage family permanently by putting them in debt of over a million dollars; a debt that I knew they could never repay.

City thought that he was punishing me by leaving me, but when the Columbians start this war with the Savages, I would be the one that had inflicted the ultimate punishment.

KEANDRE 'MONEY' SAVAGE

"Bliss!" I called for her as I entered her hotel room. I was able to get a key since the room was in my name. I understood that she was in her feelings. She had all rights to be. But I had been calling her all day to let her know that I had made a choice, and I had chosen her. Since she hadn't answered, I was prepared to make her listen.

I needed to tell her that she was right. If I wanted her, I needed to leave Zoe. I should have left Zoe the first time that Bliss had asked me to. As a matter of fact, she shouldn't have had to ask me. I may not have been ready to man up then, but I was ready now. If I had to fucking stay in that hotel with Bliss to prove it, I would.

Picking up Zoe from the hospital that morning had been eye opening for me. Who the fuck was Zoe's junky ass for me to choose her over Bliss? What the fuck had she done for me to leave her gracefully?

Not a gawd damn thing!

Fuck Zoe and fuck any other hoes. I was ready for *Bliss.*

Every Love Story Is Beautiful, But Ours Is Hood
by Jessica N. Watkins

Growing up meant turning down all the pussy in the world just for one, and I was ready to grow the fuck up. It was time.

But it might have been too late because as I looked around the room, I realized that all evidence of Bliss and Keandre were gone. All of their clothes and all of their toiletries were gone. Even the beds had been made, so I knew that Bliss had been gone since earlier, before the maids had come in for the day.

Leaving the room, I called Yummy.

"Hello?"

Pressing the elevator button, I asked, "Aye, is Keandre still over there?"

"Yeah. I've been calling Bliss. She isn't answering. She said she was coming to get him by five, and I'm supposed to be going out tonight."

"Where did she say she was going again?" I asked as I got on the elevator.

"To run a few errands was all that she said. Is everything okay?"

"Yeah," I lied. "Everything is fine."

"So are you coming to get him, because I got somewhere to—"

EVERY LOVE STORY IS BEAUTIFUL, BUT OURS IS HOOD
by *Jessica N. Watkins*

I hung up. I didn't have time to pick up Keandre. I needed to find my girl.

The next person I called was Bliss' mom as I exited the elevator and hurried through the lobby.

"Hey, Money," her mom answered.

"Hey, Marjorie. Have you talked to Bliss today?"

"Yeah. I wired her some money," she answered with a bit of attitude in her voice.

My face balled up in confusion. "Money for what?"

"She wanted gas money to come down here. She said that she was driving to Texas. What did you do?" she popped.

"*She what*?!" I fussed as I marched through the parking lot.

"She said that she was leaving. She planned to hit the road this evening and come here to Texas with me. I wired her some money through Western Union."

"Did she pick it up?"

"Yes, but I haven't talked to her. I just figured she was on the road. You know some of those highways don't have good service once you get in those mountains."

"Tell her to call me when you talk to her." I hung up and slammed my fist against the hood of my truck. "*Fuck!*"

Every Love Story Is Beautiful, But Ours Is Hood
by *Jessica N. Watkins*

I had most definitely waited too late to man up. Bliss was gone, and she didn't give a fuck about my threats. I told her that she couldn't leave the state with my son, so she had left the state *and* had left my son here. I guess I had officially hurt her for the last time.

I climbed into my truck mad at the fucking world. One thing that I always got in this world was what the fuck I wanted. I didn't ask for what I wanted, I took it. This was the first time in my life that I couldn't take what I wanted, couldn't buy it, or couldn't threaten it to give itself to me. I was out of control, and I didn't like that shit.

I was pissed off like a spoiled kid who was used to getting his way. I drove home smoking the fattest blunt. But then I realized that I was going home to Zoe, and I couldn't stomach that shit. I planned to go in the crib, get some of my shit, and stay in the hotel where I wanted to be, whether Bliss was there or not.

I walked into my place, hoping that Zoe was gone, but as always, she did the fucking opposite of what would make me happy. She was sitting right at the living room table with tears in her eyes.

"What's wrong with you?" I reluctantly asked as I closed the door behind myself.

EVERY LOVE STORY IS BEAUTIFUL, BUT OURS IS HOOD
by *Jessica N. Watkins*

She huffed and puffed. Then she wiped her face, but more tears fell in their absence anyway.

Her continued silence was irritating the fuck outta me, so I said, "Whatever, man. Fuck it."

Now was definitely not the time that I felt like dealing with her shit. I made my way into my bedroom, but I stopped in my tracks as soon as I heard her say, "I'm pregnant."

I turned and just stared at her in disbelief. Before I could find the words to say, she stood and walked toward me. Once she was near me, she slammed a piece of paper into my chest. I caught it just as she walked by and said over her shoulder, "Read my discharge papers. I'm pregnant."

"I thought you were on birth control?" I asked, still staring at the paper, reading in disbelief.

"Well, clearly, those pills aren't 100% effective," I heard her spit.

I shook my head. I was fuming. For all that I knew, her pill popping ass had forgot to take the damn pills a few times.

"How do I know it's mine?"

I turned to follow her just in time to see the disgusted look on her face.

"I'm just sayin'. We haven't been fucking that much," I clarified.

Every Love Story Is Beautiful, But Ours Is Hood
by *Jessica N. Watkins*

"But we did on New Year's, and, unlike you, I'm not a fucking hoe!" Tears filled her eyes as she stared at me with disbelief. "I know that you have been too far up in Keandre and Bliss' ass to give a fuck about me, but don't insult me. *We're* having a baby."

EVERY LOVE STORY IS BEAUTIFUL, BUT OURS IS HOOD
by *Jessica N. Watkins*

ZYSHONNE 'SHON' SAVAGE

*** *a few hours ago* ***

"Is she breathing?"

I bent down to put my ear to her mouth, praying to God that I heard something.

"No," I told her, though I wasn't sure.

When Zoe sighed with relief, I knew she was fucking crazy. I knew that there was no way she would let me get Bliss help. Zoe was so high that she wasn't thinking.

I didn't know how to check a fucking pulse, but what I did know was that I was going to get this girl some help. Zoe was straight trippin'. "Go get dressed and get the hell out of here. I'll get rid of her body... and hurry up before Money gets back."

She shot back into the house quickly, and I started to panic.

"Fuck, fuck, fuck!" I chanted quietly.

Bliss was breathing, but I couldn't assess what her injuries were. I had gone against my brothers, but that did not mean that I didn't love them niggas to death, especially

Money, since he and I had been in these streets making moves and doing the grimiest shit to take care of our families, together. Money was my heart, and I knew that Bliss was his, so as I watched her lying there lifeless in disbelief, I hurt as I assumed he would if anything happened to her.

I stared at her, in fear of how this would hurt Money, knowing that I would have to go against any bond that Zoe and I had because I was not about tie myself up in this bullshit.

Just as I continued to stare unbelievably at Bliss and got comfortable in knowing that I was about to be the next nigga to deceive Zoe, Bliss' eyes fluttered open!

"Oh shit!" I gasped.

Before I could say or do anything, I could hear Zoe's footsteps as she rushed towards the front door.

I hurriedly closed Bliss' eyes and shouted at Zoe. "Hurry the fuck! Do you want the nigga to catch us?! Get the fuck outta here!"

"I'm coming!" she shrieked breathlessly as she rushed out of the apartment and flew down the stairs.

She stepped over Bliss' body as if the girl was nothing. Her deceit was so fucking effortless. I was disgusted. I couldn't believe that she was this obsessed with Money that she was willing to stoop this low.

"I'll call you when I'm done," I told her as she rushed out of the security door.

She hurriedly said, "Okay," and disappeared with no worries.

Relieved, I bent down just as Bliss' eyes fluttered back open.

"I got you," I promised her. "Don't worry. I'm going to get you some help."

to be continued...

CPSIA information can be obtained
at www.ICGtesting.com
Printed in the USA
FSHW020525180419
57374FS

9 781543 278897